SHADOWBEAT

FASA CORPORATION
1992

CONTENTS & credits

SHADOWBEAT

Writing
Paul R. Hume
Development
Tom Dowd
Editorial Staff
Senior Editor
Donna Ippolito
Assistant Editor
Sharon Turner Mulvihill
Production Staff
Art Director
Jeff Laubenstein
Project Director
Jim Nelson
Cover Art
Dana Knutson
Cover Design
Jeff Laubenstein
Color Section
Jim Nelson
Illustration
Janet Aulisio
Joel Biske
Earl Geier
Jeff Laubenstein
Jim Nelson
Mike Nielsen
Layout
Tara Gallagher
Keyline and Pasteup
Ernie Hernandez

Published by
FASA Corporation
P.O. Box 6930
Chicago, IL 60680

INTRODUCTION

No matter what happens the beat must go on
—Andrew Brady, reporter

S hadowbeat is a sourcebook for use with the **Shadowrun** game system. In no particular order it describes rock and rockers, the popular media, journalism, and sports as they have come to be in the Sixth World, at least in North America.

Shadowbeat also provides rules and guidelines for players who want to get out there and make big nuyen and big trouble as rock stars, or who want to dig up the muck as crusading reporters. For those who like their violence gratuitous, there are complete descriptions of Urban Brawl and Combat Biker, which have never been explained until now.

Note that whenever these rules refer to a standard Success Test, the reference is to a simple, **unresisted** Success Test. This should prevent confusion with the Resisted and/or Opposed Success Tests that also occur in the **Shadowrun** game. **Shadowbeat** also introduces a test new to the game system, the Open Test. Unlike other **Shadowrun** tests, this one has no target number; the outcome is determined simply by the highest die result rolled.

Rounding out **Shadowbeat** is a section on equipment appropriate to the character types discussed in the book, as well as four characters that can serve as archetypes, NPCs, or simple examples.

In the fragmented society of **Shadowrun**, the media are also fragmented, alienated, maybe even a touch paranoid. Certainly this book seems to have fought bitterly against any unified theme or central vision, and if it sometimes seems like it is flicking from one channel to another on some manic network, well, that may be inherent in the subject matter.

IT'S ONLY ROCK & ROLL

Music is the messenger no one can silence.
—Maria Mercurial

Some of the stuff that passes for rock these days would probably produce shrieks of horror if the ghosts of Lennon, Berry, Holly, or Presley happened to be nearby. 'Course, that was just as true back at the turn of the century. The one thing anyone can say for certain about rock is that it doesn't stand still.

Tech has always been one of the things that defines where rock is going. Rockers proved that all over again when they got hold of cheap computer power, sophisticated digital sonics, and cyberware. State-of-the-art studio gear still runs to big nuyen, but for a few thousand, a budding band can turn any space into a studio good enough to pump their music into the distribution networks.

STYLE AND SUBSTANCE

Rock in the 21st century has gone through so many styles and fads that it would eat up megapulses to offer even a short list here. And with the advances in music tech in the last fifty years, a rocker can grind out product and distribute it over the Matrix whether he's got a big contract or not. Heck, whether he's got an audience or not. The test of a star is no longer who hypes him, but whether people listen.

It's no go trying to catch it and say, "this is rock." The music scene changes too fast. The days when any one sound dominated music, or even when it was split into two or three camps, are as dead as Nixon.

With modern tech, rock music can sound like anything, and most rockers get royally honked off when someone tries to shoehorn them into one pigeonhole or another. Oh, there's still commercial rock, ground out according to a formula. And don't forget that ever since the Song-O-Mat™ came along, fans can get music to order without musicians, which makes the bigger recording corps happy, at least.

Style still counts. Performing style, passion, the sound itself—these are super-vital. When anyone with the tech can sound good, the buying public has no patience for anything less than excellence.

But what makes rock really move is the message. Rockers who have nothing to say are gone today, no waiting for tomorrow. The anger, the fear, the hard-eyed regard of the predator and prey that defines a lot of life in the Sixth World finds an expression in rock. Hope, too, for future years or even for the next ten minutes. Love. Hate. Anger. Awe.

CONCRETE DREAMS

On February 9, 1964, a band called The Beatles played on "The Ed Sullivan Show," and the history of rock and roll was changed forever. On March 21, 2032, RockNet's "New Notes" played a trid by a band called Concrete Dreams, and rock changed again. The trid, of course, was *Sons of Thunder,* and this was the first public 'cast of the music of Concrete Dreams.

The Dreams combined brilliant musicianship with breakthroughs in musical technology. In those six minutes on "New Notes" they redefined the sound of rock for a generation. For the first time, people heard Warren Cartwright, switching with easy mastery from electric guitar to acoustic guitar to synthaxe;

I don't know why the frag they still call it Rock 'n' Roll after 100 years.
— Warren Cartwright of Concrete Dreams

Andrea Frost, driving that new instrument called the synthlink as she wove her ethereal vocals through the music; Moira Thornton, programmer and songwriter, producing an incredible spectrum of sounds from the keyboard synths; and the incredible drumbox work of François Nyanze.

Concrete Dreams was the main influence on rock for over a decade, with scores of imitators and wannabes following in their wake. Their advanced tech, most of it custom stuff designed and programmed by Moira Thornton, quickly became standard in the industry. The combination of her technomancy and Andrea Frost's superb neural control and artistry made cybercontrolled instruments an essential part of the music scene.

The band refused to be limited to one sound, one message. Concrete Dreams educated modern listeners to look for the meaning of the music, not just the hype.

Concrete Dreams played their last concert appearance in 2044, in the antique surroundings of Club Penumbra, site of their first gig in 2030. The place only holds about three hundred people if they agree to breathe in shifts, and the prices paid for tickets were unbelievable. The recording rights sold for a reputed five or ten million nuyen, and the soundtrack became an instant classic.

Since then, Concrete Dreams has produced one album a year, and every year, their new release reminds everybody who are the leading rockers in the Sixth World. The Dreams pursue other projects as individual artists. Cartwright's acoustic jam at Penumbra in 2049 is a good example, with a dozen musicians sitting in, ranging from novastar Maria Mercurial to a streetgrimy blues player whose real name never did get mentioned and who has never been seen since. All they had in common was the music, and that was all they needed.

ROCK AND ROLE

Rocker characters will need to sing, play an instrument, or dance. Though these game mechanics concentrate on rock music, they can adapt to fit almost any form of expression intended to reach an audience, be it literary, graphic, or plastic arts.

PERFORMANCE SKILLS

These are all Special Skills and do not tie into the Skill Web. A character can use Attributes in place of these skills, but the *Impact* (described below) of his performance will be reduced by 4. The description of each skill indicates what Attribute may replace it.

A player may want to create a rocker who has no formal training, but the character still has a Skill Rating, and still improves it using Karma, even if the roleplaying is for a character with "natural talent."

These Special Skills are also discussed briefly in the chapter **Archetype Additions**, page 84, for use in regular character creation.

Dance

The player must specify the form of Special Skill (Dance) the character has. Though dance is a complex art form, for simplicity's sake no Concentrations of Specializations are given here. Players knowledgeable about dancing might want to alter that for their own use. Typical forms of Dance Skill are ballet, modern dance, Native American dance, and various other forms of social and ethnic dancing (ballroom, Balinese temple dance, Japanese kabuki, slam, whip-trash, and so on.)

A character can substitute Quickness for Dance Skill at a +4 to any target numbers.

Musical Instrument

General skills must specify the class of instrument: winds, guitars, keyboards, strings, or percussion. Concentrations exist for acoustic, electric, synthesized, and linked versions of each instrument. Specializations govern specific instruments: acoustic guitar, synthaxe, western drums, maxophone, electric guitar, tabla, acoustic double bass, violin, dobro, synthlink, and scores of others. For example, a rocker might take the Special Skill of Guitar, then Concentrate in Electric Guitar or Specialize in Electric Bass.

Unique instruments that do not fit into the general categories described above are handled by individual Special Skills. These include ethnic instruments such as the Japanese koto or Indonesian gamelan and technoweird instruments like the throbber.

Skills govern playing the instrument, tuning it, and simple maintenance. A character can substitute Intelligence for Musical Instrument Skill at a +4 to any target numbers.

A Build/Repair Musical Instruments Special Skill is also available.

Singing

Anyone can try to sing, of course, but Singing Skill lets the individual do it on key, clearly, with the sound intended. Typical Concentrations would be Chant, Pop, and Classical. Specializations would be particular genres: jazz vocals, crooning, opera, Gregorian chant, hard rock, blues shouting, and any other known or yet-to-be-discovered style.

A character can substitute Charisma for Singing Skill at a +4 to any target numbers.

SONG-O-MATS™

Like so much of the Sixth World, commercial music lives in a permanent state of fast-forward. A lot of big recording companies are not interested in waiting for rockers to finish sweating out music that shows originality, fire, and that might even contain controversial subject matter! Instead, a simple expert system can take whatever parameters the consumers want, scan its files, and generate a musical piece guaranteed not to offend—or to offend only as much as desired—in minutes.

Some rockers (in name only, perhaps) even license companies to use samples of their licks in Song-O-Mats. Not only does one get a ready-to-sell "hit of the minute" out of the Song-O-Mat, but it will have the distinctive sound of a star performer to boot.

Zir Zemo, the Zazz star, is rumored to pull down big nuyen this way, though his label, Zazz Zone, has filed suit against the rock snoops who reported the story, so the word hasn't spread much outside the Shadowtalk nets.

The commercial record stores and pay-for-play databases are usually full to bursting with Song-O-Mat output. Hey, the Song-O-Mat never trashes synthesizer racks during a temper tantrum, never holds out for more money, and never calls in sick after a heavy night of partying. Recording executives appreciate qualities like that.

...AND IT COMES OUT HERE

Almost every musical instrument known to history has been used in rock at one time or another, and technology has been inventing new ones in the past century, ranging from the old Moogs and Syn-kets up to the latest ASIST-driven synthesizers. Instruments can be divided into four classes.

ACOUSTIC

An acoustic instrument has no electronic amplification or tonal control at all, but uses analog processes to vibrate the air and produce sound. Every musical instrument ever invented, up until the early part of the 20th century, has been an acoustic instrument.

Acoustic instruments fall into several broad categories, each category governed by a general Musical Instrument Skill.

Wind Instruments

Wind instruments are horns (trumpet, tuba, and so on), woodwinds (flute), reeds (clarinet and saxophone), and double-reeds (oboe, bassoon).

Stringed Instruments

Stringed instruments are violins, cellos, and others played with a bow.

Guitars

Guitars, banjos, mandolins, and other strings played by plucking.

Percussion

Percussion instruments are drums, cymbals, and other instruments played by striking.

Keyboards

Keyboards are pianos, harpsichords, pipe organs, and so on.

SPECIAL INSTRUMENTS

Scores of special instruments abound that are like nothing else on Earth—the koto, gamelan, glass harmonica, and bagpipes, for example. Each is probably worth a Special Skill all by itself.

Rock in the 21st century is multicultural and hungry for new sounds, and so fashions have come and gone involving ethnic and historical instruments. It is hard to find a sound that has not been part of some popular rock style in recent years.

ELECTRIC

Any acoustic instrument can be rigged for electronic amplification, and most have been at one time or another. A character plays an electric instrument using the same skill needed to play it acoustically. Concentrations in electric instruments (e.g., electric keyboards) or even specializations (e.g., electric bass guitar) are certainly possible. Generally, an electric instrument allows the musician to play games with various tonal qualities, adding reverb, altering parts of the acoustic waveform, as well as modifying volume.

Advances in technology have made questions about clarity in speakers and amplifiers fairly moot. Good sound costs as little as muddy sound, so even cheap equipment sounds good. What people pay for when they shell out for amplifiers and speakers is **VOLUME!** And they usually get it.

SYNTHESIZERS

With the development of synthesizer technology in the late 1960s, the world of music changed permanently. Instruments were no longer governed by the laws of acoustics.

A synthesizer can generate almost any sonic value, or "patch." A patch is a particular configuration that creates a sound. Patches can be made from recorded, or "sampled" sounds, or completely synthesized under computer control.

A synthesizer can generate a patch at any pitch or volume. The gizmo is limited only by the power and programming of its controlling computer and by the quality of the digital-to-analog equipment that generates the actual sound waves. It is also important to build a collection of good patches to give the synthesizer a library of hot sounds. Many musicians are hyperparanoid about someone else ripping off their sound. Some bright boy with a synth stocks it with patches from a recording, hooks up a Song-O-Mat, and next thing you know he's marketing schlock songs that sound like they're being played by Mercurial or Concrete Dreams.

This is one of the reasons passion and message have become so important in modern rock music. The technology can reproduce a sound with no sweat, but so far, only the human mind and heart can put fire into it.

A synthesizer has three types of components: a master controller, slave synthesizers, and audio output.

The master controller can be played like an acoustic instrument, or controlled by a computer program, or even hooked into the human nervous system using a synthlink. Keyboards are very common controllers, but a character with Guitar Skill might prefer a synthaxe. A synthaxe is shaped like a guitar and played like a guitar, but by itself does not make any music. Instead, it hooks up to a synthesizer array that can be programmed to sound like anything at all. Want a full symphony orchestra to sound off every time a chord is struck? For anyone who can afford a good multivoice synth, no problem.

Same deal for drumbox controllers, synthwinds, and the traditional keyboards. Using his instrumental skill, a musician plays the controller to make the synthesizers produce almost any desired sounds in response.

A character with Computer Programming Skill can use a personal or minicomputer as a controller, but because few programmers are, in fact, skilled musicians, the gamemaster may wish to require them to use a Special Skill such as Electronic Music to produce art instead of spreadsheets or PDX language code.

Slave synthesizers are the components that actually generate the musical signals, under the direction of the master controller. A controller can have one synth hooked up or built into it, or it can be connected to several synths at once (depending on its capability), driving all of them.

The audio output produces actual sound (if it is a digital-analog gate driving an amplifier and a set of speakers) or records directly to digital storage media. Gizmos like the CyberNote OMNI Terminal Input send output directly over a Matrix connection. This transmission can be written to a special computer data file, or be sampled in realtime by other Matrix-users if the host system is set up to allow that. "Listeners" never actually hear the music; it is fed directly to their brains via the ASIST interfaces in their cyberterminals. Bands comfortable with this medium report successful "live" concerts in clandestine Matrix "clubs," hacker heavens, or private systems.

OMNI

In the early 1980s a new protocol for music-data interchange was introduced for use with electronic instruments and the computers that controlled them. This was the Musical Instrument Digital Interface, or MIDI. After the usual birth pangs of a new protocol, MIDI-equipped instruments began to show up in commercial quantities in 1984.

Because the designers were shooting for a simple, open-ended architecture, MIDI proved remarkably durable, and remained the standard for synthesizer data-exchange until 2025. By then, MIDI's limitations were seriously affecting the ability of synths to take advantage of optical data technologies and the expanded computer power they provided. The result was the Optical Music Networking Interface, or OMNI.

OMNI is simply an updated version of MIDI, and, in fact, OMNI is downward-compatible with MIDI, so someone looking for a hip retro sound can use an old MIDI machine in an OMNI network.

OMNI takes advantage of the enormous bandwidth possible under optical data transmission, the extended word-framing protocols used in modern SANs, and other changes that were sheer science fiction in 1980. It also includes a command set for ASIST control-interfaces, which was the foundation designers needed to introduce synthlinks.

SYNTHLINKS

A synthlink is a master-control unit operated via an ASIST interface and a datajack. The musician controls the system with direct neural impulses.

Some rockers just jack in and stand there, zombied out, while the synth goes nuts. Others choreograph their performance: the muscular impulses of the dance produce the music. Superstar synthlink performers can combine dance and song with the control sequences. This is the magical level of performance achieved by Andrea Frost and Maria Mercurial.

Synthlinks, like synthesizers before them, let a lotta no-talent zeroes play at being musicians. Links can be preprogrammed with control sequences that anyone who isn't brain-dead can trigger. Until people like Frost started pushing the outside of the envelope and turning technology into raw, passionate art, synthlink was regarded as a technotoy with no serious musical application.

A rocker can use an instrumental skill to drive a synthlink, but dance and singing skill also trigger the control sequences. Basically, all a chummer's gotta do is "think" the music, and it happens. Anyone who can hum a tune can hear it played by a full orchestra, or a rock ensemble, or a massed koto consort, or whatever their synthesizer is set for.

WAX

"Wax" is music biz slang for the recording industry (sort of a retro-nostalgia thing). Even when "phonographs" were still the norm for recorded music, people talked about "vinyl" and "wax," despite the fact nobody had used those materials for years. Now, with recordings digitized on MCDs (minicompact disks) or stored on chips, no connection at all exists between the term and the reality, but it still persists. So when a rocker records a new album and it novas the charts, people talk about "good wax."

Wax in **Shadowrun** is a mix of corporate giants and one-man bands. Through downloads over the Matrix, a rocker can make a recording available for a few cents. Before the Grid, if a musician wanted to get his product out to the public, he shoveled out big bucks to get records pressed, distributed, and advertised. Now, he uploads the recording to a pay-for-play bulletin board. Every time someone downloads it, he gets some money. If a million people download it, he gets a goodly amount of money.

A small-scale, pay-for-play service, the equivalent of a private record label in 20th-century terms, charges 5¥ for a download of a one-hour recording. The rockers usually get .5¥ per download. In this kind of market, a million-seller pays the artists 500,000¥ directly. This does not happen often.

Mass distribution of MCDs and chips is the land of the giants and involves advertising, promos, tours, and so on. This is where the big waxworks play. A one-hour album from a big recording corp costs about 20¥, whether purchased in a store or downloaded off a net. The artists still get royalties. They also get major fees and other bennies from the waxworks. A million-seller in this arena can net the rocker 4,000,000¥, on top of the other goodies.

DISKS, CHIPS, AND DOWNLOADS

Recordings are always—*always!*—in extended-spectrum sound (ESS). There's just no point in using anything less, and people will not spend money on anything else. Digitized ESS recordings eat up 3 megapulses (Mp) for every minute of music. So a one-hour commercial recording needs 180 Mp of storage. A standard Matrix access (1 Mp per second) can download that in three minutes, and a high-speed Matrix connection can do it in a tenth of the time.

An MCD can hold up to 500 Mp, and of course optical storage chips can hold gigapulses (Gp = 1,000 Mp) of data. Both formats are popular. Prices for storage media are in **Gear**, page 99.

CONCERTS AND CLUB DATES

Live appearances are the fuel that keeps wax going. People are bombarded by thousands of new recordings every year, so they want to know what they are getting before they shell out for wax. Every twink with a ten-yen synth and a digital recording unit can load his musical junk onto a net. Why drop any cred listening to some pimply wannabe's delusions of grandeur?

Music trid channels, freebie download offers, and the old standby, radio broadcasts, help push rockers, either because the jocks find a sound they think will go over big, or because the big waxworks pay for a specified number of broadcasts in a given market. Of course, some media outlets belong to a corp that also sells wax. In that case, no problem with the broadcast coverage.

But nothing sells wax like a live concert. Start-up bands live and die on club dates. A lot of small bands make pilgrimages from city to city, playing the clubs, loading their wax into the local rocknets, and praying they'll collect enough cred to keep going until that day when a big-name agent or talent scout discovers them. For most, of course, it never happens.

Big-name rockers can fill arenas with tens of thousands of fans. The waxcorps stage tours featuring their top sellers every year, and make it a media explosion in every city they hit.

A really neat side effect of the distribution technology for wax is that a rocker with a loyal following can make a living free of the corporate waxworks. Even if the star chooses to contract with a company to distribute disks and chips, he can control the terms of the agreement instead of becoming a corp puppet. This leads to the rather strange phenomenon, in 20th-century terms, of top-rank stars playing small club dates instead of megahype concert tours.

In a sense, concert tours are out of fashion with major stars. They are what rockers on the way up have to go through to get major commercial distribution. Once a rocker arrives at the top, he can cut his own terms with the waxcorps, and playing backstreet clubs like Penumbra or Underworld 93 in Seattle is a sign of artistic (and financial) independence.

Some novastars do the big tours, but only because they want to. Maria Mercurial's upcoming world tour is an example of that. The silver lady has made it clear she is staging the tour to get her message into the face of the fat cats worldwide, up close and in person.

IMPACT TEST

Right, so a rocker has skills, instruments, and songs to sing. That's just the price of admission. The main event happens when the pieces all come together and music comes out, whether it be a back-room studio somewhere or dead center in a stadium seating fifty thousand screaming fans.

When a rocker performs, he must make a test to determine *Impact*. A single series of appearances is measured as one performance, requiring a single test. It is not the idea to make a test for every song in a concert or club set, much less for a tour with dozens of concert appearances. The same goes for recordings. Don't make an Impact Test for every song. One test measures the Impact of the whole piece.

The Impact Test uses an *Open Test*, a game mechanic new to the **Shadowrun** system. *Impact* is the measured result of an *Open Test*. Unlike other tests in **Shadowrun**, the Open Test has

no predefined target number. The Open Test is made and the result determined by the highest die rolled, in effect setting what would have been the target number. For example, a rocker wails out a hot reggae-blues shout number. He has a Singing Skill of 5, so he rolls 5 dice. He scores 6, 6, 4, 3, 1. Rerolling the two sixes, he gets 6 and 2. Rerolling the six again, he gets a 4. 6 + 6 + 4 is 16, the number used to represent the performance's Impact. Impact measures the passion, the commitment, that the rocker puts into the performance. In a sense, it has nothing to do with skill or successes, though a skillful musician is more likely to keep his performance controlled enough to let his passion speak clearly to an audience.

A character using an Attribute instead of a Musical Skill for a Performance Test reduces his Impact by 4. This also applies to the Impact for group performances, if **any** member is using an Attribute instead of a Skill.

GROUP IMPACT

When a band is playing, make one test for the whole group, with the following choices: Use the Skill Rating of the member with the lowest Skill, OR use a higher rating, up to the Skill of the member with the highest rating, but reduce the Impact of the performance by **double** the difference between the Skill Rating used for the test and the lowest Skill Rating involved.

For example, Steelmind is a band with three members. The lead synth player has a Musical Skill of 6, the highest in the group, and the throbber player has a 4, the lowest.

When Steelmind plays, the rockers can either use a group Musical Skill of 4 or a Skill of up to 6. If the player rolls 4 dice for the test, the Impact is unchanged. What he rolls is what he gets.

If 5 dice were rolled, the Impact would be reduced by 2. That is, 5 (the skill used) minus 4 (lowest skill in group) is 1. Double that for a 2.

Similarly, if the band used its maximum skill of 6, the highest skill rating among its members, it would reduce the Impact of the performance by 4.

REHEARSALS

Performances don't just happen, or at least, not usually. Live concerts require rehearsal, and recordings involve retakes, editing, hours of pre- and post-production work.

The time to write and arrange music, rehearse, and so on, varies according to the scale of the performance. The time required increases for fancy shows with lighting effects, choreography, and tour logistics. Ditto for recordings, which involve actual recording, negotiating distribution, editing, and the whole nine yards.

REHEARSAL TIME TABLE	
Performance	**Base Time**
Club date	10 days
Recording a single	10 days
Commercial album (about 1 hour of music)	60 days
Major concert	90 days
Concert tour	180 days

The main skill used to coordinate rehearsals is the Special Skill of Musical Production. Any Performance Skill can be used as well. Make a Success Test with a Target Number 8 if using a Performance Skill, a Target Number 4 if using Musical Production. Divide the Base Time by the number of successes. Failure means the full Base Time is required to prepare for the event or session.

Unrehearsed performances or concerts, for which the performers have **not** spent the necessary time preparing or have skimped on production values, lose 4 points of Impact.

KARMA AND IMPACT

That little extra edge that comes from luck and experience makes for hot music. Rockers can use Instant Karma to improve their Impact. Players may add additional dice to the Impact Test at a ratio of 1 die for every 2 points of Karma their character possesses. So, 2 points of Instant Karma adds one extra die to the Impact Test, 4 Karma Points add two dice, and so on, up to a maximum number of dice equal to the Skill Rating used in the test. No additional Karma can be spent on Impact.

IMPACT MODIFIERS TABLE	
Group Skill	Subtract twice the difference between the skill rating used and the lowest skill rating in the group.
Band includes a Sasquatch	+3
Band/Rocker is not rehearsed/ under-rehearsed	4
Band/Rocker using Attribute instead of skill	−4
Synth Quality (See **Gear**, page 93)	
Monovocal synth	−4
4-voice synth	−2
12-voice synth	+1
16-voice synth	+2
24 or more-voice synth	+3

COMPOSITION

If a rocker wants to get into songwriting without performing on his own, use the following rules.

Any Performance Skill can be used to compose a song, or else the character can use the Special Skill (Musical Composition). The Base Time to compose a song is ten days per minute of the final composition. Make a standard Success Test with a Target Number 4 if using Musical Composition, or 6 if using a Performance Skill. Divide the Base Time by the successes rolled to determine the actual time. If the test fails, the song has an automatic Impact of 1.

If the test succeeds, determine its Impact as previously described, using the same dice. Compare the die results against the indicated target number for time computation as in any standard Success Test, and also determine Impact from the highest-scoring single die in an Open Test.

For composing a song, the writer receives only 10 percent of the usual royalties for a recording. Most rockers in the Sixth World write their own music for their performances, and the money for that performance includes the fees for licensing the music. The rocker does not get paid once for writing the music and again for recording it.

Longer pieces such as operas, symphonies, and musicals can be written this way, too. Increase the Target Numbers by +4 and use a Base Time of 15 days per minute to perform the piece. If the test fails, the piece needs more work or else has not found a producer willing to spend the nuyen to mount such a large work. A second test, adding +4 to the Target Number, is necessary to try and get it produced. The market is so skimpy for this kind of work, that the piece will not get any distribution unless the Performance Rating (see below) is Exceptional or better. If the test is completed, but the Performance Rating is lower than Exceptional, then try, try again.

The composer gets full distribution money when he finally gets his magnum opus sold. Newbie musicians should probably avoid three-hour oratorios unless they have some other way to pay the rent while struggling to make their mark.

PERFORMANCE RATING

Once complete, a character must discover whether a composition or a performance soars or crashes and burns by determining the Performance Rating. For compositions, assuming the composer is not performing his or her own work, the test will determine whether or not the song is "saleable." The character, or legal representative, makes an Etiquette (Music Business) Test against a Base Target Number 14, minus the Impact of the piece. The piece then sells for 500¥ multiplied by the number of successes generated in the Etiquette Test. This final nuyen amount can be Negotiated, using the usual **Shadowrun** Negotiation procedure. The Base Time for such a sale is three months. Successes from the Etiquette (Music Business) Test can be used either to increase the price of the sale (by multiplying those successes by 500¥) OR to reduce the Base Time required to accomplish the sale. The player can split total successes generated between price and time as desired.

For actual performances, recordings, or tours, determine the Impact as described previously. Multiply this result by the rocker's Charisma. If dealing with a band, multiply the Impact by the average Charisma for the group. This number is the Performance Rating.

For example, a four-member band has Charisma scores of 4, 6, 6, and 8 (Elves are pretty popular in rock these days!). This is an average of (4 + 6 + 6 + 8)/4, or 24/4, for a 6. The band generates an Impact of 5. Their Performance Rating is 30. If it is a single-song performance, add the composition's Impact to the Performance Rating. If it is an album, long-form concert, or tour, the gamemaster should determine the average quality of the material (the compositions) and assign it a value from 1 (rehashed drek) to 10 (wrenchingly stunning), which is added to the Performance Rating.

If the Performance Test dice come up all ones, then the Performance Rating is also a 1 (an "Abysmal" rating), no matter what the rocker's Charisma.

HIT OR FLOP?

Basically, a high Performance Rating means a successful performance. A low rating means an ordinary job at best, maybe even an awful one.

Some storytelling and common sense are called for here. A pick-up band of wannabe rockers with a Charisma of 3 can always roll some incredible Impact and get a "novastar" result. This is going to be good for them, but no one is going to spend millions of nuyen promoting a flash in the pan. The usual response to this kind of performance is good word-of-mouth, an increase in bookings, some nice money from the distribution on the recording (if one was made), but not a world tour! See **Status** in the following section for a means of measuring career progress for rockers.

Similarly, when a top star turns in a scummy performance, it usually means a rash of nasty reviews, losses in sales, even lost status, but not the end of a career. Rock fans love comebacks.

Consistency is the key to success or failure. A professional rocker with a Musical Skill of 6 and an average Charisma of 4 is usually going to turn in ratings in the mid-30s. This translates into an average performer who occasionally manages to play exceptionally.

A top-ranking rocker who works at his art, with a skill of, say, 8, and a Charisma of 6 is going to hover in the "Exceptional" range, with ratings of around 60 most of the time.

Real novastar performances only occur when everything comes together and the inspiration, represented by a high Impact, strikes like lightning from above.

PERFORMANCE RATINGS TABLE

9 or less:	Abysmal. A flop. Bombs on distribution. Status is reduced. If status is already "Newbie," then Booking Target Numbers (see below) are increased by +4 until an Exceptional or better performance is turned in. Distribution Factor 1.
10 to 21:	Poor performance. Lack of skill and/or passion is obvious. This would reduce future contract offers, make critics wonder if the performer is losing his or her touch, and so on. Add +2 to Booking Target Numbers (see below) until an Exceptional or better performance is turned in. Distribution Factor 1.
22 to 36:	Average performance. Everyone's happy with it. Distribution Factor 2.
37 to 60:	Exceptional performance. Reduce Target Number for next Booking Test by −1. Distribution Factor 3.
61 to 96:	Incredible performance. Next booking is automatic. Distribution Factor 4.
97 or more:	Novastar material. Producers cluster around, contracts are offered, and at least 15 minutes of fame are guaranteed. Next booking is automatic. Status is increased. Distribution Factor 5.

CASHING IN

Most rockers are in the field for something besides the money, but money doesn't hurt. How does a player character who rocks keep the rent paid?

ROCKER STATUS

When using the **Shadowrun** rules to create a rocker character from scratch (p. 53), a player can use Tech nuyen to purchase status. The rocker types listed below show the amount of Tech nuyen it costs to purchase that status. If a character does not buy a status as a rocker, he is presumed to be a "newbie." See also the **Archetype Additions** section, pp. 84–6, for more on status.

Status provides a basic lifestyle (if the rocker is not pulling down income from other activities—this is still **Shadowrun**, after all), determines how much money distribution pulls down for a performance, and gives a basis for figuring out how easily the rocker can get bookings, and what he gets paid for them. It also deals with the degree to which a rocker is recognized on the street.

Following are the six types of rocker status and the information needed for generating these characters.

Newbie

Tech ¥ Cost: Free (You lucky dog, you.)
Lifestyle: Street
Booking Test: 6
Booking Fee: (100¥ x Performance Rating)/2
Distribution: 50¥ x 1D6
Recognition: None. Nobody is going to recognize this null.

The name says it all. No rep, no records, nowhere to go but up. (Talk about room for growth.)

Anyone who starts a rocker career without buying a status during character creation is automatically a newbie.

A club date is for one night. The rockers are expected to be at the club from 6:00 PM to 1:00 AM.

Opener

Tech ¥ Cost: 500¥ (Such a deal.)
Lifestyle: Street
Booking Test: 5
Booking Fee: 100¥ x Performance Rating
Distribution: 100¥ x 1D6
Recognition: 14

Local rock fans sorta know who this rocker is, though no one's going to be walking around singing his songs or anything. The term "opener" refers to the show-business practice of booking cheap local talent to play before a featured performer comes on stage. Club dates and recordings pay better than when the rocker was a newbie, but otherwise this isn't much different.

Seller

Tech ¥ Cost: 1,000¥
Lifestyle: Low
Booking Test: 5
Booking Fee: 200¥ x Performance Rating
Distribution: 150¥ x 1D6
Recognition: 10

The rocker is starting to get good sales on recordings and may even be recognized in towns where he is playing. Club dates are still at night, but the rocker is not expected to be there until 9:00 PM. Sideline jobs playing pick-up for social events, jamming on recordings of other bands, and so on, provide a steady enough income to support a Low lifestyle.

Solid

Tech ¥ Cost: 10,000¥
Lifestyle: Middle
Booking Test: 4
Booking Fee: 300¥ x Performance Rating
Distribution: 100¥ x 2D6
Recognition: 8

A solid rocker is a pro who makes his living from his music. He can support a Middle lifestyle with gigs as a studio musician, as an arranger, by writing commercials or other fluff music, and assorted pick-up work.

Club dates are for 1D6 days, and the rocker has to be there from 9:00 PM to 1:00 AM.

Star

Tech ¥ Cost: 100,000¥
Lifestyle: High
Booking Test: 3
Booking Fee: 500¥ x Performance Rating
Distribution: 200¥ x 2D6
Recognition: 6

A star is just that—a celebrity in the rock business. Recording contacts, royalties from hit songs, and personal appearances all contribute to a High lifestyle. Club bookings are up to 1D6 days, usually two sets per day. Concert tours are a possibility, and last for 2D6 + 6 weeks. Multiply the booking fee for a concert tour by the number of weeks it lasts. For example, a twelve-week tour would pay 2,400¥ x 2D6 x Performance Rating. If the rocker generates a rating of 30, that translates into 72,000¥ x 2D6. Tours are exhausting, averaging a concert every three days, with the rest of the time spent traveling, setting up, rehearsing, giving interviews, and so on.

Novastar

Tech ¥ Cost: 500,000¥
Lifestyle: Luxury
Booking Test: 2
Booking Fee: 1,000¥ x Performance Rating
Distribution: 300¥ x 2D6
Recognition: 5

A novastar is one of the top rated-rockers in the world. He or she lives like a star, only higher on the hog. Bookings and contracts are almost automatic. Club dates and concert tours are handled the same way as for stars.

LIFESTYLE

The rocker gets a lifestyle free as part of his Status. Income from recordings, bookings, personal appearances, contacts with waxworks, all pay an income that takes care of the rent.

A character with outside income, or who decides to spend some of his cash from the career on a higher lifestyle, only needs to pay the difference between this lifestyle and the one he wants (see **Shadowrun**, p. 148). For example, a solid rocker gets a Middle lifestyle free as part of his Status. If he wanted to live a High lifestyle, he'd only have to pay 5,000¥ a month to make up the difference.

Because most elements of a lifestyle involve perks from the waxworks or life on tour, where accommodations are booked for the rocker, it is not possible to live a lower lifestyle and pocket the difference as cash.

Low-status rockers get a Street lifestyle. That is, zip. If they want to live comfortably, they're gonna have to hustle up the nuyen.

Booking Test

When a rocker is looking for a booking at a club or with a recording company, he must make a Booking Test. The Base Time to find a booking is 30 days for a club date and 90 days for a recording contract or tour. Tours are not available to rockers with a status lower than Star or to those who have not previously acquired a recording contract during the game.

The player can make the Booking Test using Negotiation Skill or the Special Skill of Musical Production. He can also use Performance Skills at +2 to the Target Number.

The number of successes rolled reduce the Base Time to find a booking or other contract. A failed test means the rocker has hustled for the entire Base Time without securing a booking.

To keep things simple, assume that a rocker cannot go looking for another booking until he finishes the one he already has. This is not an entirely accurate reflection of the situation, because most rockers have to scramble to keep their calendars full and their credsticks happy. If the players and the gamemaster can work out a method of keeping schedules straight, by all means go for it. Obviously, a rocker who manages to book himself into two clubs on the same date is going to be in trouble. (But, then, that's what troll bodyguards are for.)

Booking Fee

This is the fee a rocker gets for a booking. The fee for a typical club date varies according to the status of the rocker or band, per **Rocker Status**, p. 13. Above-average performances can lead to extended bookings. Similarly, successful Negotiation Tests can extend bookings or increase the basic fees. Of course, rockers who blow their negotiations can actually lower their fees.

Distribution

Multiply this figure (determined by status) by the Performance Rating of the recording. The resulting amount is what the rocker collects from sales of the recording. For example, a group of newbies scores a rating of 32 on a recording, which is average. Roll 1D6 and multiply by 50¥. Say the roll is a 3. That will get them 150¥ x 32, or 4,800¥, for their work. The money is divided among all the members of the band.

Strictly speaking, distribution pays off over a three-to-six-month period, and the gamemaster may divide the amount into equal payments over that period if he wishes. Income after the initial sales goes into maintaining the lifestyle that accompanies the rocker's status.

The rate described above applies to a complete album, one hour or more of music. For a single or a mini-album that is significantly less than an hour long, the distribution payments are proportional to that amount.

Recognition

Whenever it is possible that a rocker might be recognized, the rocker must **fail** a Recognition Test, using the Recognition Target Number for his rocker type. If the rocker makes a successful test, then the individual has behaved too much like his star-persona and is recognized. The rocker player can make a Recognition Test when he wants the character to be recognized, or the gamemaster can require one, perhaps especially when the rocker does **not** want to be recognized!

If the rocker performs or does something else that makes him or her recognizable, it can reduce the Recognition Test Target Number. If the rocker is physically distinctive or dresses in some kind of trademark glitter, recognition may be automatic. Similarly, a disguise, or simply dressing in street clothes or keeping a low profile can add to the target number. If the rocker is in a crowd that just does not listen to modern rock, people who think music started with Mozart's *First Concerto* and ended with McCartney's *Third Symphony*, then the players can skip Recognition Tests.

UP AND DOWN

Whenever a rocker gives an Abysmal performance (Rating 9 or less), his status goes down. In a group, **everyone's** status goes down if they turn in an Abysmal performance.

If a rocker is at newbie status and gets an Abysmal result, then his target number for bookings goes up. Until he gets a booking and turns in a performance that is at least Exceptional, life is going to be rough.

Similarly, whenever a performance rating is 97 or higher, the rocker (or band) gains status, improving by one grade. A newbie band would be upgraded to opener, for example.

If a novastar gives a Novastar performance, the only result is the increased payoff. People expect the best from the best.

STATUS AND BANDS

If the members of a band are not all equally well known, the band has the status of its most famous member, and the payment to a band is based on its most famous member. If the group turns in a Novastar performance, all members advance. If they blow it, they all slip.

Individual members of a group use their own status if they are trying for individual bookings and for dealing with possible fan recognition.

As for lifestyle, a high-status member of a band can maintain lower-ranked members of the group as his guests, as described in **Shadowrun**, p. 148.

MONEY OR MESSAGE? (OPTIONAL)

This is an optional rule for gamemasters who have a problem with rockers who combine making a fortune with recording incredibly meaningful songs.

When a rocker generates a Performance Rating, he must decide how many points will go toward the message, the social commentary that makes his music distinctive, and how many will apply to the commerciality of the music. These are Message Points and Money Points.

Only Money Points apply when calculating booking fees and distribution payoffs. For example, a rocker turns in an Exceptional performance in concert, with a rating of 74. He decides to put 60 into Message Points, and the remaining 14 go into Money Points.

If the rocker is a star, he will only get 7,000¥ for the concert (Booking Fee 500¥ x Performance Rating 14 = 7,000¥).

Social Effects of Rock

Message Points get the audience to do something in response to the music: adopt an attitude, agree with a point of view, whatever. The player and the gamemaster need to agree on the desired results beforehand. Even the greatest rocker in the world cannot single-handedly decide the outcome of an election, foment a general uprising, or make the audience go out and kill somebody. He cannot make someone give up an informed and deliberate opinion, though he might improve the chance of persuading that person to change his mind. A rocker certainly could not use music to convince a bunch of goons who are about to kill him that they really don't want to.

But he can hose up a publicity campaign, or promote one, praise or ridicule an establishment or individual, get a mob mad enough to riot if they are provoked, or calm down a riot enough to let negotiations proceed.

•30 message points will not change much, but will at least make people willing to listen to the rocker's message.

•60 points just barely achieves the desired result.

•90 points will completely achieve the desired result.

•120 points or more will achieve the result, with extra benefits.

For example, a rocker is involved with a group of shadowrunners who discover a corporate plot to create major social disruptions in a neighborhood to enhance sales of their security equipment. A decker in this kind of situation would look at trashing necessary computer resources to prevent the plot. A samurai would organize armed resistance or start trying to kill off the officials responsible. A reporter would be out there trying to get the story into the newsnets.

A rocker might stage a concert in the neighborhood, using his Performance Rating for Message Points, to get the inhabitants to pull together to resist the plot.

At least 30 Message Points would prevent total chaos, helping people keep it together in the face of the damaging crimes planned by the corp. They would also be open to proof from the runners that they are being manipulated.

With 60 Message Points, the locals would resist responding to the corp campaign the way the company expects.

Ninety Message Points would give the locals heart and even help them organize defenses or protests against the intrusion, especially if they had some support, say from a bunch of wiz-hot shadowrunners. In any case, they would certainly refuse to fall for the corp plot, and would not buy the security weapons the company tried to push after the first incidents.

With 120 or more points, the performance would inspire public shows of solidarity against the corp, and average folks would face down hired rioters and help each other out in the face of danger or even death. Local resources would become available to the shadowrunners, individuals normally afraid to talk to the press will open up on camera, and so on.

The scale of this kind of campaign depends a lot on the rocker's status. A newbie or opener will not be able to sway a national audience. As a rule, a Status of Opener or lower can only influence an audience at a live performance, and the effects are limited to the immediate neighborhood of the concert.

Solid rockers can influence a city through concerts and broadcasts or recordings.

Stars and novastars can even influence national events. Political candidates have been sponsoring concert tours for years as part of their campaigns.

As always, the gamemaster, not the game system, has the final say on performance effects in the game.

MAINTAINING A LIFESTYLE

A rocker has to come up with a minimum number of Money Points each year to maintain the lifestyle that goes with his status. If he doesn't, his status will go down, unless he starts paying for the lifestyle himself.

Because lifestyle is supported by distributors out of the profits from commercial successes, no money comes in if the rocker turns all his energy to social commentary.

If the rocker does not pick up the payments on his lifestyle, then his Status is reduced by one level. Following are the costs for maintaining various lifestyles.

•Street lifestyle doesn't cost a thing. Such generosity.
•Low lifestyle = 100 Money Points/year.
•Middle lifestyle = 200 Money Points/year.
•High lifestyle = 300 Money Points/year.
•Luxury lifestyle = 400 Money Points/year.

METAHUMANS AND ROCK

So far, most of the previous discussion could cover rock in the dark ages around 1991 as easily as rock in the happening world of the mid-21st century. Does anyone think that the changes in technology, not to mention the presence of magic and metahumans, isn't going to be a big deal in rock?

No fear, chummer.

The rich mix of species and races in the Sixth World has had its effect on rock, same as everything else.

ELVENROCK

Because of their Charisma, elves are a very big deal in rock. Not only do the most charismatic elves sweep all the shrieking fans into little heaps, but the ones raised speaking Sperethiel, the so-called elven language they use in Tir Tairngire and allegedly in the Irish elflands of Tir Nan Og, seem to have a natural bent for poetry and music. (What else could be expected from a language with a dozen declensions, some of them used only in poetry?)

Only a few of the lah-dee-dah elves from the Tir play for mass markets, which may come as no surprise. Bootleg recordings of "elvenrock," music in Elvish for elven audiences, are a lucrative black market item between Tir Tairngire and its neighbors. Usually, when an elf gets the urge to be a star on the big scene, he has to hustle into a sprawl to get his career rolling. Natch, Seattle is the big magnet for runaways from the Tir.

But even a rough, tough, old sprawl-bred elf still has that incredible Charisma. Coupled with musical talent, watch out. Easily a third of the top-ranked rockers in North America today are elves.

SASQUATCH ROCKERS

There's another Awakened species now showing up in rock in increasing numbers. Again, perhaps it's no surprise that it's the sasquatch. Even before the U.N. decree of 2046, sasquatches were showing up in some bands, especially the ones formed in the NAN territories, where they were already considered people.

The decree, backed by laws in most member nations, eliminated the drekky practice of capturing sasquatches and using nasty behavior modification to try to make them perform, which, sad but true, was occurring in some areas.

There are no solo sasquatch performers. They don't seem to get any kick out of performing unless surrounded by a group. But put them in a band, and the furry guys can make things jump.

If a band has a sasquatch in it, the following rules apply:

•Don't figure the sasquatch's Charisma into the band's average rating. That is, if there are four members of the band plus the sasquatch, use only the four other rockers' scores to figure Charisma.

•Increase the Impact Rating of the band's performances by +3.

Sasquatches don't do rock for the money, though if money is coming in, the metahuman rights folks are watching close to make sure the sasquatch gets his rightful share. Sasquatches who hit it big, like "Hairy Krishna," who plays with Starfire, usually feed their incomes into funds designed to help protect and reclaim the wilderness.

A sasquatch joins a band because he likes its members, their music, and what they have to say. So roleplaying, rather than nuyen or tables or die rolls, is what will inspire a sasquatch to link up with a rocker. Someone who wants to start out with a sasquatch as his friend and fellow rocker should, at the very least, have to purchase the non-player character as a Buddy when creating the rocker character (**Shadowrun**, p. 53).

GOBLIN ROCKERS

The downside of the Charisma thing: orks and trolls do not usually make it big in mass-market rock. That doesn't mean plenty of goblin rockers don't play for a goblin market, but there's no big money there, and their stuff doesn't get played on RockNet. A lot of the music in this community is powered by rage, music of the oppressed. It doesn't have much good to say about normals, elves, and dwarfs.

Even ork/troll bands that break out of the ghetto and hit the big-time charts usually have an attitude. Darwin's Bastards went platinum with their home-brewed recording *Do We Not Bleed,* but their next album, *Breeder Blues,* was not comfortable listening. Audiences can take only so much direct abuse, even when the complaints are justified. *Breeder Blues* fizzled despite heavy promotion. Still, public interest in the group revived after the incident involving a Humanis shock squad in Dallas. The score at the emergency room was four broken legs, two concussions, and one shocked squadder who needed a jump-start while he was still in the ambulance. On the DB side: two minor contusions and throbber player "Gristlehide" Brannigan took a nasty knife slash requiring a dozen stitches. If Darwin's Bastards could meet the public even halfway with a slightly less confrontational message, their powerful music might still grab a permanent slot in the big leagues.

MAGIC AND MUSIC

At first glance, it might seem odd, but magic does not mix into the rock scene as much as might be expected. Some of the reasons make more sense when you think about it, and a nasty moment in recent history explains the rest.

Rumor has it that more than a few hot rockers have had a little help from the magic arts when it comes to their Charisma. A lot of fans frown on this, saying it feels like magical invasion of their headspace. Some call it phony, like lip-synching and stand-in singers on albums. So if there's any truth behind the stories, the rockers in question want it kept strictly in the shadows.

Things have been particularly uptight since the ham-handed fiasco by the now defunct Eight Immortals. In 2048, the 8-I were caught using a couple of wizards to hype up concert audiences for their neo-Maoist raga-metal sound. The drek flew hot and heavy, and lead singer Tony Li and his magical hirelings pulled down sentences for magical assault. Anything that even hints at a rocker using magic to control audience response is the kiss of death.

The suspicion of magical mind control, along with the heavy price tag on top illusionists, has also damped down enthusiasm for magical effects on concerts. With the exception of the neoCeltic

*You dirt, you specks
You flecks of scum!
We'll scrub you humanz
Our time has come!*
—"Cleanup," by Trollgate

band Til Es Hault, none of the star-ranked bands on the circuit today use magic as part of their act, for reasons discussed below.

MAGICIAN MUSICIANS

At least two novastars are out of the broom closet as practicing magicians. Sandra Willowfall, the elven bass player for Til Es Hault, is a trained mage. And Harvey Voice of Rivers, of Thunderdance, is not just a wizard on the keyboards. He's also a full-blooded Shoshone and a shaman of that tribe.

Willowfall spins powerful illusions during Til Es Hault gigs, fantastic displays that complement the stories their songs tell. The group's use of overt magic in the act is the exception that proves the rule, and the reason people accept it may be because of Willowfall's role in exposing the Eight Immortals' abuse of magic in 2048.

Because Voice of Rivers considers magic a religious discipline, he does not use his powers in his musical performances.

Considering the kind of money a magician can pull down either punching a clock or running the shadows, it is not surprising that very few of the spook squad go into rock. Besides, being a hot magician is a full-time job. It's not easy for someone to master the arcane at the same time he's playing club gigs or traveling all over hell and gone on a concert tour.

That's why people like Willowfall and Voice of Rivers are exceptions in the music biz. They're in it because it is what they want to do, maybe more than they want the power they were born with. The same goes for any of the baby rocker mages working their way up the ladder, who turn away from the gift of magic to chase the music only they can hear.

ASTRAL ROCK

Despite all that, never let it be said that magicians don't go meltdown for a hot performance. The astral vibes of a high-power performance are awesome to behold, according to the magefolk. One doesn't find magicians hanging out on every street corner, even these days, but any live appearance by a performer who gets behind the music and wails is likely to attract more than the average share of wizards.

When the artist has some juice himself, and is aware of the astral scene, he can pick up a cult following among the magi. The street razors who tried to rumble nasty at an Enoch Ian Keys gig caught on to that trick. Half the clientele of the grimy little Barrens club proceeded to lay them out in a display of spell-tossing that almost lit up the sky. Keys is an astral adept, and though he's no great shakes as a musician, he is popular with local magicians because of the intensity he gives his performance in astral space.

No matter how spectacular astral rock may be, it is a limited-demand market. There are not enough magicians to turn an "astral rocker" into a novastar, and, of course, there's no wax in astral rock at all. Some rockers who have played gigs to audiences of magicians say the scene is too dead for them. Think about it: most of the audience is either lying there snoozed out in their seats, or staring, half out of it, at the stage, with their bodies running on auto while they send their headware into astral mode. Not an inviting prospect for a mundane rocker.

BROADCASTING

It's simple. With the technology available today, we're everywhere.
—Arthur M. Cavanaugh, Senior VP, Marketing, ABS

Cavanaugh came up with that little gem in an interview on a Public Broadcasting Network talk show. You know, the "open forum" type of thing where everyone who supports the official party line gets to explain how diverse their views are. But just because it got said by a suit on a propaganda show doesn't make it a lie. Okay, usually, that *does* make it a lie, but this time, Arty somehow managed to glue the fork in his tongue together long enough to say something true.

Technically, a lot of "broadcasting" in 2050 is not really broadcasting at all. It is piped over cable, accessed through the Matrix, downlinked from the satellite nets—anything *but* transmitted omni-directionally. But people get used to using the same old words, and it seemed kinda silly to say cablecast, satcast, matcast, and so on. It's not like it matters to the viewer how it gets into the trid. So "broadcasting" means any kind of popular trid transmission. Same way that folks still use "TV" whether they are talking about flat imaging or 3-D holovision.

TRANSMISSION SYSTEMS

AM, FM, and TV/3V are still broadcast over public airwaves. Really broadcast, that is. Anyone with a commercial receiver can pick them up. Public air broadcasts are free trid. There are no user fees, because most of them sell commercial time to make their money.

There are hundreds of other channels coming over cable, satellite, and the Matrix. Some of them belong to the majors or to independent operations doing mixed programming just like the majors, but on a smaller basis. Some specialize in movies, sports, news, or whatever. Most of these are pay channels that charge for delivery to the viewer's home. Usually, it's a flat monthly fee, sometimes a pay-per-use. Watch an Urban Brawl game, pay for that broadcast. Watch it again, pay again. Hit the instant replay option if you're watching a multi-tasking cable or Matrix channel, and you pay a service fee for that.

TERRESTRIAL BROADCASTING

This is transmission via omni-directional electromagnetic signals from a ground-based transmitter. Good old radio and television, in other words.

Commercial radio operates on the AM and FM bands. TV broadcasts on the VHF and UHF bands. VHF broadcasting operates on channels 2 through 13, UHF from 14 through 80. An average metroplex area has ten to twenty TV stations transmitting, and anywhere from twenty to eighty radio stations.

In a metroplex area, each major network operates a transmitting station or has an affiliate. That accounts for seven TV channels, one for each major. The rest are affiliated with smaller nets, or else are local independents.

Outside the NAN and Québec, stations are licensed by the ITCC, a "self-regulating" agency run by the major networks. The theory is that this puts broadcasting regulation into the free market. In reality, it means the majors can keep anyone they don't like from getting access to the airwaves. So what is offered on local stations is mostly gonna be advertising, reruns of old network shows, and movies.

Free broadcasting is everywhere. Makes sense. If someone wants to watch cable or a Matrix hookup, he needs either a legal connection, which means he also needs a SIN, or he's gotta have the tech to steal a connection. But a TV broadcast doesn't care if the viewer's got a SIN or not, and it doesn't require a tech to punch an On button.

CABLE TRANSMISSION

An optical trideo-data cable can route two hundred separate TV channels and get hookups all over the metroplex. Cable transmission is a lot cheaper than setting up a transmitter and the ratings game is less important. As long as people pay to have a channel hooked up, the station makes some money even if the viewers are not watching. So most of the available cable channels will be in use in a sprawl, usually one hundred to one hundred fifty of them. On the downside, the cable provider is the sole legal access to the cable system. If the provider will not permit a broadcast onto his cable, it does not go out. At least, not legally.

Big sprawls may have more than one cable system. Seattle, for example, has two: Cable A operated by Photo-3 Cable Connectors, a Fuchi subsidiary, and Cable B, operated by Optical Media Systems, a local firm.

Big extraterritorial enclaves, like the Renraku Arcology in Seattle, have their own in-house cable system. Metroplex cable services are routed into the corporate system, where the enclave authorities can decide what broadcasts to pass on to their users. Corporate programming is also available on these systems, of course. Renraku, for example, sells its in-house programming to Optical Media as part of the Cable B basic-service lineup.

Some cable stations stick to the old-fashioned single-program format. Everyone who accesses the channel sees the same thing. Some premium services offer select-a-trid programming, where subscribers can pick from a library of films, regular programming, or continuous news reports, all on the same channel. Many channels also have selectable language and/or subtitle tracks, so that a viewer may watch the same show in Standard English, Japanese, one of the NAN languages, or even the local dialect of City Speak. Though this technology

was real hot around the turn of the century, it is on its way to being replaced by Matrix-based broadcasting, which is even more flexible.

Cable is installed in virtually 100 percent of registered trideos, that is, trids owned by someone with a SIN. And it is bribed or boosted into trids for a whole lot of SINless folks, too.

SATELLITE TRANSMISSION

Satellite transmission is a crazy mix. About 100¥ worth of off-the-shelf tech from Radio Shack will let anyone who can follow an instruction vid put together a receiver dish. The problem is sorting through the available channels and decrypting scrambled signals.

A communications satellite carries about thirty transponders. One transponder can either receive input or transmit output. Transponders use 4:1 output compression, meaning the output from one transponder actually has four program feeds on it. The receiving gear down on the ground unpacks the signal from the transponder and lets the viewer pick which feed he actually wants to watch. This means that a typical comsat, using maybe twenty-five of its transponders for output, is transmitting one hundred channels. Only a handful of these carry organized programming. Most are switched around as needed to handle network feeds, news stories, and such.

Switching channels on a satellite dish is not like clicking the trid for transmissions or cable. First, the dish has to be aimed at the right comsat. Then the viewer has to pick the transponder, then choose the particular feed he wants off that transponder signal. Most home-control units have a microprocessor to handle the scut work: Tell it what you wanna watch and it tells you if it can find it or not. Public-access databases with programming information are part of the basic Matrix service in most areas, and they keep an up-to-date ephemeris on the commercial birds and their transponder schedules so that it's possible to search for a particular show without having to be an astronomer.

The usual listing for a full-time satellite channel looks something like: Vidsat-31:4-1. That's the name of the bird (Vidsat-31), the transponder number (4), and the signal component to unpack for that channel (1). Music-lovers will spot this particular address as the code for Rocker Stars, the Seattle-based music trid and rock-news station.

Lots of satellite feeds are unscrambled. Free and clear. But premium sat feeds are not, so there is a lot of protection against pirate receivers. The usual drill nowadays is that a legit receiving unit has a Matrix interface running in realtime with the satellite feed. A program on the comsat corp's system synchronizes the encryption of the signal at the broadcasting ground station with the decryption circuits at the viewer's receiver. The viewer is billed based on connect time on the Matrix. Any decker worth a even a tenth of a yen can either crack the encryption or steal access to the commercial system, and there is a thriving market in black box samplers that will unscramble satellite feeds for less adept viewers.

A few satellite channels do real, "free" broadcasting: commercials and more commercials. Some corporations and governments bankroll satellite stations for propaganda purposes. Both UCAS and CAS law have interesting loopholes that give satellite broadcasts a lot of freedom: the content of broadcasts can only be regulated under the laws of the originating corp or country. So there is no legal basis for trying to regulate satellite broadcasts of

HOME RECEIVERS

Almost every household in 2050 has a "trid." That's short for trideo, of course, and means both 3-D holovision and "three-way" access: broadcasts, cable, and telephone. Oh, there are still TV/3V receivers that are not part of a trid, and still telephones that do not get broadcasts, and so on, but in living rooms all over North America, the trid is what you find.

The broadcasting standards for North America went through a real shakeout about forty to fifty years ago, as high-definition flatscreen formats and then the earliest holocast tech competed for market share. With the implementation of an ultra-fast digital-packing algorithm in 2008, HDTV could finally work on the existing U.S. channel bandwidths, and in 2024 Renraku's Digital-XScan holo protocol was adopted by the major networks.

BASIC TRIDEO

Anyone with a Low lifestyle or better has access to a basic trid unit and services. The lease on the unit and the subscriptions for the services are covered by the cost of the lifestyle. An average unit is about the size and shape of a laptop computer, except for the TV/3V display field, which is a 50 to 90-centimeter diagonal (about 20 to 30 inches) for flatscreen displays and about a cubic meter for 3V. Low-class homes usually have smaller units, and in poor homes, or out on the streets, you find real antiques with problems like no holo, or no Matrix hookup. Just flatscreen.

Naturally, SINless trid-users need a gimmick to receive anything except broadcast services. No SIN means no legal comm code for phone calls, no passcode for municipal Matrix services, and so on. Basic services are, however, available at Middle lifestyle or higher for SINless folks. Presumably they are greasing the right palms as part of the payments. There's also flat-out stealing, or *boosting*, which is described a bit later on.

In general, a home trid unit has:

•A receiver for commercial radio and TV broadcasts.

•A cable hookup and access to basic cable channels: public access channels and free cable stations. Additional services can be switched on or off by the distributor at any time.

•A telephone.

•A public access Matrix terminal hardwired into free public databases. The terminal is not cybercapable: a "tortoise." The terminal can also be used to dial out to any other Matrix systems for which the user has access. The bandwidth on basic Matrix service is one megapulse per second. (Figure that this is comparable to the I/O rate for file transfers, way too low for things like simsense transmission or decking.)

OPTIONAL TRIDEO FEATURES

It is possible to pile lots of extras onto the trid. The right Lifestyle will offer some of these possibilities as part of the perks. Each of the following descriptions of optional features lists the Lifestyle that includes it. If a feature is listed as available at Middle lifestyle, for example, that means Middle or better.

All these features require that the user have the appropriate basic trid service first. For example, a vidphone connection is not much use without basic phone service.

If an option requires a SIN, an (S) appears after the Lifestyle level. That means the option is available only if an individual has a real SIN, a very good fake, or if he is at the next higher Lifestyle,

---

ultra-violent sports or pornography. And as long as sponsors contract and produce their commercials in the country or enclave of origin, they are also exempt from prosecution. Though it is possible to pressure advertisers to discourage them from underwriting pornographic, violent, or otherwise undesirable broadcasting, the corporate stranglehold on the legal systems in North America has so far kept the governments from closing the legal loophole. The law does, however, prevent these programs from being re-transmitted from ground-based systems; only a dish can pick them up.

About 40 percent of all trideo-users in North America have satellite access, either through a home dish or via cable feeding from a central dish in their condo, enclave, or development.

MATRIX TRANSMISSION

Matrix access may eventually replace the other transmission systems. After all, if it's digital, it can travel over the Matrix. Whether things go that way or not, a standard trid unit with a high bandwidth modem can access all sorts of signals via Matrix: print, sound, imaging, 3V, even simsense.

Packet switching for high-speed modem access is fast enough that a user can even access several services at the same time over a single comm line, if using High-Speed Matrix Access on his trid (see **Gear**, page 88.)

Matrix "broadcasting" is really just telecommunications, with the user able to select any available program, or programs, at will. It grew out of the commercial computer network services of the 1980s, when technology for realtime vid transmission was adding on to the things a modem could provide. As home systems able to handle the requirements for Matrix broadcasts reached the marketplace, a few commercial stations started playing with it. As of 2050, an estimated 27 percent of all homes have a Matrix-capable trideo unit.

where the necessary bribes are all part of the service. Thus, a SINless shadowrunner who wants a high-speed matrix access connection ("free" at High lifestyle) either has to have a good phony SIN or else be whooping it up at Luxury lifestyle. Or he can simply boost the service if he knows a good tech or decker. Features that do not require a SIN need not be boosted. Oh, you can knock over a shop and steal the equipment, but that hardly takes any tech savvy, now does it?

Besides the features listed here, a trid unit can come with all sorts of attachments that can also be added later: audio playback units, simsense decks, VCR (vid-chip recorder) and holovid players, automatic soykaf makers, personal computers, and much more. Anything that can be added on and works without tapping into the telephone, cable, or Matrix is no big deal. Figure that a typical unit in a High-lifestyle habitat will have one to three of these optional toys, and a unit in a Luxury lifestyle squat will have three to six of them.

FAX
Basic Service: Matrix or phone
Lifestyle: Middle

This isn't the same FAX people used in the late 20th century, but its descendant by about four generations. FAX is the commercial standard for graphics storage and transmission. It virtually replaced all other print and graphics peripherals, and the resolution of a typical unit is about that of a very good laser printer from the year 2000. A standard FAX can bitmap and print a standard A4 (letter-size) sheet of print or graphics output, or scan in a hardcopy image that size, in .5 seconds. A high-speed FAX can produce output in .1 second.

This unit can transmit FAX to other trids or freestanding FAX machines or to FAX chips in personal computers. It can print out FAX data as it is received or store it in datafiles for later browsing and/or printing.

No SIN is necessary to use FAX, though SINner services may be needed to get a phone line or Matrix hookup in order to send and receive faxes. Middle lifestyle trids come with FAX built in, but anyone can buy a FAX unit and plug it into their trid, computer, or whatever.

HIGH-SPEED MATRIX ACCESS
Basic Service: Matrix
Lifestyle: High (S)

The high-speed matrix access offers extremely high bandwidth connection to the Matrix, 10 Mp/second or higher. Besides allowing much faster file transfer, the connection is suitable for high-speed realtime Matrix access. Simsense broadcasts are available over this unit, and it can plug into the LTG using a cyberdeck. This lets the user access any LTG or RTG without having to beat the phone company IC, because he is calling from a legal access node. It lets the player skip the tests on p. 100 of **Shadowrun** for switching into different LTGs or RTGs.

On the downside, trace programs get a –4 target number modifier to tests for backtracking the access path of someone plugged in through a legal node. Of course, if that chummer's using someone else's trid, no sweat.

LARGE FIELD HOLOPHONE
Basic Service: Phone (and vidphone)
Lifestyle: Luxury

This item is a full-field holoscan and holoprojection phone attachment. Basically, it allows users who have this option to get full-body holos of other users with the same attachment. The callers see each other in 3V, as if they were really face-to-face. The feature itself does not require a SIN, but it only works on a phone circuit that has the vidphone service feature (see below).

LARGE TV/3V DISPLAY
Basic Service: None required
Lifestyle: High

This includes any large display up to the life-size option, in other words, a large wall screen or large-volume 3V projection unit. A life-size flatscreen unit occupies an area about two meters square, and a 3V occupies an area about three meters square and two meters high.

The large display works fine with any video or holo output, including signals from broadcast TV, so it does not require any particular basic service hookup.

MULTISTATION TRIDEO
Basic Service: Any or all
Lifestyle: High (S)

Multistation trideo provides not only multiple trid units on the site, but multiplexing connections and high-speed packet-switching connections to the various networks, which allow each unit to operate independently of the others. A viewer can be watching one cable access and talking on the phone on one unit, while his buddy is FAXing some sample data to a prospective buyer, accessing the Matrix, and watching the satcasts of the Freestyle Semifinals from Bangkok on another.

High lifestyle gets up to three units. Luxurious lifestyle allows six. Additional units have to be bought, as do units wanted by those living other lifestyles. Multistation connections for SINless users have to be stolen individually, that is, a separate boost for each unit to be served.

MULTIPHONIC SOUND
Basic Service: None required
Lifestyle: High

The multiple speakers and microprocessor-driven acoustic tuning of multiphonic sound provide absolute fidelity. The listener is one meter from the edge of the stage at a Mercurial concert, or smack in the *middle* of the choir for the "Ode to Joy" in Beethoven's Ninth Symphony. Of course, this works for any other playback units plugged into the trid as well as for broadcasts.

PREMIUM CABLE ACCESS
Basic Service: Cable
Lifestyle: Varies (S)

This is access to pay cable channels.

Middle lifestyle gets access to three pay channels.

High lifestyle gets access to all monthly subscription systems and three pay-per-view systems.

Luxury lifestyle gets access to any and all cable channels.

Stealing cable access requires a separate boost for each channel.

PREMIUM MATRIX ACCESS
Basic Service: Matrix
Lifestyle: Varies (S)

This is access to Matrix channels that carry entertainment programming. More accurately, it is access to the local switcher service. Matrix channels can carry simsense as well as TV/3V and other data formats, but receiving simsense requires the High-Speed Matrix Access option as well (no problem for normal High-class units, as they get both features free).

High Lifestyle gets access to three Matrix channels.

Luxury lifestyle gets access to all available channels.

Stealing Matrix access requires a separate boost for each channel and a boost of High-Speed Matrix Access if sim is desired.

PREMIUM MATRIX INTERFACE
Basic Service: Matrix
Lifestyle: Luxury (S)

This is a cyberdeck interface built right into the trid. This feature is used by the execs and double-dome R&D boys to access the Matrix from home. It is a legal deck, natch, so it doesn't have the cybercombat features or fancy reactions of a street unit. But it does give normal Matrix access to a user armed with legal passcodes.

SATELLITE RECEPTION
Basic Service: None required (Matrix for decryption schemes)
Lifestyle: Varies

Getting satellite reception is no big deal. Off-the-shelf tech handles that. However, stealing it requires some technical smarts because the signals are usually encrypted.

No SIN is needed to get satellite broadcasts, as shown in the boosting rules, below. It is also possible to get satellite access legally, on the same basis as premium cable access. In this case, the broadcaster gives the user a decryption system or key.

SIMSENSE INTERFACE
Basic Service: Matrix (and premium matrix access and high-speed matrix access)
Lifestyle: High

A Dir-X simsense unit (see p. 97) is built right into the trid and lets the viewer plug into simsense broadcasts via a datajack, chipjack, or induction electrodes. Trodes give lousy signal resolution, and sim through a trode is like taking a shower in partial heavy armor, but it's better than nothing.

It is possible to obtain the interface unit itself without a SIN, but access to premium matrix access that offers simsense broadcasts is another matter. That must be purchased (if the buyer has a SIN) or boosted.

VIDPHONE SERVICE

Basic Service: Phone
Lifestyle: Middle (S)

The telephone circuit is coded to carry imaging signals as well as voice. The trid unit is equipped with a camera pickup in order to transmit vidphone signals. The received image can be displayed either on the TV screen or on a separate vidphone screen that is part of the phone unit. It is also visible on the flip-up or pull-out screens that are available on many personal phones.

BOOSTING TRIDEO SERVICES

SINless folks need trid, too. Even non-persons may want to make a phone call every now and then. And the broadcast channels in summertime are nothing but reruns, for Ghost's sake. Being stuck watching those is cruel and unusual punishment.

Null perspiration, chummer. What the wonders of technology can create, the wonders of technology can steal.

Boosting trid service and its features requires a Success Test. Each service has a boosting target number (see Boosting Table, below) and the relevant skill needed for the test. If the booster passes the test, he has successfully boosted the service for a number of months equal to the successes rolled.

For example, boosting basic telephone service has a Target Number 8 and requires Computer Skill (or the Decking Concentration). Your friendly neighborhood decker makes a Computer Test, scoring 3 successes. The phony telecom code he slipped into the LTG directory database will last for three months before some busybody watchdog software spots and deletes it.

If the boost attempt fails, the gamemaster should make the test again, secretly. This time, he uses the Traceback Target Number from the Boosting Table to see if the booster has avoided detection. If this column shows "None," no traceback can take place. If this second test does not yield a simple success, the service provider has detected the attempt to boost services and traced the location of the pirate trid unit. Many providers have a policy of letting failed boosts go through, that is, they let the booster make the connection, so as not to warn the thieves that their evil, antisocial shenanigans have been detected. For this reason, the gamemaster may want to make the first boosting test secretly also.

Attempting to pirate trid services is a misdemeanor for people with SINs. The fine is 500¥ for each count. Oh yes, if any one boost attempt fails and is traced back, **all** boosted services will be detected, because they are all keyed to that particular trid address. Each boost is another misdemeanor count.

SINless boosters may get fined, just like honest citizens. That's if they're lucky. Depending on local ordinances and the corporate policy of the service provider, their trid can be confiscated and they may get a little summary justice from the offended corporation's police (anything from a bad beating to a bullet). In Seattle, whose voter base has a significant population of bleeding-heart liberals, killing the SINless for a misdemeanor is not allowed. Company towns are less forgiving, not to mention what can happen when the local trid-provider happens to be a front for yak or Mafia operations! It is worth noting that in Chicago, where the Mafia has its finger in most municipal pies, trid boosting is a relatively rare offense.

BUYING TRIDEO SERVICES

Yes, it's possible to get trideo legally. Check out the prices in the **Gear** section, page 99. The table below provides a quick reference to services available with the various lifestyles.

TRID SERVICES

Lifestyle	Services
Low	Basic trideo (commercial radio/3V; basic cable; telephone; public access Matrix terminal).
Middle	As above, plus FAX, vidphone, three pay cable channels.
High	As above, plus high-speed matrix access, large TV/3V display, multistation trideo (up to three units), multiphonic sound, simsense interface, all subscription cable plus three pay-per-view cable channels.
Luxury	As above, plus large field holophone, multistation trideo (up to six units), premium matrix interface, all cable channels.

BOOSTING TABLE

Service	Target Number	Boosting Skill	Traceback Number
Basic Phone	8	Computer	18*
Basic Matrix	12	Computer	18*
Basic Cable	6	Electronics B/R	None
High-Speed Matrix Access	16	Computer	24*
Multistation Trideo	12	Electronics B/R	14
Premium Cable Access	6	Electronics B/R	12
Premium Matrix Access	14	Computer	18*
Premium Matrix Interface	18	Computer	24*
Satellite Reception	8	Electronics B/R	14
Vidphone Service	12	Electronics B/R	12

*If a decker performs this boost via a cyberdeck, subtract the deck's Masking Attribute from the Traceback Target Number.

THE NETS

Lotta different masks. Always the same faces behind 'em.
—Jon Botha, Freelance Vidsnoop

Do you realize that in the 1960s corporations began going on a shopping spree? At that time, 80 percent of the approximately 25,000 media outlets in the United States were independently owned. By 1980 the percentage was reversed: fifty companies owned more than 80 percent of the broadcasting and publishing industry.

When the sharks finished off the little fish, they started on each other. By 2020 it was down to twenty-three corporations. With a few changes, mostly minor ones, that tidy little oligopoly has persisted for the last thirty years. Today, twenty companies control almost all the major networks of communication in the so-called civilized world.

And what is the result? Mainstream media caters to the butt-end of the lowest common denominator. What passes for news is usually sanitized, trivialized, and guaranteed not to offend either the government or the corporate establishment. Oh, if a network sees a chance to nail some politico's hide to the wall after he gets caught fragging the public, it may decide to score some points. Stories that expose dirt on a competitor are also likely to survive. Anything else the least bit controversial is watered down to nothing or simply spiked.

And as for other programming, the hottest sportscasts on the nets involve people pounding each other into snail snot. I suppose we should be grateful that, in theory, any deaths in a game of Urban Brawl or Combat Biker are accidental. Still I sometimes wonder if the real killer sports that get beamed in from Aztlan are simply less hypocritical. Both are using death and injury to sell products. The Azteks are just more honest about it.

—So Who Told You?, by Mullins Chadwick, Putnam-Izumo Publishers, New York, 2044

TRID NETWORKS

The major trid networks operate over all the broadcast media. They maintain the fiction of "free 3V," and pay for their operations by running commercials. An average hour of programming on a major has about 25 minutes of commercials. That's not counting shows that are nothing but ads with some entertainment wrapped around them.

The majors also operate premium access channels for a fee, and of course, they advertise their pay services heavily on the free channels.

THE ITCC

Public control over broadcasting was pretty much demolished in the privatization wave at the turn of the century. Government finally gave up in 2022, and the Internetwork Transmission Control Council took over from what was left of the FCC. The ITCC is a "self-regulating oversight body for the responsible management of the communications industry." It says so right in its charter.

The ITCC is the majors, and the majors are the ITCC. They're in charge of regulating themselves and their independent competitors, too. The result is a tight, self-perpetuating little oligarchy whose main job is keeping competitors from making trouble for the majors.

There were rumors that the ITCC charter was part of a deal between President William Jarman, who was running for his third term, and the networks, which were a big piece of the remote-vote system that put Jarman back in the White House in 2024. Natch, that's just spiteful sour grapes spread by Jarman's opposition.

Like most big corps, the majors came out of the economic collapse following the Computer Crash of 2029 ahead of the game. The ITCC today operates in the UCAS, CAS, and California Free State as the regulatory body for all media transmission. They have influence in the NAN and Québec, mostly from the economic clout their corporate affiliates have in those countries, plus the propaganda they can beam in from ITCC stations on the borders or via satellite.

THE MAJORS

Any network with a seat on the ITCC is a major. There are two major North American nets that are not ITCC members, and both are mouthpieces for their national governments (the NAN and Québec).

The majors operate freely across national borders, thanks to the mess of interlocked trade agreements among the North American powers. Most international broadcasting regulation is smoke and mirrors anyway. With almost unlimited cable feeds, satellite availability, and Matrix transmissions, it is pretty hard to keep people from watching anything they fragging well please. The following are generally agreed to make up the majors:

ABS (American Broadcasting System, UCAS)
CBC (Confederate Broadcasting Company, CAS)
NABS (Native American Broadcasting System, NAN)*
NBS (North American Broadcasting System, UCAS)
NN (NewsNet, formerly Turner Network Television, CAS)
OTQ (Organisation Trivideo de Québec, Québec)*
PBN (Public Broadcasting Network, UCAS)
*Not an ITCC member

ABS

ABS is a subsidiary of Transnational Communications, which also owns assorted faxnews services, databases, and recording companies. Transnational was recently the target of a successful takeover by Morgen-Tek GmbH, a Cologne-based operation that produces all manner of technical goodies, and which is a leader in nanotech research. Morgen-Tek is itself a major subsidiary of Saeder-Krupp. Rumors that ABS will be changing its logo to a dragon with a credstick are doubtless exaggerated.

CBC

CBC is an independent corporation, but 18 percent of the voting stock belongs to Mitsuhama, and Yomiuri controls another 20 percent. Fuchi bought into Confederate Studios, CBC's Atlanta-based sim and film operation, three years ago. Fuchi wanted a CAS market outlet to bolster its top-dog role in sim. CBC was loud in its praise of the buy-out, claiming that Fuchi was "revitalizing the entertainment industry in the Confederated American States." So we can assume the takeover had the blessing of the big boys back home.

NABS

Controlled by a consortium of NAN governments, NABS is like the old Public Broadcasting Systems in the U.S. But if it cannot keep the different factions on the Sovereign Tribal Council happy, it risks crippling budget cuts. The network also has commercial sponsors, but does not, by the terms of its charter, allow script approval or other open control to sponsors.

For all its faults, NABS is one of the nets that allows major journalistic freedom to reporters and affiliates. The top news management insists on solid documentation for controversial stories, and reporters who commit flagrant felonies while getting their story may find it spiked if diplomatic paybacks arise.

NBS

A wholly owned subsidiary of Ares Macrotechnology. NBS is the stuffiest of the nets when it comes to news and editorial policy. The corporation is always right. The government is the wise ally of the corps. Do what you are told and it will all turn out right. Trust us.

NN

When Atlanta billionaire Ted Turner died a number of years back, his will set up Turner Network Television as the controlling company in an interlocking restructure of his corporate holdings. This threw down a challenge to the big corps that were busily achieving a choke-hold on the media, even back then. "This network will stand as a bastion of the free press in a world where freedom is increasingly under attack."

NewsNet is the modern incarnation of the Turner Network, and the crusty old guy's brilliantly paranoid net of legal and financial defenses is still working. NewsNet is the only major that is independent of higher corporate ownership or government control. Its stock portfolio even boasts significant chunks of voting stock from other majors.

That's why NewsNet has the biggest, most controversial news division of any of the majors. And with a SWAT team of lawyers second to none, NewsNet is not afraid who their stories might hurt. A lot of pabulum still goes out on their broadcasts, but it is the only major that also offers good, muckraking, investigative reporting.

OTQ

The Organisation Trivideo de Québec was cobbled together from assorted affiliates and stations that became nationalized under President Celinne DeGaulle when the Republic was just getting off the ground. The Québeçois government figured, correctly, that the only way they could get away with secession was with strong control of news inside their borders and a loud propaganda voice outside.

Since then, OTQ has remained in control of all legal broadcasting originating inside the Republic. There are no legal independents in Québec at all, but plenty of pirates, many of them broadcasting from just across the borders from UCAS or Algonkian-Manitoo Council territory.

OTQ runs commercial trid as well as government-funded broadcasts, but all their news shows are government-subsidized and subject to official censorship.

The Bob Channel! News and info for and about folks named Bob!
— Joke ad that received 1,200 responses

PBN

The old PBS was broken up and privatized in 2005. A couple of local stations found the funding to keep going as independents, but most were snapped up by commercial buyers glad to promise to maintain "significant educational and public interest content" in return for bargain basement prices on the station's license.

PBN came along twelve years later. It was funded by the U.S. government and a consortium of corporations. Its main job was to pump out "educational" broadcasting to keep the cits well-informed of the official position on how things were going. Any oldies out there may remember that in 2017 they weren't going real well. The country was still reeling from the assassinations of 2016, and the Soviets were still making noises about how it was all the U.S.'s fault. Weather strikes generated by Howling Coyote's Ghost Dancers were hitting all over North America, and a series of quakes was rattling the Northwest. We know now, of course, that they were building up to the blowoff of the Cascade volcanoes. The *America* spaceplane disaster had everyone asking if the U.S. still knew what the frag it was doing with high tech.

PBN ran a series of glossy specials that toed the government party line and praised Jarman to the skies. It put high-priced wage mages and scientists on the air to show how the Ghost Dance was small stuff and its effects were merely the result of natural patterns in the environment. Anthropologists proved that the Native American cultures could only benefit by cooperating in the government's relocation and reeducation programs.

Objective scientific journalism, you see.

PBN also runs lots of art shows, with only a half a dozen breaks to acknowledge the corporate donations that make it all possible.

A lot has happened since PBN went on the air, but not to worry, PBN hasn't let that change its style. It's still a free and open forum for anyone who holds opinions that the ITCC and the UCAS gummint approve of.

THE INDIES

Every trid market has local independents, the *indies*. Indies have business facilities, assigned operating frequencies or cable nodes, and licenses. They are under ITCC rules, and if they want to stay legal, they play by those rules. That keeps 99 percent of the indies in line. The left-overs walk the line on ITCC regs, and have some kind of edge that keeps their license from getting zapped.

Natch, some "independents" are owned body, soul, and cable hookup by the majors. Ain't free enterprise grand?

COMMERCIAL INDEPENDENTS

Commercial independents do the same kind of trid programming as the majors. Just smaller, with reruns, syndicated feeds, and local programming. And commercials. Most operate on transmission channels, but also do cable feeds. A few have branched into Matrix access.

SPECIALIZED INDEPENDENTS

Like chess? How about sports? Weather reports? Shopping? There's probably a specialized indie to suit every viewer's taste.

Some of these are two-bit feeds of stock trid, which pay for themselves by serving as filler for the local cable company. Stuff like Chessvid fits that bill.

Then there are the 24-hour commercials, the home shopping nets. They pay for themselves, and then some.

The pay-per-use nets don't, of course, have to sweat commercials and ratings. The film and sim channels, like Fuchi Realsense Theater ("*If it's Fuchi, it's really real*") and Home Theater Organization pay the bills lotsa different ways. A basic membership in these premium services buys a limited number of views per month. To get anything else, or any special shows they put on, the viewer pays a surcharge. Pricier memberships carry free access to all the goodies. These guys also carry commercials. Just money from home, s'right?

It's the same deal with the sports and battle channels. Battle channel ratings, and publicity, are a big deal with the corps. Helps justify the cost of those little corp wars, y'see.

PUBLIC AFFAIRS INDEPENDENTS

Public affairs stations are run by either the local government or funded by private money. The government stations are local copies of PBN. Seattle's Channel 6 (KPUB) is a typical example. Local talk shows, stuff on arts around town, reports from metroplex contractors like Lone Star, and government-approved news.

The privately funded public affairs channels are more interesting. Some are outlets for the sponsor's agenda, and boil down to corporate propaganda stations. A few are backed by foundations or private fortunes. These can be real mucknets, where all the dirt the big boys want hidden gets hauled out and thrown onto the airwaves. Some of these channels also offer "outlaw" trid, stuff that usually only shows up on the pirates.

In the middle ground are the public-access channels on cable. Because the local cable provider and the metroplex government control public access, they can keep anything really controversial off the net. Some places, that's exactly how it is. Other sprawls, other customs, though, and where the climate is a little looser, even runners can get on PA cable and push their stories, if they care to step that far out of the shadows.

Public affairs indies that push the outside of the establishment envelope don't last too long as a rule, unless they've got a lot of nuyen and a lot of clout backing them. Seattle Spy, on Cable B, is an example. Seattle Spy is backed by the Insight Foundation. Of course, no one is quite sure who's backing that. Rumors have pegged its money to everything from a great dragon to the High Lord of Tir Tairngire to space aliens from Andromeda. The Foundation has been a big campaign contributor to a dozen metroplex Congresspeople from all three major parties, and so far has managed to stand off attempts by the ITCC to lift Seattle Spy's license.

THE PIRATES

Any broadcasting operation that does not have a license is technically a pirate. There are two major types of pirate operation: remote and local.

REMOTE PIRATES

Remote pirates are usually legal somewhere, and broadcast via satellite. They format their programs as if they were a regular network operation, and anyone with a dish can pick up their signal.

In the UCAS, at least, it would be possible to make a case that most remote pirates are not pirates at all. In the Revised Telecommunications Act of 2027, the UCAS government washed its hands of the whole problem of trying to monitor and control satcasts from overseas. If the content of a program is legal in the country of origin, the UCAS does not challenge it. This legislation mostly provides the government a way out of an impossible situation without looking too chicken, since even if the contents of a 'cast are wildly illegal, there's not a frag of lot the UCAS can do about it. As far as the ITCC is concerned, the money for satcasting is too good to give up over minor points like morality. So there are no controls worth mentioning on the contents of satellite transmissions. Pirate injection into satcasts is another matter, of course. Using facilities without paying for them is…is…why, it's evil!

It is still illegal to re-transmit kill shows and similar raw fare over ground-based transmitters, cable, or Matrix systems in the North American countries other than Aztlan. Occasional attempts by various interest groups at getting that restriction off the books have so far been beaten in the various governments, and the ITCC is staying neutral on this one. For now, it's an impasse.

So, these "legal pirates" are feeding in programming that is illegal on local broadcast nets. That can be "subversive" programming, according to however the local set of prejudices define subversive. But a lot of it is porn so raw or violence so bloody that even the battered ethics of the UCAS draw the line.

With the Telecom Act of 2027 to protect them, some sponsors have figured out that they can push their commercials to the sickos who like this sort of thing by setting up a local office in the country where the stuff originates, and contract their advertising there, and voilà: no legal recourse in UCAS. So in between the screams, you can see commercials for all sorts of things.

And some local pirates, for money or for fun, pick up satcasts and feed them into local ground-based nets. So even poor old SINless trash with nothing to sustain them but a boosted cable feed can pick up the best in porn trid, with a little bit of luck.

LOCAL PIRATES

Local pirates have something they want to say, and they are, by Ghost, gonna say it. They may use a short-range transmitter on VHF/UHF bands, operating out of a truck to avoid triangulation. Lots of pirates sneak a feed into the cable network. Whole lotta optic out there, waiting for enterprising chummers with the right tech. And like we said earlier, pirates with a taste for big audiences can find an unused channel on a satellite transponder and put their stuff on that.

Pirate stations move around a lot. They put a feed into the system, the legit operators find it and rip it out again. A few days later the pirates are back on another channel. The trid guides on local databases are usually crawling with shadowtalk, letting people know where the pirates are this week.

This is where someone can find the underground politics, the neoanarchists, the revolutionaries. With the tech available off the shelf, it doesn't take that much to hoist the Jolly Roger on trid these days.

Broadcast Piracy

Most broadcast pirates transmit over short-range equipment on unused channels. The authorities will not usually bother trying to hunt them down unless the pirate material interferes with commercial broadcasting or is somehow "subversive." When some broadcast does tick off the ITCC or the local corps, they'll have tracers working overtime trying to locate the scoundrels.

The transmitters for pirate broadcasting are street-tech and often equipped with some ECM that makes it possible for even a stationary transmitter to operate for some hours before it is located. Of course, the better the transmitter, the more it costs.

From a gaming standpoint, tracing a broadcast signal can be handled one of two ways: as hunter or as hunted.

If a player character operating a pirate station wants to avoid being located, he makes a standard Success Test for Electronics or another appropriate tech skill. The Target Number depends on how hot the broadcast is, and how eager is the establishment to get the pirate off the air. Add an additional number of dice equal to the ECM Rating of the pirate's transmitter to the Target Number.

For a quick result, multiply the pirate's successes by 1 hour to determine how long it will take to home in on his location. If he fails the test, the heat will locate him in 1D6 x 10 minutes.

To make things a little less certain, the gamemaster can roll 1D6 for every success the pirate scores, then multiply the result by 10 minutes. That figure, which he keeps secret, is the actual time it will take the ITCC or other heat to locate the transmitter.

A stationary transmitter is cake, once located. Security forces will arrive in minutes. A mobile transmitter can live to fight another day, but it must go off the air for at least 24 hours. If it sticks its head up before then, automated tracers will locate the transmitter in minutes. The gamemaster can, of course, decide that the authorities will drop the trace in less than 24 hours or else keep it going longer. Much depends on just what the pirate was doing that so attracted the big boys' attention.

LOCATION AVOIDANCE TABLE

Broadcasts have little political content	6
Broadcasts are highly political but have no specific facts	8
Broadcasts contain illegal material	10
Broadcasts include detailed stories that embarrass authority	12

Target Number Modifiers

Transmitter is mobile	−2
Pirate is using commercial channel	+2

Gamemasters or player characters might also make a test to locate a pirate transmitter if they need to find the pirate for some reason. This uses the same standard Success Test against Electronics Skill. The Target Number is 6 plus the ECM Rating of the transmitter, if any. The Base Time is three hours to locate a stationary transmitter and six hours to locate a mobile one. Divide the Base Time by any successes from the test. If the test fails, the searcher must spend the full Base Time in fruitless scanning before he can try again.

The tech for homing in on a signal has improved, but the principle remains pretty much the same. The searcher gets several readings on a signal from different locations, then plots a common point of origin to locate the transmitter.

It used to take multiple scanners operating together to pull this off. Modern technology allows a single unit to do the job. A transmission sampler (see **Gear**, p. 91) computes the likely locations for a transmitter as long as it can pick up the signal for a significant part of the search time.

Using a single transmission sampler in a fixed location is the slowest way to search for a pirate. And if the guy goes off the air for more than an hour, it is not possible to complete the task. If he starts broadcasting again, the search must start over.

Multiple sampler units reduce the Target Number. Two units at different locations or two mobile units reduce the number by −1. Three units are worth −2. More than three units will not change the odds that much.

However, anyone with lots of resources can run multiple tasks at the same time. This explains why the ITCC can find a pirate faster than a poor, dishonest shadowrunner, who can only afford the tech for one search at a time.

The usual method for trying to locate a signal in 2050 is to fit rigger drones with transmission samplers. The rigger just has to keep the units in the air until the transmitter is located. He can also dispatch one or more of the drones to the site of the transmitter once it is located, which is handy when searching for a mobile transmitter, as it permits identification of the vehicle. That way, if the transmitter goes off the air, the searcher still knows who was using it.

Rumors that the ITCC uses armed drones to summarily take out mobile transmitters that have offended them are sheer libel. If we ever discover the true identity of the muckraking pirate broadcasters who assert this falsehood, they may expect the most stringent legal action. Boom.

Cable Piracy

Cable piracy requires a physical link to the cable network at a signal injection node. Legal injection nodes exist at studios that are licensed to broadcast on the cable system. They are usually heavily guarded physically and tested regularly for illegal feeds. Not much help there.

Fortunately, optical signals require fairly regular boosting, though nowhere near the frequent boosts they needed in first-generation optical systems. A pirate feed to the cable system can be inserted at any of the thousands of booster units around the sprawl. All it takes is a cable signal-formatter. It is a misdemeanor to own one of these without an ITCC license, of course.

Installing the formatter takes a standard Electronics B/R Test with a Target Number 4. The base time is 120 minutes.

Input to the pirate formatter can be by direct hookup, which means running a cable to it from a playback console, or by using

a transmitter broadcasting to the formatter. That's the usual drill, since it lets cable pirates operate at a distance from their cable-access point.

Finding a pirate cable feed is a long, drawn-out process. On average, the authorities check each booster point in the system every few months. Once a pirate feed is installed, it will be 2D6 weeks before the authorities find and rip it out.

If a cable pirate puts out some really outrageous stuff over the network before the end of that time, things will heat up appropriately. In this case, the pirate must avoid being located the same way a broadcast pirate does. When the trackers locate his signal in the cable net, however, all they find is the signal formatter, not the pirate himself. Unless the drekhead is sitting on top of the formatter, of course.

This search involves a series of network sampling tests coupled with physical checks on the cable equipment. The pirate can use either Electronics or Decking Skill to fight the sampling because he can combat the interference equally well by playing games with his signal or by messing with the search software active on the cable net.

Satellite Piracy

Satellite piracy requires a ground station and transmitter. It is the hardest form of piracy to track down, because the pirate transmitter can be anywhere within line-of-sight of the satellite—and that's a loooong line, chummers. Satellite uplinks used to be rare enough to make the hunter's job easier. Only so many places could pull it off. Nowadays, the tech is on the street, and pirate signals bounce around the satnets with abandon.

The usual protection against pirate signals is the use of encryption protocols on the transponders. These let the satellite lock out signals from unauthorized transmitters. Any decker worth the name can steal the latest access codes for a would-be satellite pirate, though recently the satellite companies have begun increasing the security on their systems.

The usual method is to crack the code scheme by trial and error. To do so, the pirate must have a computer hooked up to his transmitter to try different decoding schemes. The job calls for a standard Computer or Electronics Success Test.

The target number for this test depends on the computing power the pirate has on hand.

If he's using a PC (personal computer, not player character), the base Target Number is 12, with a −1 to the Target Number for every 100 Mp of memory the machine has. The minimum Target Number when using a PC is 6.

If the pirate has access to a mainframe, the Target Number is 4.

The Base Time to crack the encryption is 100 hours, divided by the successes, as usual.

Once the pirate is in business, he generally can expect 2D6 days of access before the codes change again.

THAT'S ENTERTAINMENT

Wasteland? Heavens, no, we've gone far beyond that!
—Sheila N. Griggs, President, Entertainment Division, CBC

Formula writing is the rule in broadcast entertainment. At least one popular adventure series on NBS has no writing staff at all: just an expert system accessing a database of the last 110 years' worth of TV and trid scripts, audience surveys, and ratings drek. It correlates this data with the sponsors' sales figures, market-study parameters, and a library of their available commercials..Turn the crank and, voilà, out comes the perfect script to enhance sales that week, commercials and all. So what if the scripts are almost interchangeable.

There's even a rumor that the network feed got hosed one night and mixed the last half of one episode with the first half of another. Only thing is, hardly anyone watching noticed the switch in plot lines.

ACTION/ADVENTURE

The big theme for action shows on the majors this season is corporate security operations. "Protector" brought in big ratings for ABS last year, and so this year we have clones like "Bright Lights" (NBS) and "Shadowbreakers" (CBC). The corp-heat shows look like a good bet to replace mercenary shows as the hot format in action/ adventure. "Money Warriors" (ABS) is still in the top twenty, even though in its seventh season, but other merc shows are losing ground in the ratings.

Every week viewers can tune in to see a lot of sensitive, socially responsible *shaikujin* using a remarkable array of high-tech weaponry to blow away drooling, BTL-crazed shadowrunners.

That's assuming they don't switch to, say, "Tyee!" (NABS), the SSC-produced docudrama series about Thunder Tyee's campaign in the Northwest during the Ghost Dance War. That show allows people to watch sensitive, ecologically aware NAN guerrillas use a remarkable array of old-tech weaponry to blow away bloodthirsty, bureaucratic U.S. forces. Not to mention the spectacular (and bloody) special effects when the power of the Great Ghost Dance descends on the treacherous white-eyes, usually about ten minutes before the end of the show each week.

Magic plays a big role in action series. Most shows feature a stereotypical magician as a supporting character. Shows with magicians as the central character usually go over like week-old nutrisoy with the folks out there in trideo-land. The typical sidekick mage is a cold-hearted fragger with a vulnerable side that he only shows to the series hero. This type of character is called a "spock" in the trade, after some ancient show that used the same stereotype. Shamans in shows written for anglo markets are usually comic relief, or else working for the villains. They're skulking, dirty, and into nasty depravity as part of their power. Some NAN shows have a brave, hearty shaman as hero, but more often he's some wise-looking old fragger who keeps the brave, hearty warrior-hero headed on the right track with his good advice.

GAME SHOWS

Nobody likes a showoff, so "hard" quiz shows don't sell. Trivia quizzes were big once, but are fading fast. Gambling games are still popular. The newest wave makes "contestants" crawl through something slimy to get a (snowball's) chance (in Hell) to win A ZILLION NUYEN (or whatever). They're wiz-flash hits.

"Lucky Lady" (ABS) is a high-ratings gambling show that uses computer-generated blackjack hands. "Galloping Cubes" (CBC) mixes craps and trivia questions. The format is simple: take a casino game, modify it to fit the game-show format, and plunk it on the air.

All my life, I've wanted to be a winner. This is my last chance.
—Contestant on Pit of Slime

If game show participants aren't lucky, they better be tough, 'cause the other hot format is "pain for gain." Contestants perform humiliation gigs, like firehose duels dressed in water-soluble costumes on "What Goes Next" (NBS). Or the search for the winning token in the hog wallow that always wraps up "Farm of Fortune" (CBC). Now that's a laff-riot.

An obvious gimmick that developed from the combination of TV and telecommunications in trid are shows that randomly call home viewers and let them play. Ever since "Do You Feel Lucky?" (NBS) broke ratings records for the format back in 2038, about half of all game shows use this hook to keep viewers from changing channels. Hey, if you aren't watching, you can't play, right?

ABS broke new ground last season, along with some doors and maybe a few local ordinances, by combining the goo-games format with home players. "Knock, Knock" pits randomly selected home viewers against contestants in the studio. Vidphone hookups only; they will not call a set that doesn't have one. "Knock, Knock" uses a randomized set of "horserace" games combined with some truly inane trivia questions to determine who wins. If the studio players lose, they get the usual slime-in-the-face treatment. What is fun, though, is that *sometimes*, when a home player loses, they hear a knock-knock at the door, and a horde of goons from the show storms in and trashes their place. And the great part is, the home players had to agree to hold the show blameless from any damages, *on the air*, before they were allowed to participate. Gotta love it.

LETHAL GAMES

Win one of the typical network shows and you walk away with ten to twenty thousand nuyen worth of merchandise, taxable local currency, or corporate scrip from the sponsors. Maybe get a crack at a big prize (50,000 to 100,000¥). There are other shows with higher…*much* higher…purses. Besides blood sports, Aztlan introduced lethal contests for high-cash prizes two years ago.

"Suerte y Muerte" is a gladiatorial "amateur hour," with ordinary cits, condemned criminals, and such fighting each other to take a crack at one of the show's contract fighters, and a 100,000¥ purse in tax-free Aztechnology scrip.

"Golden Glory" drops twenty contestants in a specially booby-trapped, hostile zone (rural or urban, either way makes for good trid as far as the producers are concerned). Anyone who gets out alive within 24 hours splits 25,000¥ in gold and gets a crack at the Hero Glory meet at the end of the season. One million nuyen to the survivor. The sole survivor. "Golden Glory" goes through a lot of contestants and it is an open secret that some of them are shanghaied onto the show.

SITCOMS

Things haven't changed much since "I Love Lucy." Take some funny characters and put them through the mill. Humor, though, has gotten a little more brutal since Lucille Ball's day. "'Zappenin' inna Barrens," on CBC, has a guest star each week whose character gets geeked in some amusing fashion by the funny-nasty SINless psychopaths played by series regulars. Last week, Faye Drummond played the lady from Resource Allocation investigating soy-distribution fraud. She ended up as protein extender, fed through the comestibles processor unit while the laugh-track roared.

Medium-pornographic sex comedy is coming back into fashion this season, and OTQ's "Sans Reproche" is a good example of the format. The show's farmboy-twit hero from the Gaspé stumbles through the most hair-raising sprawl vice spots without ever quiiiite figuring out what is going on.

Minor bureaucrats and irritating low-level managers are fair game in mainstream sitcoms, but anything that reflects negatively on the top echelons of government or the corporations is O-U-T. Major sponsors routinely get script approval, and controversy doesn't help sales, as far as they're concerned.

These days, any kind of genuine social comedy, on a par with the old classic "All in the Family," is going to be a shoestring production running on an independent or even a pirate net. "I Hate My Boss," Pat Yasuhiro's razor-edged comedy about a low-grade sarariman family, looks at the tribulations of Marco Marconi at the hands of Mr. Shogayu, who could be a nasty, upper-level suit from just about any corporation in the world.

As far as the major nets and their sponsors are concerned, "I Hate My Boss" is trash, with no popular appeal. So then why did Photo-3 Cable Connectors register 1,500 complaints when they cut a pirate feed of "I Hate My Boss" off the wires? Oh, yeah, malcontents and juvenile pranksters, just like it said in the press release.

Magic, especially magic that goes sour, is all over the sitcoms. A lot of the mundane population's fear of magic shows up on the trid. Even Yasuhiro falls into the stereotype. Marconi, on "I Hate My Boss," always has major problems with Jagger, the very badass wage mage who trails around in Mr. Shogayu's entourage.

Two new shows this season are "Down the Tubes" and "Glerethiel Morkhan Shoam." The first show is on CBC and is all about the funny scrunges in an underground trogtown under Atlanta. They always have these big plans to rip off the normals,

2 NITE ON OTQ   SANS REPROCHE

ACCESS 3206-02-34515
ccessing
onnect –Welcome to KA-POW! KA-POW!
nter System ID Number: !!!!!!!!!>

KA-POW! KA-POW!

VOLUME XX • NUMBER 12 • SEPTEMBER 2053

IN YOUR FACE ISSUE!

hoi

Stargazers, we've been busy getting

the goods on the *latest* and *greatest*

folks that Shadowteens like you have

asked about. A dreamteam of *too-wiz*

rockers and *sub-zero* newsnet stars is

lined up in our PROFILES library.

Call *PROFILES NEW ALL* ★

KA-PROFILE! JACK Q ★ TRID REPORTER

Jack Q. is a tridsnoop, a muckraking reporter on the independent networks, and the cutest thing we've seen on a screen in months here at KA-POW! KA-POW! Jack carries the latest tech out into the streets to tell all of us at home what's really hot. Jack wants to bring you Stargazers all the facts and figures. When a lover-looker like this is the one on the trid, KA-POW! KA-POW! knows all sweet Sixth-World-teens will be watching those nightly newsnet shows…weeeell, unless the news is opposite something really hot on RockNet.

Jack takes his work seriously. In our indepth interview with this newshunk, he had this to say: "Someone has to bring the truth out where people can see it. I intend to do just that. Whatever it takes.

"The system always has something to hide: the corporations, the government, the policlubs, the cops and the robbers. I don't care who it is. Their decisions affect our lives, no matter how we feel about it. They aren't shy about keeping their secrets, either. Sometimes, it's like a war zone out there. Maybe that sounds like paranoia talking, but you know what they say: even paranoids have enemies."

(Access "JQ-IN-TR-VUE" on any KA-POW! KA-POW! access node for the whole interview, Shadowteens. 3¥ for the text download and only 5¥ for full trid replay.)

"People used to have the 'right' to know, now they have an urgent need to know! To know who is running their lives, who is telling them the truth and who is lying."

Jack Q.—Vidsnoop with An Attitude

Attributes:
Body: 2 (3)
Quickness: 3 (4)
Strength: 2 (3)
Intelligence: 4 *(Ooh, and brains too! To die for, Shadowteens!)*
Willpower: 3
Charisma: 6 *(Love that smile, Jack!)*
Essence: 1.2
Reaction: 3 (5)
Initiative: +1D6 (+2D6)
Dice Pools:
Defense (Armed): 1
Defense (Unarmed): 5
Dodge: 4
Skills:
Bike: 4
Etiquette (*): 3
Etiquette (*): 3
Firearms: 6
Interrogation: 4
Interrogation: 8 (Specialization: Trideo Interview)
Leadership: 3
Leadership: 7 (Specialization: Trideo Reporting)
Stealth: 4
Unarmed Combat: 5
Special Skills:
Portacam: 6
Cyberware: *(Wiz metal makes the man, readers. See what it's done for Jack?)*
Datajack
Dermal Armor (1)
Muscle Replacement (1)
Skillwires (3)
Smartgun Link
Wired Reflexes (1)
Skillsofts: (All at Level 3)
City Maps (Datasoft)
Etiquette (*)
Etiquette (*)
Etiquette (*)
Electronics B/R
Electronics B/R (Concentration: Video)
Contacts:
Independent Network Affiliation
6 Contacts (*)

Gear:
(2) Line Taps
Ares Predator II [Heavy Pistol 15 (clip), 6M2, w/3 extra clips FirePower ™ ammo and Built-in Smartgun Link]
Armor Jacket (5/3)
Auxiliary Memory Module (1,000 Mp)
AZT Micro25 Microcybercam
AZT Micro30 Steadicam Wrist Mount
Bug Scanner (6)
Data Codebreaker (5)
Doc Wagon Contract (platinum)
Fine Clothing
General Products Steadicam™ Shoulder Mount
High Lifestyle (4 months prepaid)
Ingram Smartgun [SMG, 32 (clip), 5M3, w/3 extra clips regular ammo]
Jammer (5)
Laser Microphone (6)
Lined Coat (4/2)
Micro-Recorder
Mossberg CMDT/SM [Shotgun 8 (clip), 4M3, w/2 extra clips Stun rounds replacing 2 clips regular ammo]
Narcoject Pistol [Light Pistol, 5 (clip), as toxin, w/3 extra clips]
Pocket Computer (100 Mp)
Secure Short-haul Transmitter
Shotgun Microphone (5)
Signal Locator and two Tracking Signals
Sony CB5000 Cybercam with Smartcam Adapter (+1 Impact)
Walther Palm Pistol [Hold-out Pistol, 2 (Break), 3L1, w/explosive ammo]
Wrist Phone w/Flip-up Screen & Video Interface
Yamaha Rapier

Jack sez: "The Etiquette skills and contacts a reporter chooses should fit his or her expertise as a reporter. Choose your own. A crime reporter should have Etiquette skills in the law enforcement and criminal subcultures, with contacts in those areas. A reporter covering corporate activity should have Corporate Etiquette and contacts."
(Can this man talk or what, Shadowteens?)

KA-PROFILE! AUDREY W. ★ CYBERSNOOP

Audrey has a headful of hot wares and a nose for news. But what this lady covers isn't just the latest pep rally for the school BBS. She packs metal in her fists as well as her bod, and goes wherever a story takes her.

"I don't carry a camera. I am the camera."

Audrey has cyber that would make some samurai drool. And she's got some of that samurai attitude, too, that's subzero with today's teens. She scans her top-line Chiba eyes over the scene just like Denise Doral in her last supersim, *Reporter On the Edge*. Too wiz!

In our typically indepth KA-POW! KA-POW! interview, Audrey has this to say: "The facts are all that matter. If you have the facts, everything else falls into place. So I get the facts, whatever they are, whoever they hurt."

Truth can be a tough cap to swallow, Shadowteens, but this is one tough lady, and she can take it—or dish it out!

(For the full story download "AUD-W-TALKS-2-U" on any KA-POW! KA-POW! access node.)

"Cold? Maybe, but you try and stay 'warm' wading through the slime out there day after day!"

Audrey W: Cybersnoop with An Eye to Die For

Attributes:
Body: 5
Quickness: 6
Strength: 4
Intelligence: 4
Willpower: 5
Charisma: 6 *(Those looks never came out of a vat!)*
Essence: .15
Reaction: 5 (6) (+2D6)
Dice Pools:
Defense (Armed): 1
Defense (Unarmed): 1
Dodge: 6
Skills:
Driving: 2
Electronics B/R: 1
Electronics B/R: 3 (Concentration: Video)
Etiquette (*): 4
Etiquette (*): 2
Firearms: 4
Interrogation: 2
Interrogation: 6 (Specialization: Video Interview)
Leadership: 1
Leadership: 5 (Specialization: Video Reporting)
Special Skills:
Portacam: 5
Cyberware:
Boosted Reflexes (2)
Cyberears with Hearing Amplification, Select Sound Filter-4, Recorder Interface
Dr. Spott Smartcam
Eyecrafter Opticam Package
Headware Memory (200 Mp)
Smartgun Link
Contacts:
Major Network Affiliation
5 Contacts (*)
Gear:
(2) Line Taps
Ares Predator II [Heavy Pistol, 15 (clip), 6M2, w/3 extra clips Firepower™ ammo]
Armor Jacket
Auxiliary Memory Module (1,000 Mp)
AZT Micro20 Microcamcorder
Bug Scanner (6)
Data Codebreaker(5)
Doc Wagon Contract (platinum)
Fine Clothing
Ford American
General Products Steadicam™ Shoulder Mount
Ingram Smartgun [SMG, 32 (clip), 5M3, w/3 extra clips of regular ammo]
Jammer (5)
Lined Coat
Micro-Recorder
Pocket Computer (100 Mp)
Pocket Phone w/ Flip-up Screen
Secure Short-haul Transmitter
Signal Locator and two Tracking Signals
Sony CB-5000 Cybercam
Video Maintenance Kit
Voice Identifier (3)

Audrey sez: "Who you know is important, and so is how you know them. A reporter has to pick her social skills and contacts with care. It's the only way to properly manipulate people to get at the story."

KA-PROFILE!

DARKVINE ★ ELF on the RISE

He came out of the land of magic, Tir Tairngire, two years ago. You may have heard his magical harping on downloads from Doctor Roxx Magical Musical Mystery Board or KA-POW! KA-POW!'s own New Sounds in Town service. He is Darkvine, and this elven rocker's career is beginning to move.

Handsome as a fairy-tale prince, Darkvine talked to our interviewer between sets at Seaghdhe's Pub, a bit of ancient Celtiana in the University district. "True, fair one, it is a different way of life here than one finds in the shaded byways of the Land of the Promise. But only in the lands of mortals does the blood run hot in the music. I don't regret my choice. Especially when such fair flowers as yourself grace the world without Tir Tairngire." Really, Shadowteens, no one talks prettier than an elf. Catch Darkvine's sound now, because this rocker is definitely D-Vine!

Darkvine: Elven Rocker

Attributes:
Body: 4
Quickness: 4
Strength: 3
Charisma: 8 *(Do you believe they still make them this good, Shadowteens?)*
Intelligence: 3
Willpower: 5
Essence: 6
Reaction: 3 (+1D6)

Dice Pools:
Defense (Armed): 1
Defense (Unarmed): 1
Dodge: 4

Skills:
Etiquette (Media): 4
Etiquette (Street): 4
Firearms: 4
Negotiation: 3

Special Skills:
Musical Instrument (Harp): 5
Singing: 4

Gear:
Body Microphone
Cheap Celtic Harp
Microphone and stand
Ruger Super Warhawk [Heavy Pistol, 6 (cyl), 6M2, with 12 extra rounds Firepower™ ammo]
Small Amp
Small Speakers

Rocker Status: Opener

(Download "D-VINE-HARP-TALK" for the full interview with Darkvine, Shadowteens. 3¥ for trid of the interview, 5¥ for a full-polysonic transcription of a Darkvine set!)

"The magic is in the music, and the harp can weave spells more subtle than any wizard's."

S

Sheena M.: Rocker Star

Attributes:
Body: 3
Quickness: 4
Strength: 2
Charisma: 6
Intelligence: 3
Willpower: 2
Essence: 3.5
Reaction: 3 (4) (+1D6)
Skills:
Bike: 3
Electronics B/R: 3
Etiquette (Media): 4
Etiquette (Street): 3
Firearms: 4
Negotiation: 3
Unarmed Combat: 4
Special Skills:
Musical Composition: 4
Musical Instrument (Guitar): 4
Musical Instrument (Specialization:
Synthaxe): 8
Singing: 6
Cyberware:
Cosmetic Surgery
Datajack
Smartgun Link
Synthlink Interface
Wired Reflexes (1)
Gear:
Ares Predator II [Heavy Pistol, 15
(clip), 6M2, w/3 extra clips
Firepower™ ammo]
Armor Clothing (3/0)
Assorted Microphones, stands, booms
Autosynth (Rating: 8)
Club Acoustic Modulators
Doc Wagon Contract (platinum)
Fine Acoustic Guitar
Fine Synthaxe
Fine Synthesizer (24 Voice: +3 Impact)
Fine Synthlink Deck
Fine Wardrobe
HK227 SMG [SMG, 20 (clip), 5M3, w/3
extra clips of regular ammo]
Home Recording Studio
Lined Coat (4/2)
Mixer (10 inputs, 3 outputs, built-in
DDO and polycorder)
Multitrack Sampler (12-track)
Stadium Amplifier
Stadium Speakers
Wrist Computer (100 Mp RAM)
Wrist Vidphone
Yamaha Rapier
Rocker Status: Star

hield Wall cut their first album in 2046, headed up by veteran rockers Sheena M., Jay K., and their friend Doris, a Sasquatch who hails from the chilly reaches of the Algonkian-Manitoo Council.

Since then, the band has taken off like wildfire, and Sheena is one of the stars who shine on the rest of us today. During Shield Wall's ultra-wiz concert tour last year, Sheena talked to KA-POW! KA-POW! in her dressing room at the Kingdome.

KK: Sheena, how does it feel to be the lead axe in a band as hot as Shield Wall?

Sheena: Well, Mark, it's too wiz, natch, and Jay, Doris, and I, and all the members of Shield Wall, want to thank readers of KA-POW! KA-POW!, and all our other fans, who have made life such a thriller for us.

KK: Well, with music like yours, the pleasure's all ours. How has the tour been going?

Sheena: Well, its rough playing eight cities in three weeks, but the way people take to the music makes it worthwhile.

KK: Wasn't there some kind of problem in Dallas?

Sheena: Arrgh, don't remind me. Some local hate group got it in their head that Doris was casting spells on the audience with her music, and there was a demonstration, and cops, and…it was an ugly scene. Shield Wall has always had a strong message to deliver, which is that we are all children of the Earth. Sadly, there're some folks who feel threatened by that.

KK: Has Shield Wall had to back off on "message" music since its commercial success?

Sheena: No, thank Goddess. I don't think we could have accepted that. Our producers and distributors have never even suggested changes of that type, so maybe we were lucky. You hear stories about some labels, natch, but Nine Spheres isn't like that.

KK: Seattle is your last stop on the tour. What's next for Shield Wall?

Sheena: Would you believe…an opera?

KK: You're farcing!

Sheena: Seriously, Jay has this concept for a fusion Menotti/Celtic Metal sound, built around some Algonkian myth cycles, and the way it's been developing, we're looking at a full-scale rock opera at this point. Our agent is out lining up production now, and we should be ready to start cutting wax in about six months if the Lady smiles.

(Download SS-SHEENA-STAR for the full text of our interview with rock star Sheena M. 5¥ gets you the interview in full trid repro. Only 15¥ for our exclusive recording of the Kingdome concert.)

KA-PROFILE! TEDDY X ★ WAXMEISTER

"Don't try to tell me

how to write my songs,

and I won't tell you how

to balance your credit

sheets, okay, Mr. Suit?"

Teddy X: Rocketing Ratings Rocker

Attributes:
Body: 6
Quickness: 6 *(Teddy's dates say he has fast hands—and he picks a mean axe, too!)*
Strength: 5 *(Ooh, Teddy, where's a guitarist get those muscles?!)*
Charisma: 6
Intelligence: 4
Willpower: 3
Essence: 5
Reaction: 5 (+1D6)
Skills:
Drive: 2
Electronics B/R: 3
Etiquette (Street): 4
Firearms: 4
Negotiation: 5
Special Skills:
Electronic Music: 2
Musical Composition: 4
Musical Instrument (Guitar): 6
Cyberware:
Datajack
Smartgun Link
Gear:
Armor Clothing
Body Microphone
Browning Max-Power [Heavy Pistol, 8 (clip), 4M2, w/2 extra clips regular ammo, Built-in Smartgun Link]
Club Amp
Club Speakers
Fine Electric Guitar
Lined Coat
Mixer (built-in direct digital output and polycorder)
Rocker Status: Seller (Includes Middle Lifestyle)

TEDDY

is a rocker with a future. You've heard his new hit album, *Priest of Princes*. If you haven't, Shadowteens, then punch up download request TX-52003-POP on KA-POW!KA-POW! right now! Only 5¥ for sounds that'd cost you the big Two-Oh in any waxshop in town. This special offer is available for a limited time, so jack that chip and Dee Ell!

Teddy was gigging at Club Penumbra when we interviewed him, touring under a promo sponsored by Aurica/Pollux, who've distied his last two recordings. His take on newfound fame?

"Sally, it's wiz to have folks finally listening to my music. Everyone knows it can be rough starting out as a rocker, and I'm just grateful to Aurica/Pollux for having faith in me and my sound."

Late Breaking Flash: Since that little talk, we've heard that Teddy and A/P have had a parting of ways, after Teddy's controversial song, *Those Who Spin the Webs*, drew fire from the stixfolk in LOUD, the Legion of UCAS Decency. You know the LOUDmouths don't love KA-POW! KA-POW!, readers, and we aren't chillthrilled by them either, so we'll leave that lying there. Happy side of things is that Teddy took his sound over to Turner Music, and is hard at work on his next album under the wing of the Atlanta-based waxworks. So A/P's loss is Turner's gain.

or con them, or whatever, but you know those trogs: they're just so dumb, they frag it up, every week, and hilarity ensues. Lots of gags about living in the sewers, too, but then, they really prefer it down there, after all. Mothers of Metahumans has mounted a major campaign all over North America to boycott the sponsors of "Down the Tubes." Hope it works, 'cuz this show is ugly.

"Glerethiel etc. etc.", is, of course, Elvish. It is supposed to be a pun meaning "Keeper in the Monkey House," "Inbreeding Causes Stupidity," and a third-level meaning that is untranslatable but pretty filthy. It is produced by a studio in Tir Tairngire (where else?) and has this local nobleman in Portland trying to keep order in his area, which is mostly populated by humans. The humans on "Glerethiel Morkhan Shoam" act and talk a lot like the orks and trolls in "Down the Tubes," and the level of humor on the two shows is about the same. "Glerethiel" is filmed in English (with some of the gags delivered in Elvish) and available on a couple of cable nets and satcasts. The scary thing is that elf wannabes eat the show up just because the main characters have pointed ears, even though it takes the nastiest kind of racist shots at humans, other metahumans, and, in fact, anyone who isn't an elf.

SOAPS

Society, science, the world itself have all changed like mad over the last forty years. But nothing can change the soaps. Almost all are aimed at the low- and mid-level corporate class, and plots are a mix of hardworking corporate values, personal conflicts, and an occasional threat to that stability by the sinister SINless elements.

A classic example is "Until Tomorrow," in which Violet Hogan's long-lost brother Martin has shown up on their condo doorstep. Street-flash, cybered Martin threatens to spill the beans that he and Violet grew up in the Barrens as SINless kids unless she and hardworking sarariman spouse Ted help him steal the prototype of a new chip from Ted's office. Fortunately for the Hogans, Ted's boss, Joe Prentice, is a sensitive manager. When Ted comes to him for help, Joe and delectable security chief Amanda Webb set up a trap for the nasty Martin, promising that Ted and Violet will not be punished, though of course a transfer to a low-security position is pretty much mandatory for someone with a less-than-dependable spouse like Violet. Amanda, crisply efficient despite her violent attraction to Joe (fans say their love scene in the computer center hit new heights of network romance), has her own problems. After turning down the leering advances of sinister wage mage Ivan Merov, she has been getting nothing but grief from the wizard's boss, William Candless. Of course, Candless is also Joe Prentice's big rival for the VP slot opening up at the company, and is…Well, it goes on and on.

The soaps are about the only format that claims corporate managers are not always noble, selfless, dedicated suits. But a major exec who is a real evil fragger is usually a secret front man for a terrorist organization or perhaps a rival corp. He, or she, is always painted as someone who does not deserve high rank, in the role of an ungrateful traitor to proper corporate values. Not the kind of person who'd ever turn up in a real company, natch.

TALK SHOWS

Chat shows have guests who come on to push their latest thing: a sim, a trid show, a computer program, whatever. Cute inside jokes and mild gossip are their stock in trade. The old-style chat show where the host parks it behind a desk isn't very big these days. Most chat-show hosts have some gimmick, like CBC's inane "Baking with Aunt Sally," where the celebs on the show help kindly old "Aunt Sally" whomp up her carbo-death goodies. Gee, junk food and junk trid in one heaping helping.

Topical talk shows claim to handle hot news topics in an open forum. Usually the topic is whatever sensational nut-fringe group or non-story the host can get approved by the head office. Jermaine Jerard, in Seattle, is the current leader of the ratings pack for this kind of fluff journalism. Ever since an episode on his "Heavy Hitters" show (NBS) last year, when a street shaman's conjured spirit shoved Jerard's head into a holocam during a "debate" between corporate security goons and some so-called shadowrunners, people have been watching to see if anything that funny will happen on the air again.

Whichever format they use, talk shows can also have an attitude. Many are on the United Christian Broadcasting System, where, whatever the format, the shows all have a conservative church mindset. NewsNet does a number of topical shows, and most of them go for the guest's jugular on public affairs matters. Carried to the extreme, there is stuff like "Revell's Yell," on CBC, where Bart Revell spends most of the air time screaming accusations at his guests.

Call-in shows are very big, of course, with vid- or holophone hookups bringing callers right into the studio picture. Talk-show staffs are adept at lousing up the connection for a caller whose views don't jibe with program policy, which allows the host to scream abuse at the poor geek before they cut the line.

3V GUIDE

Seattle: pretty typical Sprawl, s'right? Well, they got fourteen broadcast channels, over two hundred channels on the A and B cable nets, plus Matrix access broadcasts, sats, the whole bit. So how do the folks out there in trideo-land figure out what's on when? Same way as anything else in the Sixth World, chummer: ask a 'puter.

Most places have a public database with trid info on it. The fanciest ones have hypertext options that preview shows for those who can't make up their minds what to watch. Like, no honest cit would even think of turning the fraggin' box *off*, right?

The nice thing for those with, shall we say, exotic tastes in trid, is that the 3V Guide databases are in Bluenode country, where the IC never freezes up. It's dead easy for the local pirates to drop their shadowtalk in right next to the legit file entries.

Now, we ain't got the RAM to cram a whole week's listings into this book. We can't even show all the channels available in Seattle. But we can show excerpts from a typical evening of viewing pleasure, just to give the idea.

CHANNEL GUIDE

BROADCAST CHANNELS

[4] KOMA (ABS)
[5] KONG (NBS)
[6] KPUB (Seattle Metroplex Public Affairs)
[7] KORO (CBC)
[8] NABS/SSC
[9] KSPS (PBN)
[11] KSTS (Independent)
[12] NSSL
[13] KKRU (Independent)
[22] KTXX (Independent)
[32] KNUS (NN)
[40] KHMC (Home Megastore Channel)
[54] KUCB (United Christian Broadcasting System)
[67] OTO/Seattle

>>>>>[S'right, little chummers, be ready for the Enochophones marathon. All their trid hits back to back, coming at you on Big World TV over UHF 65. You never know when we'll be coming to your neighborhood.]<<<<<
　　—Blank George (06:37:52/04-03-53)

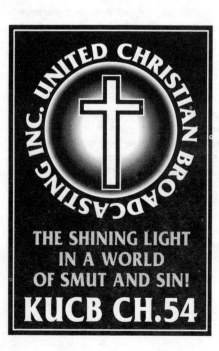

BASIC SUBSCRIPTION SERVICES

[AW] Ancient Wisdom (CA34/Matrix 4206-2264407/GalStar 2:19-2)
[CHV] Chessvid (CA48/Matrix 5206-6472414)
[GON] God's Own Network (CB12/GodSat Alpha 1:1-1)
[HMC] Home Megastore Channel (CA23/Matrix 3206-SPENDIT)
[NOS] Nostalgiavid (CB74/Matrix 2206-OLDTIME)

[SEX] Surging EXtasy Channel (CB101)
[PA1] Public Access 1 (CA79)
[PA2] Public Access 2 (CB50)
[PA3] Public Access 3 (CB115)
[REN] Renraku Broadcasting (CB43)
[ROK] Rocker Stars (CB19/Matrix 5206-9284743/Vidsat-31:4-1)
[UNC] Uncle Don's Kidvid Channel (CB67)

>>>>>[Public Pronunciamento #51-213. The Executive Cell of the Information Adjustment Sub-Cabal has shifted Truth Channel to Matrix LTG 5206-3404088 following the fascistic raid by Fuchi cyberstorm-troops last week. Neoanarchists are hereby directed by the Free Seattle Communard Army of Necessary Revolution to access this node for the truth the scum-corps try to suppress.]<<<<<
　　—#4234532 (18:57:17/04-03-53)

>>>>>[Deathstar-9 coming in pirate tonight on Cable B122 if the netcops don't spot the feed. It's splatter time, chummers, so click it out on your trid. If ya can't find it there, swish your dish to satfeed Deathstar-9, anywhere on transponders 1–3. Check out the program listings for the fare that the square don't care for.]<<<<<
　　—Bloodyguts (08:43:22/04-05-53)

PREMIUM SUBSCRIPTION SERVICES

[¥M¥] Moneyline (Matrix 7206-7920594)
[FRT] Fuchi Realsense Theater (Matrix 1206-GO FUCHI)
[HOT] Hotspot Simcast (Matrix 7206-SEXYNOW)
[HTO] Home Theater Organization (CA2/Matrix 8206-1155306)
[TBC] The Battle Channel (CB119/Matrix 1206-BIGGUNS)
[WSB] World Sports Broadcasting (CB36/GalStar 2:15-3)

>>>>>[Booknet is feeding to Juno 1:29-2 and by next week should have a Matrix feed hanging off the public library again, after we figure out their new trace algorithms. All you wiz-kids stay with us, we got the updates from the MITM symposium from last April ready to go.]<<<<<
　　—Librarian Libertarian (12:18:56/04-03-53)

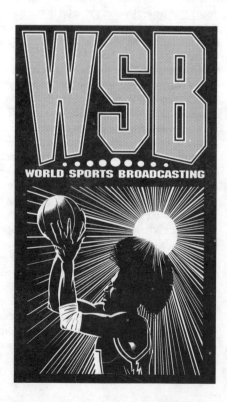

[REN] Crimson Files. Tales of the Red Samurai. Hayashi must choose between duty to his family and duty to Renraku.

>>>>>[If they don't mop up the bug (and Stickyfingers swears their tech won't crack this one), check out CB109. Live and direct, the closed session meeting of the plex Congressional Subcommittee on Revenues. See what the gummint don't want made public as they set YOUR taxes for next year!]<<<<<
—The Big I (22:54:19/04-03-53)

19:30

[5] **Kill The Dead (R).** Mark Hunter (Alan Bixby) must confront a coven of ghoul demons.

[7] **Revell's Yell.** Guest: Penelope Harris, director of NACLU's Atlanta office

[9] **Congressional Scorecard**

[NOS] Astro Boy (R)

>>>>>[Got wiz news, chummers! Vidsat-31:12 is beaming a simulfeed of four episodes of "I Hate My Boss." Its a secure scramble. Going to a UCAS think-tank doing a fed-funded study on subversive media. The decrypt algorithm's stashed at Club Deck and Matrix Madness.]<<<<<
—Matrix Ghod (09:22:41/04-02-53)

20:00

[5] **Swift and Sure.** Real exploits of Urban Militia units across the UCAS.

MAR.15 *WSB "URBAN BRAWL" EXCLUSIVE*

NEW YORK SLASHERS VS. SEATTLE SLUGS

URBAN BRAWL BONANZA!

ISSV PRE-SEASON CHALLENGE MATCH

---

[6] **Lone Star Report**

[7] **Shadowbreakers**

[8] **Tyee!** Chief Thunder (John Three Arrows) must elude a flight of cybernetic hunter-killer drones. Jones challenges Screaming Falcon to a duel. Can even the Power of the Great Ghost Dance save the freedom fighters?

[12] **Glerethiel Morkhan Shoam.** Count Tiriel's plans for Festival Night are disrupted when Homer moves his in-laws into tents on the Dancing Green and starts digging latrines in the Sacred Grove.

[22] **Money Soldiers (R).** Sarge tries to get the platoon back in the groove after a disastrous fall season.

[AW] **Healing Drum**

[NOS] **Madonna: A Retrospective**

[SEX] **Nostalgia Theater.** Behind the Green Door. Marilyn Chambers (1978, Holovized)

[PA1] **Have You Seen...** Missing persons search show.

[PA2] **I Know What I Like.** Ted shows us the really good parts of the Renaissance.

[PA3] **The Stuffer Gourmet**

[REN] **Way of Kendo**

[ROK] **Wiz Sounds:** Featured artist: Nerve Tonics

BROADCAST PROGRAM GUIDE

18:00

[4],[5],[6],[7],[11],[12],[32],[67] News

[8] **Medicine Hour.** Guest Shaman: Joe Onesalt

[9] **Perspectives On the Day**

[13] **Around Our Zone**

[54] **Words to Live By** with Rev. Ivan Fropp

[AW] **Tales of Atlantis.** Zannor leads a raid against the Crimson Citadel and learns the lesson of compassion.

[NOS] Leave It to Beaver (R)

[PA3] Metahuman Rights Review

[HTO] Movie: Coalsack Invaders. Sci-Fi. 2 hours.

[WSB] Australian Football

Baking with Aunt Sally, Channel 7, 18:30 Pictured: "Aunt" Sally Nemeth

>>>>>[Sunset starts the frolic on Deathstar-9. Transponder 2 carrying live feeds for "Golden Glory." Twenty lambs to the slaughter, taking that big drop into the killzone. Twenty-four hours stayin' alive in 300 square klicks of the Libyan Desolation. Rumors say one of the players is a ringer, vatjob ninja on loan from the yak. And the local bedouins get a bounty for every head they bring in. Gonna be a good one.]<<<<<
—Bloodyguts (08:47:15/04-05-53)

>>>>>[Whyn'tya take your drooling somewhere else, snuff-freak? If the damn government had any guts, they'd blow that stinking Azzie death machine out of orbit.]<<<<<
—SPD (14:32:53/04-05-53)

18:30

[4] **Basketball:** Washington Bullets at Boston Celtics

[5] **NBS Sports Dynamo** with Rod Malcom and "Crusher" Jenks

[6],[32] Local News

[7] **Baking with Aunt Sally**

[12] **This Week on Council Island**

[NOS] I Love Lucy (R)

[REN] Arcology Today

[TBC] Mitsuhama vs. Oldfield Petroleum. Company strength. West Virginia War Zone. Live Warzone coverage.

19:00

[5] **The Odd Coven (R).** Felix takes out the trash, only to discover it was Oscar's medicine lodge. The sloppy shaman plots revenge on his hermetic roommate. Hilarity ensues.

[8] **Let's Learn Lakota**

[9] **Wall Street Watch**

[11] **Sports in Review.** Special guests: Lancebikers Jed Gold and Katy Morgan

[12] **Potlatch**

[13] **Nova-HOT:** Music Trideo

[AW] **Hour of the Magi**

[NOS] Mr. Ed (R)

[PA2] Home Recycler Almanac

20:30

[6]   Seattle Eco-report

[12] Salish Language Programming

21:00

[4]   **Protector.** Captain Stone (Vince Hammond) and the Global Transport security elites face off with their old enemies, the Devastators.

[5]   **Bright Lights.** Corporate Security Director Hatchet (Tony Lamont) must confront BTL use by Dr. Inga Swensen (Brenda St. Jacques). Will corplaw or love carry the day?

[6]   **Here For YOU.** With Governor Schultz

[7]   **'Zappenin' inna Barrens.** Dirty Gus (Phil Trudeau) gets hassled by the cable access inspector (guest star: Jackson Downes) when he and the kids boost some prime trid.

[13] **Movie: Elven Lords.** Fantasy. Laeghaire Falconson, Caprus ua'Sidhe (2051)

[22] **Movie: Cybercop II.** Action. Ted McEwan, Brandi Chaser (2042)

[PA3] **In with the New:** The Nachtmachen Manifesto.

[REN] **Ikebana with the Master**

[WSB] **TransPacific Freestyle Finals.** Live from Bangkok

>>>>>[Check out Deathstar-9 on the cable feed or do the dish for 1-2. Court Ball from Aztec Stadium, Tenochtitlan vs. Monterey. Ortiz is still plenty steamed after the last game against Monterey, and sez, "This time, Xomotec leaves the Court in a bag." Grudge match, chummers.]<<<<<
  —Bloodyguts (08:51:37/04-05-53)

21:30

[6]   **New in Town.** Scheduled: Hemlad Consortium's new plastics plant

[7]   **Down the Tubes.** Snuurk starts courting Velveeta until they both remember she's his daughter. Warthog's plan to keep the Grungebusters out of the tunnels backfires.

>>>>>[Sweet Mother Gaia, isn't there some way to get this piece of trash off the air? Watch the funny trogs commit incest. What'll those CAS bleeders use for laughs next!?!?!?!]<<<<<
  —Otho (00:02:56/04-01-51)

>>>>>[Not long now. The Sons of Sauron are working on it.]<<<<<
  —New Breed (03:09:22/04-01-51)

[REN] **Company Calisthenics**

22:00

[7]   **Mosby's Raiders.** The Grey Ghost harries Grant's troops in the Shenandoah.

[13] **Tech Trak Tonite.** Fang, of the Devastators, shows off his new dental work.

PAID ADVERTISEMENT PAID ADVERTISEMENT
FRIDAY MARCH. 22
LIVE AT THE SEATTLE BALLROOM
EMO AND THE SPASTIC WAR MACHINE
PAY PER VIEW ONLY ON "ROK"
PAID ADVERTISEMENT PAID ADVERTISEMENT

[22] **Your Home Is Your Castle.** How to turn windows from defense nightmares into effective mantraps. Plus: Range tests of Chesterton Arms new line of combat shotguns.

>>>>>[Public Pronunciamento #51-213: Addendum A. The Executive Cell has authorized the Councillor of Resource Redistribu-

"SWIGGLY'S"
The hottest "talk" line in Seattle.
"only 6¥ a minute or 100¥ a month"
1-976-LUVU

tion to deliver a report to the public outlining fiscal elements of the Necessary Revolution on the Truth Channel in this time slot.]<<<<<
  —#4234532 (19:03:29/04-03-53)

22:30

[AW] **Beyond Myth.** Scheduled: What the Gnostics Really Meant

23:00

[4],[5],[6],[7],[8],[11],[12],[32],[67] **News**

[22] **Movie: Ramboid VI.** Action. The perfect fighting machine, driven by the brain of the perfect warrior. (2048)

23:30

[12] **Our Totems, Our Souls**

[PA3] **Arise Humanity!** The Policlub Humanis Forum

>>>>>[The hooded scum go down tonight! We of the Sons of Sauron pledge death to the Humanis fascists.]<<<<<
  —New Breed (03:12:52/04-01-53)

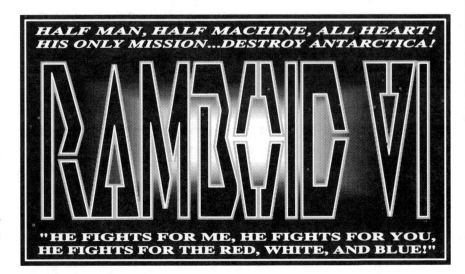

HALF MAN, HALF MACHINE, ALL HEART!
HIS ONLY MISSION...DESTROY ANTARCTICA!
RAMBOID VI
"HE FIGHTS FOR ME, HE FIGHTS FOR YOU,
HE FIGHTS FOR THE RED, WHITE, AND BLUE!"

AND NOW THE NEWS

All the news that's fit to print.
  —Motto of the New York Times
Anything that fits is news.
  —Al Bennett, Producer, NBS National News

News in the Sixth World is a flexible critter.

To the big networks, it is hot visuals, punchy story, human appeal, and all that jazz. A little controversy goes a long way, but mustn't upset the legal department. And of course it can't tick off the sponsors. Gotta keep sales happy, too.

To a pirate net with neoanarchist tendencies, it is the down and dirty truth that will move the people to rise and trample the chains of corrupt corporate and government rule underfoot.

This section does not presume to define news, or reality, for that matter. What it does do is describe the way a reporter gathers and presents news in the world of **Shadowrun**.

NEWS BEATS

A *beat* is a news story. A reporter working on a story is "on a beat." Putting a beat together takes three things:

•Pix: Love it or hate it, journalism these days is a visual medium. Print reporting survives on the Matrix nets, but for a beat to nova the ratings, it needs pictures, pictures, and more pictures. So a snoop needs to be hot with a portacam or else have a hot camguy on his or her team to get those shots for the network feed.

•Proof: A beat needs documentation to back it up. No proof, no news. No one wants to risk getting sucked into the tangled jungle of the libel laws. Documentation can be lots of things: Hardcopy. Matrix files. Interviews. Eyewitnesses. Experts. The people get lied to a lot, so they like to see a lot of proof on a story.

•Punch: A beat has punch when a reporter ties it all together and puts it in the public's face. That's the snoop's job, whether he's out in the field, where it's happening, or in front of a camera back at the studio. Ready to go the distance to nail down the story and tell it.

STORY BEHIND THE STORY

Shadowrun operates on two levels, like any roleplaying game.

For one thing, it is a game with rules that make it possible to measure how a reporter is doing. Does he get trid he can use on the nets? Can he prove what really happened? How well does the story do in the ratings? For all this, there are tests and target numbers and all that stuff.

The big questions for a reporter are now: Who, What, When, Where, Why and How much will it cost me?

—Newswatch *magazine*

But **Shadowrun** is a *roleplaying* game. Players are supposed to be caught up in an adventure. And if they're not, the game designers are all gonna have to find honest work. For roleplaying purposes, this section looks at what it's like to be a snoop on a hot beat. How does his role differ from a samurai on a run? Sometimes maybe it doesn't.

It is assumed here that players will be interested in beats that bring hidden things out into public view. Investigative reporting, **Shadowrun** style: scandals, murders, bribery, and skullduggery. That's what sells the news. Digging out the truth will mean danger, maybe even some shadowrunning, and there are lots of ways the opposition can try to shut down a nosy reporter.

It is also assumed that most player-snoops will be tackling stories that pitch them against the same "bad guys" as other shadowrunners: unscrupulous corporations, organized crime, social injustices, tyrannical street gangs, crooked politicians, terrorist policlubs, maniacal magical threats, fanatics of every stripe—all the delightful folks lurking in and around the shadows of the Sixth World.

There are street reporters, gadflies who go looking for scandal, who put what they find out on pirate nets, often without proof. Often without pay! Obviously, they have some kind of private agenda because they sure aren't in it for the money.

The more typical newsie does do the job for money, though he probably has other reasons as well. After all, there are safer ways to make a living. Maybe he's just hungry for fame on the network news. Maybe he's a danger junkie with a social conscience who feeds both impulses at once. He may actually hope to make a difference in the world.

A lotta shadowrunners spend their time waiting for Mr. Johnson to call and tell them what to do. But a snoop needs to go after stories on his own, motivated by his own goals, not the demands of faceless employers. Oh, a producer may send a snoop out on assignment, but this is usually one-story coverage: a fire, a riot, a shopping mall opening. **Shadowbeat** deals with the muckraking reporter who is driven to look behind the scenes and follow a beat into Hell itself, until he gets the whole story.

THE BEAT SHEET

The Beat Sheet is a record players can use as a snoop puts his beat together. When the snoop *files* his story (see p. 51), the entries on the Beat Sheet help measure its results, in the ratings and in the world.

PIX SECTION

The *Pix* section keeps track of footage that the snoop shoots while he's out on a beat. You get pix by making Pix Tests (see below). The section has space for the entry's timestamp, Impact, fake number, description, and file number for the pix.

• **Timestamp:** The date and time the pix were taken. This can be a detailed timestamp, like "14:02:05/04-15-51" (2:02 P.M., April 15, 2051), but all that is really necessary is a count of the days the character has spent on the beat, and maybe the approximate time. On day 1 of a beat, the timestamp might be "1/10 A.M." There needs to be some idea of when the pix were taken when the snoop *files* the story (see **On The Beat**, page 51).
• **Impact:** Measures how effective the pix are in terms of visual impact.
• **Fake Number:** For faked pix, this records how good the fake job is. Careful, chummers! Get caught faking news even once and credibility turns into toxic waste.
• **Description:** Tells what the shot was, where it was taken, what it is about.
• **File Number:** Notes when the pix are used in an on-the-air report.

PROOF SECTION

The *Proof* section keeps track of documentation on the story. The two kinds of proof are interviews (with ratings and other rules stuff), and actual pieces of information and documentation that the snoop digs up. These always have an *Impact* of "R" (for "Real").

The Proof section has room for the same kinds of entries as the pix section.
• **Timestamp:** Same as for Pix section.
• **Impact:** For Proof that has an Impact Rating (remember that "real" proof is simply rated with an "R").
• **Fake Number:** In case the snoop uses faked proof. Don't mess with it, chummer!
• **Description:** Tells what the proof is.
• **File Number:** So that the snoop can note when he files the proof, that is, when he reveals it on the air.

PUNCH SECTION

When a snoop files a report on a beat (see **Filing the Story**, below), he makes a *Punch Test* to measure how well the story goes over on the net. He has to record the pix and proof he used in the report. Usually he files everything he has accumulated up to that point, but he may hold back material for later use.

The Punch section has room for the file number, the target number, and successes rolled. These numbers are important when determining the overall effectiveness of the beat and its final ratings.
• **File Number:** A "1" for the first report the snoop files, a "2" for the second, and so on. When the snoop files, note the File Number in the pix and proof sections, so a record exists of when he used the material.
• **Target Number:** The Target Number for the Punch Test (see **Rating the Beat**, p. 53).
• **Successes:** The number of successes from the Punch Test.

SIGHT AND SOUND

To build a solid beat requires pix, and to get them, a snoop has to be where the action is. He needs interviews, he needs background, he needs cameras, recording gear, satellite uplinks, and Matrix terminals.

Sounds like a reporter has to chug around loaded down with tons of stuff, right? Hey, get with the century, chummer.

Imaging isn't on film anymore, not even on mag-tape. If someone's using old tech, his portacam loads a CD. Professional gear stashes digitized trid on a memory chip. If a guy's got a jack, he doesn't need bulky manual controls. The biggest thing on a state-of-the-art portacam is the lens, and for the right price, that can shrink, too.

Then there's the few, the proud, the heavily modified. Cybersnoops go into the vat and come out as living camcorders. They're carrying top-flight cyberoptics with specialized trid interfaces, ears that record everything they hear, and a head full of memory for storing the data. Cybersnoops are made to order for assignments where someone with visible trid-gear would draw unfriendly attention.

I AM A CAMERA

Anything that happens within camera range of a snoop is trid fodder. So all the guy has to do is be there, right? Sorry, that's incorrect, but thanks for playing.

Shooting trid that captures the facts, that moves viewers, that tells the story—it ain't automatic and never has been. The snoop's gotta know where to point the camera, how to spot action before it starts, and have the lens ready to pick it up. That's what newstrid is about.

So there are two sides to this trid stuff. On the storytelling level, a snoop has to record everything that happens, unless he turns his portacam off or someone takes away his toys. Painful that last, if he's a cybersnoop. Laser scalpels can be nasty.

Just being there *can* be enough. A snoop who goes along on an adventure can pick up a story just by running his portacam. If a bigwig brags about his clever (and illegal) plan in front of a snoop, he is on the record. If a corpcop abuses his authority while a snoop is around, odds are the cop is destined for stardom on the evening news. In cases like this, where the trid *is* the story, the gamemaster can decide that no fancy tests or target numbers are needed. Newsies can run as part of a regular team without getting into all the bookkeeping.

For folks who like it all nailed down and numbered, we provide Pix Tests.

PIX TESTS

The Pix Test does not measure the power or composition of a single picture, but the overall footage shot during a whole scene or sequence. It is not a standard **Shadowrun** test, but is instead the same kind of Open Test used to determine the Impact Rating of musical performances, p. 10. There is no preset target number. Instead, the player rolls his portacam skill dice (see page 84). Note the highest die roll scored, resolving any sixes. This number, the highest die rolled, is the *Impact Rating* of the tridshot. This number may be modified by various conditions (see **Pix Test Modifiers**, below).

For example, a character with a Level 6 portacam makes a Pix Test. He rolls 6, 6, 5, 2, 1, 1. Re-rolling the sixes, he gets 4 and 5. The Impact of the test is 11.

When making a Pix Test, record its Impact. As the scene progresses, if anything happens that causes a modifier to apply, add that modifier to the Impact as it happens. If the Impact falls to 2 or less because of modifiers, then no usable trid was shot during the scene.

Making Pix Tests

At the beginning of a scene, make a Pix Test to see how much good trid the reporter can shoot. A "scene" is a chapter in an adventure, or any major change in location or action during an adventure. A snoop can only make one Pix Test in a given place or situation.

If nothing much is going on, this is called *stock trid,* and is less valuable in building the beat.

If the scene has considerable dramatic impact, the gamemaster classifies the Pix Test as *dramatic trid,* which gives the beat more punch and is much more important in the ratings. Riots, fires, scenes of pathos or excitement are typical dramatic trid.

If something dramatic and unexpected happens during a sequence in the story, make a separate Pix Test for it. This is *action trid.* Modifiers that apply during the action sequence do not affect the stock or dramatic trid the action sequence interrupted. Action trid is is what makes for wiz ratings on a beat. Combat, a rescue, a spectacular spell (if its results are visible), or any other dramatic incident that stands out from the background are all typical action trid.

The gamemaster can refuse to allow a Pix Test, by the way, if there is nothing going on that has any major visual impact. A Pix Test that does not have something to do with the story is no use either. A sudden fight or a dramatic chase that has nothing to do with the beat is nice trid, but not news. It may do for filler, but does not contribute to the beat. And, of course, if the camera is off for any reason, the snoop cannot make the test.

Sadistic gamemasters can always make the Pix Test a secret, so that the snoop will not know if breaking into a run will ruin his footage. This should worry a snoop as much as heavy wounds worry a samurai. Maybe more. Wounds can get fixed, but missed news is gone forever.

Pix Test Modifiers

Modifiers to the Impact are added to the highest die roll. The Pix Test Modifier Table gives some typical modifiers. If something else crops up that might affect the Impact, the gamemaster should feel free to assign it a value using the ones given here as a guideline. Keep in mind that the way to "convert" a standard **Shadowrun** modifier to an Impact Modifier is by *subtracting* it. A +2 to a target number, which makes something *harder* to do, will become a –2 to the Impact, making it less effective. A –2 to a target number, making it *easier* to score, will be *added* to the Impact, making it more effective.

PIX TEST MODIFIERS TABLE

Type of Trid	Modifier
Stock trid	–1D6
Dramatic trid	–1D6/2
Action trid	No modifier

Visibility Conditions	
Full Darkness	–6 (using Low Light imaging)
	–4 (using floodlights)
High Glare	–4
Mist	–4
Low Light	–2 (using low-light imaging)
	–0 (using floodlights)
Smoke/Fog	–6

Situation Modifiers	
Covert Trid	
Regular Portacam	–4 (must be hidden physically)
Mini-Portacam	–2 (must hide camera)
Cybercam	–1 (must avoid obvious actions)
Gyrostable Portacam	Up to Rating (see **Gear**, page 89)
Snoop Moving	–1 to –4
Snoop in Combat (noncombatant)	–2
Snoop in Combat (combatant)	–4
Snoop damaged	Subtract target number penalty from Impact
Smartcam	+2 (see **Gear**, page 90)
Karma	+1 die per 2 points of Instant Karma

Type of Trid

Because Pix Tests measure overall dramatic impact, and not just the technical quality of the shots, it matters whether the subject matter is exciting or not. Stock trid reduces the Impact of a shot, as does dramatic trid, to a lesser extent. Impact for action trid is not reduced at all.

Visibility Conditions

Professional portacams are equipped with selective filters, image processors, and lenses, allowing the operator to switch from normal light to low-light or thermographics at the flick of a switch, or the twitch of a nerve if he's jacking the camera. For that reason there's only one set of modifiers. The camera will be able to compensate for any of these lighting conditions.

If the snoop is using some cheap, amateur rig that has no compensating filters, he cannot get any pix at all except in normal light.

Notice that visual conditions are rougher on the Pix Test than on Fire Combat. All that's necessary in a firefight is to see something well enough to hit it. Newstrid has to be a lot more detailed.

Snoop Movement

As with firing a weapon, getting movement and getting good trid can be mutually exclusive. It can be difficult to assign penalties for movement, because the Pix Test covers footage shot during a scene or sequence. If the snoop is moving slowly, concentrating on his shot, there is no penalty. If he is moving normally or through a crowd, apply a –1 or –2. If the sequence involves movement at a run, over broken ground, or through thick growth, apply a –3 or –4.

This can be a pain to judge in long sequences. The guy was not moving when the test was made, but next turn he is sprinting along. In this case the Impact should be reduced. But if the snoop took a –4 to the Impact for movement when he made the test, then more running later in the scene would not affect his score. He has already "paid his dues" for that.

A gyro-stabilizer for the portacam can reduce the effects of movement (see **Gear**, page 88).

Snoop In Combat

Since a new Pix Test can usually be made when a snoop finds himself in the middle of a fight, this modifier is pretty easy to apply. If the snoop just shoots trid during the fight, the test gets a –2. If he takes an active part in the fight, it is a –4 to the Impact.

As with movement, gyro-stabilizer gear can reduce the penalty for shooting trid under combat conditions (see **Gear**, page 88).

Snoop Damaged

Like anything else, shooting trid is hard to do when the snoop is hurting. The target number penalties for physical or mental damage do reduce Pix Test Impact.

Covert Trid

Shooting trid without being obvious about it is easier for cybersnoops than for snoops using external gear. Using a mini-portacam is the middle ground. Shooting covert trid with regular equipment means the snoop has to hide himself, using Stealth. Using a mini-portacam, the snoop can be in the open, hiding the tiny camera in his hand, or inside his clothes, or in a briefcase, and so on. A cybersnoop isn't showing any obvious trid-gear, but he has to avoid obvious "staring" or other body language that tells people what he is up to.

Karma

A snoop can improve chances of a Pix Test and get an extra die for the test for every 2 points of Instant Karma spent. No test may be improved by more than 2D6. One lucky tridshot does not a story make.

For example, Tom Turner is a cybersnoop tagging along with a runner team that owes him a favor. They've got a contract to deliver black market medical supplies to the Underground, where a nasty mutant virus is tearing through the local orks.

The team meets a gang of armed, nervous orks in a back alley of the Barrens. Deep shadows lie everywhere, and hazy mist twirls slowly through the garbage piled in stinking heaps all around. Pretty ordinary stuff in **Shadowrun**. Tom shoots some stock trid to give the story texture. He'd like to add some floodlighting to get better imaging, but when he starts to unsling the portable lamp, half a dozen big guns swing in his direction. Maybe he'll let the Pulitzer wait awhile. One of the orks slides a false wall aside. The orks and the runners step into the pitch-black hole. "Move it or stay behind, snooper," a hoarse voice hisses sharply from the darkness. Aw, drek! Tom breaks into a trot and scrambles downs into the hole.

The Pix Test for this scene is only stock trid. The snoop has a Level 7 portacam, so roll 7 dice. The results are 6, 5, 3, 3, 2, 2, 1. Rerolling the 6 scores a 5, for an Impact of 11. But the scene suffers from low light (−2) and mist (−4). That drops the Impact to 5. Floodlights would have made it a 7, but the orks didn't seem to go for that idea. The gamemaster judges that the rapid movement into the access hatch is another −1, so the Impact of this stock shot is now 4. Because this is stock trid, the gamemaster also rolls 1D6 and comes up with a 5, which reduces the final Impact of the footage to −1. Oh well…

Emerging from the access tunnel, Tom steps into a makeshift clinic. A few weary members of different races are trying to care for more than a hundred feverish, moaning plague victims. Just in front of him, an elven woman, her fair-skinned face drawn tight with fatigue and strain, sponges sweat from a young ork's forehead as he whimpers hoarsely for his mother. Across the aisle, a shaman crumples, having called on his powers once too often in a desperate attempt to banish the infection from one more patient.

The gamemaster decides this Pix Test is for dramatic trid. Roll 7 dice (the snoop's portacam rating). The dice score 6, 6, 4, 4, 3, 2, 1. Rerolling the sixes, he gets a 6 and a 5. Resolving the 6 again, he rolls a 4. The shot has a base Impact of 16. The light is dim, but not so bad as to impose a modifier, so this is one heck of a tridshot. Because this is dramatic trid, the gamemaster rolls 1D6 and divides the result by 2. The roll is a 1. Rounding fractions down, the Impact Modifier for dramatic trid has no effect (a −0).

Tom is still walking slowly and carefully through the rows of makeshift cots, scanning his cybercam dispassionately across faces twisted with disease or slack in the final rest of death. He whirls sharply when the shooting starts. Looks like those medical supplies got boosted from some dangerous people. A squad of yak enforcers have burst into the tunnels, shooting wildly. Tom tries to keep his camera-eye focused on the action as he swings the automatic shotgun to his hip and starts firing.

This calls for a new Pix Test for action trid. Roll the portacam-7 dice again. This time the results are 6, 6, 4, 3, 2, 1, 1. Reroll the two sixes. A 6 and a 4. Roll the 6 again, and get a 2. The highest die roll in the bunch is 6 + 6 + 2, or 14. But the snoop is busily engaged in shooting guns as well as trid, so reduce the Impact by 4, for a 10.

INTERVIEWS

Interview Skill is a Concentration of Interrogation, and Trideo Interview Skill is a Specialization. If someone wants to be a hotshot reporter, he or she better get one of these.

An on-camera interview can count as either an extra Pix Test or, if some really hot data turns up, as proof. It is hard to say which, as it depends on what the interview subject, the *interviewee*, knows and how effective the Interview Test is. Interviews can also provide specific clues in an adventure and can be part of legwork.

An interview that is not on-camera can still produce proof if it is really effective (5 successes or more), but does **not** count as a Pix Test.

An interview is not an official interrogation, and it's not a magic spell. No matter how brilliant a snoop is, he's not going to get a full confession out of someone in an interview. Anyone can walk away from an interview, any time, with a "No comment." Pulling a gun (or combat spell) on someone to make them talk is not an interview. Information extracted under duress is not valid as documentation. It is also a no-no on the legal newsnets, as well as felonious assault, a weapons violation, and so on.

Live•13

INTERVIEW TESTS AND IMPACT

Most interviews are Standard Interview Success Tests, using the Social Skill guidelines on p. 153 of **Shadowrun**. The target number is usually the interviewee's Willpower, but the gamemaster may decide to substitute Intelligence or Charisma because of the circumstances. An interview with a hostile subject who is actively trying to stonewall the snoop would probably use the former's highest mental attribute, as he tries to dodge the questions using his wits (Intelligence), charm (Charisma), or bloody-minded stubbornness (Willpower).

Successful interviews have an Impact, whether they count as proof or just as pix. The Impact is figured the same way for an interview as it is for a Pix Test. Most types of interviews have modifiers to the target numbers, but these do *not* affect the Impact of the interview. So if the snoop has an Interview Target Number of +4 and rolls a 9 as his best result, his Impact is 9, not 5.

CASUAL INTERVIEWS

Whenever a snoop is at a scene where something happened in front of witnesses, or where people are reacting to an event, he can try casual interviews. This is a *single* Interview Test, no matter how many people the snoop is talking to. Successes mean that something useful has come up, even if only another usable Pix Test.

The general scene controls the modifiers and the base target numbers for the test. A crowd that is afraid of reprisals or hostile to the snoop will add penalties to his target number. A friendly crowd that is excited about being on trid will improve the target number.

A snoop with the right Etiquette Skill can use it to try to get a hostile crowd to chill out a little before he starts with the questions. Make the Etiquette Test against the same target number that the Interview Test will face. Reduce the penalties for the Interview Test by 1 for every two successes with this test. This will *not* turn penalties into bonuses, but it can knock a point or two off the modifiers for a hostile, frightened crowd.

The average Willpower in most crowds is usually 3, since that is the average Willpower for everyone. A bunch of runners might average a 4. A crowd of trained magicians would have an average Willpower of 5 or even 6.

The results of the interview depend on the successes from the Interview Test.

Successes	Result
1–2	This means the snoop didn't get any extra information, but if the interviews were on-camera, excerpts from them count as an extra Pix Test. The best die roll from the Interview Test is its Impact.
3–4	One of the interviews produced information or minor clues about the event. This is the same kind of info a runner can get from Legwork in the adventure. The interview also counts as a Pix Test.
5 or more	The interview turns up an eyewitness, someone whose account of the incident can be used for Proof (see **What Is Truth**, below). A witness this good can also provide clues about what happened, as far as running the adventure is concerned.

But, it doesn't matter a hoot how many successes are rolled if the interview subjects don't know that much! The best an eyewitness can do in this kind of situation is identify someone involved in the incident, maybe remember what was said, or verify that some corporate logo was visible on a piece of gear.

The gamemaster should not allow casual interviews where nothing newsworthy has happened. That is, a player can't send his snoop out looking for eyewitnesses to random events. The gamemaster is not obligated to make up hot news stories on the fly because some rules lawyer says his snoop is going to wander the sprawl doing casual interviews until he finds an eyewitness to a hot beat.

If time is a factor, figure that it takes 1D6 x 10 minutes to finish casual interviews, then make the test.

For example, Ace Simms from NABS News arrives at an ugly scene in Renton. The site is a predominantly ork neighborhood. A drive-by shooting by a human go-gang has just taken place. Two people are dead in the street and the crowd is mostly meta and completely outraged.

Sad but true, a human snoop in this case is going to be viewed with hostility by the orks. Talking about this kind of thing on the trid isn't that cool either. The fraggin' breeder punks may come back.

That makes the Target Number 3 (typical Willpower) + 4 (hostile attitude) + 4 (result harmful to NPC), for an adjusted Target Number of 11. A comic facing such an audience would commit suicide.

Ace makes a point of letting the crowd hear his impassioned commentary on the savage crime, and, with the gamemaster's permission, makes an Etiquette (Street) Test to see if his rhetoric calms the crowd down. He gets one success, so his Interview Test has a target of 10, not 11. Better than nothing.

Ace scores a very creditable three successes in his interviews. He gets a few crumbs of information ("I think I've seen one of them hanging around the Humanis meeting hall uptown, but I don't know no names. Red-headed kid.") and a gut-wrenching interview with the mother of one of the murder victims (the best die scored an Impact of 21, which suggests something that powerful).

FRIENDLY INTERVIEWS

This involves an interview intended to let someone put his views across and to make him look good. It can be a hype job, the kind of things reporters do to pay the rent. A successful friendly interview can turn out to be proof, or at least another Pix Test.

Because the interviewee is cooperating in the interview, his attributes are not really the right basis for a Target Number. Instead, the gamemaster sets a target based on how relevant the interviewee's expertise is to the beat. The snoop makes his Interview Test against that Target Number. If he gets any successes, determine the Impact just as for a Pix Test.

If the interview involves a Knowledge or other skill, add the subject's score to the Impact. Otherwise, add the subject's Charisma or Intelligence, whichever is higher.

It requires five successes to make a friendly interview into proof. Otherwise, treat a successful interview as an extra Pix Test. The snoop can spend Karma to buy successes to raise the total successes for the interview up to 5, if he wishes (see **Shadowrun**, p. 149). In this case, the Impact of the proof is based on the highest actual die result. For example, the snoop gets three successes, and his best result is 9. He can spend 4 Karma Points to buy the two automatic successes he needs, and the resulting proof will have an Impact of 9 (see **What Is Truth**, below).

A snoop can get only one extra Pix Test this way, but it is up to the gamemaster to decide how many Friendly Interviews the snoop can arrange in his search for proof. As a rule, one friendly interview in a given area is all one can arrange. That is, if a snoop goes to one expert on magic, he cannot get other experts on magic to give interviews for that beat.

Getting a friendly interview with someone who can provide direct testimony about the beat has to be roleplayed (see below). The only way to get an eyewitness report is to find an eyewitness. Rounding up some agreeable expert for a background interview is easier. If the snoop uses a Contact for the interview, or someone who is active in the adventure and willing to give an interview, then it takes an hour or two to set things up and conduct the interview. Otherwise, he has to use an appropriate Etiquette Skill to locate an interviewee. Roll a standard Etiquette (4) Test with a Base Time of 24 hours.

The gamemaster can rule that a friendly interview is not relevant to a beat. A friendly expert on Economics may produce one heck of an interview, but it won't have much to do with a beat concerning gang violence.

Friendly Interview Target Numbers

Direct Testimony: 3

The interview subject is revealing material tied-in directly to the story, of which he has first-hand knowledge. He is an eyewitness, in fact: a company man discussing his last hit, or a media figure revealing BTL orgies among the simsense crowd.

An Interview Test is not always required when using eyewitnesses. If their testimony flat-out proves that the story is accurate, the information is automatically proof (see **What Is Truth**, p. 47).

Background Testimony: 6

The subject is a recognized expert. His information is not directly connected to the story, but it is very relevant: a doctor discussing the effects of toxic waste spilled by the corp the reporter is after, or a Lone Star detective discussing the criminal record of an alleged Humanis hit man.

General Background: 8

The subject is a recognized expert, but his information is not directly relevant to the story. An example might be a professor discussing the Humanis Policlub in general, or the resident of a town polluted by a toxic spill talking about what life is like in a polluted area.

For example, Ace is chasing down material for his follow-up story on the Renton shootings. He arranges an interview with a professor of political science at Pacific U. to discuss the history and platform of the Humanis Policlub. This is general background for his story, so the gamemaster assigns it a Target Number 8. The snoop scores two successes, which means the interview is not proof, but the reporter does get some good trid out of it. The best die roll for the test was 17, and the professor has Knowledge (Policlubs) Skill of 6, making the Impact of the interview a 23.

HOSTILE INTERVIEWS

These are interviews with NPCs who know something that the snoop wants to find out. Again, this is not interrogation, so no one is going to reveal their deepest darkest secrets, unless they want to. In a hostile interview, presumably, they don't want to.

The Base Target Number for a hostile interview is calculated using the rules on p. 153 of **Shadowrun**. These rules would normally make it almost impossible for the reporter to get anything out of an interviewee. But a careful, or lucky, reporter can set things up to improve the odds, even with a hostile subject who wants only to say, "No comment, snooper." See **Hostile Interview Modifiers**, below. Once the mods are calculated, make the Interview Test and see what happens.

Successes	Result
1–2	You can use the interview for a Pix Test, but you get no real information.
3–4	The interviewee has given away a big clue to the story. The interview is also usable as a Pix Test.
5 or more	The interviewee lets something slip that is Proof.

Dice rolls are no substitute for good roleplaying. If the player running the snoop can get some information by conducting an actual interview, then great. Pitch out these boring rules and go for it!

Setting up a hostile interview depends on roleplaying. A snoop cannot just phone a bad guy and ask him to answer incriminating questions on a national newsnet. Karma has limited uses. The snoop can use Karma to reroll failures, but he cannot buy successes in a hostile interview (see **Shadowrun**, p. 149).

Unless the snoop digs up lots of new information, he can only get one hostile interview out of an interviewee. Crashing through the same guy's door every time the snoop digs up a new clue is going to get pretty old, pretty fast.

"Hey Slug, what time ya got?"

"1650, boss. Why'dya wanta know?"

"Oh, the snoop's due at 1700."

CRASH! "Mr. Johnson! Have you any comment about your company's scandalous record on littering? The people have a right to know!"

"Hey, Slug, yer watch is a little slow."

Hostile Interview Modifiers

Covert Intimidation: –2

Openly threatening an interviewee or trying to beat the information out of him invalidates the interview for both legal and media purposes. This is 3V, not 3rd Degree. Obvious torture, threats, or blackmail will not do.

But maybe that heavy-set "technical apprentice" with all the chrome is picking his teeth with a half-extended spur, off-camera. Maybe the news team's decker has turned up a bit of embezzling by the interviewee. These things can help to establish an open and honest dialogue between the reporter and the subject.

Magic Used: +4 to Target Number/–8 to Impact

If a snoop uses magic to force a confession, no matter how subtle the spell, the fact will certainly get out and compromise the value of a hostile interview. Magically extracted confessions have no legal standing and they scare the drek out of the viewing public. So even though a spell may force information out of the subject, it makes the interview nearly useless for journalistic purposes.

Remember that the target number measures how hard (or easy) it is to get a usable interview, not just to get information. That's why the number gets worse if the snoop uses magic. And it really louses up the interview for use on the air, which is why the Impact is reduced so drastically.

Secret Information: –4/–6/–7

If the snoop springs information during the interview that the interviewee did not know he had, it reduces the Target Number by 4. For example, producing testimony placing the subject at the scene of a crime or perhaps decked information (even if it was obtained illegally) can shock the interviewee into lowering his guard.

If the reporter has been a busy little muckraker, and has multiple information bombs usable in one interview, the shock value starts to wear off. An additional piece of information is worth a –6 to the Target Number, and a third is worth a –7. Any more just bounces off the interviewee. Shock is nature's own little anesthetic, after all.

However, if the snoop uses a piece of proof this way, and does not get at least one success on the Interview Test, then he *loses* the proof. Having blown his surprise, the bad guys will somehow manage to come up with a way to discount this proof before he can use it.

Surprise: –4

In the finest tradition of the immortal Geraldo and other pioneers of trideo-journalism, crashing into the interviewee's turf or ambushing him on the street with cameras humming can throw the victim…er…subject off-balance and cause him to reveal things he normally would not.

In an armed society, and that certainly includes the Sixth World, it's a good idea to be a bit careful about catching people by surprise. Especially if the snoop's own trideo record proves he was using force to get close to the subject.

For example, Ace pushes through the door marked Private as his "security contractor" flattens two Humanis goons who try to stop him. Inside the office of the local leader of the Humanis Policlub, Ace fires a barrage of questions about the 500¥ paid to a red-headed street ganger. A ganger who was busted last night—carrying 500¥ that has been traced through the Matrix to an account opened by the local Humanis chapter. "Any comment, chummer?"

The Humanis big shot has an Intelligence of 4. He is hostile to the reporter, and the information involved would be disastrous to him. Normally that would give a +10 penalty to the interview and a Target Number of 14, which would make things tough for Ace. In this, case, however, the following factors modify the number further:

•Ace has revealed two pieces of secret information: tracing the payoff to the policlub, and Red's capture by Lone Star. That's good for –6.

•Ace has taken him by surprise: –4.

•A samurai leans in the doorway, holding a goon face-down with a boot on the neck. Covert intimidation, good for –2.

This drops the Target Number to 2. Ace makes 5 successes, and catches the politico on chip as he blurts out, "You'll never make it stick, trog-lover. You can't prove we paid Red to burn those Renton orks!" "Funny," snaps Ace, "no one mentioned the Renton shootings. What makes you think that's what Red was busted for?"

PRESS CONFERENCES

These are interviews the snoop gets in public, interviewing the same subject with lots of other snoops. Lots of times, a press conference is PR drek anyway, and offers no chance of getting anything meaty. If the gamemaster believes the snoop can get concrete information out of a press conference, though, he can allow an Interview Test, treating the situation as either a friendly or a hostile interview, depending on the circumstances, the speaker, and so on.

Interview Test Target Numbers at press conferences are at a +2 penalty.

LEGWORK INTERVIEWS

With this type of interview, the snoop uses the interviews, even a random street interview, to do some legwork in an adventure. It is no different than using an Etiquette Skill. Obviously, such interviews are only useful if the gamemaster has clues that can be obtained through legwork.

These interviews have no value as pix or proof.

WHAT IS TRUTH?

The one thing that's certain about the media is that nothing is certain. A hotshot editor with state-of-the-art gear can fake trid of the president standing naked in Times Square doing a Mercurial imitation, and the prexy's own mother would swear it was the real thing. Matrix documentation—drek, we all know the kind of surgery a decker can do on data. With some nasty ASIST tricks and the right medication, he can even program eyewitnesses to order. They could be put on hot coals and would still swear their story was the real thing.

So how to prove that a story is real? First, the snoop must nail down proof as solidly as he can. If he is using faked stuff, he needs the best he can get, and hope to Ghost he don't get caught. Because the other thing that makes the public believe the truth of a news story is the charisma and credibility of the reporter.

A reporter who gets caught pushing a story with faked proof picks up a bad rep almost impossible to lose. One hose-up can end a career. When truth is so fragile, getting caught fragging with it will bring the mob howling for blood. Think it through: they *know* their world is a toy for the techies, for the corps, for all sorts of people. They can't do anything about that. But they can do something about a trid reporter. Like they can stop watching. Ratings death. Ciao, chummer.

NOTHING BUT THE REAL THING

Two kinds of proof are available on a beat. First is what's gathered under the rules, using interviews. It has an Impact Rating, it can get stale, it didn't cost the snoop anything except a few die rolls.

The other kind of proof can be anything, but it has to *prove* something. Someone went out and got a file, a witness, a document. Such proof does not come by making a few die rolls, however. Characters usually risk death to get it. Maybe go on a little run into the shadows. Maybe break the law, or at least bend it some.

This kind of proof doesn't get old. It ups the ante on the story, and makes ratings skyrocket.

FIRST PERSON

When backed by trid or other records, eyewitness proof is the strongest for selling a story to the public. People believe other people.

Sad but true, a witness is fragile. It's not possible to lock him in a safe or stash him on a chip. Witnesses can't be faxed or photocopied. If a snoop has an eyewitness, he may have to make sure the chummer stays in one piece until he can file the story. That can be tricky. Witnesses can be scared off, bought off, or killed off. They can change their story, or someone can change it for them.

Event Reprogramming

High-level ASIST technology, combined with the right medication and biofeedback, can reprogram specific memories. This is not just brainwashing. The victim's brain gets dry-cleaned, pressed, and starched.

Such brain-straining requires a programmable ASIST biofeedback (PAB) unit. These come in several levels, ranging from units that fit into a briefcase up to some that require clinical facilities to control the subject's environment. PABs are **very** restricted and their legal use is limited to specially licensed shrinks (who are closely monitored by the cops) and to certain government agencies (who are not). The higher the unit's level, the tougher it is to detect the reprogramming job, or to reverse. See **Gear**, p. 97, for details.

Event reprogramming can change or erase memories of specific events or specific pieces of knowledge, or plant false memories or knowledge. It does not directly change behavior patterns, but it is possible to reprogram someone to believe, for example, that he is having a deeply involved love affair with some character. The reprogrammed individual's behavior toward that other character would be the same as if they were really lovers.

The more involved the events to be reprogrammed, the greater the span of time they cover, the trickier the job is. This is a gamemaster call when it comes to assigning target numbers. Changing a simple memory of a specific event gets no modifier. To erase a day or two of memories would be a +1. Reprogramming events that covered years would be a +4.

For example, Sara was a company woman for Mitsuhama before she was assigned to a strike team that wiped out a tribe of squatters. She later learned that they'd been exposed to toxic waste from an illegal dump site. Eliminating them before they started showing symptoms that might reveal the dumping was management's solution. She contacted a top snoop with Seattle Spy, but before she could get the details to him, her former employers sent out a team of shadowrunners with an invitation to come back and discuss severance benefits.

Reprogramming a subject requires that the PAB operator make a standard Biotech Test. The Target Number is the subject's Willpower plus certain modifiers (see table below). If the test is successful, the reprogrammed memory can be either erased ("It never happened") or replaced by a false memory ("That didn't happen, but this did"). Or a completely false memory can be implanted ("Let me tell you what *really* happened"). Success also erases any memory of the reprogramming itself, and lets the PAB operator plug in suitable false memories to cover the time the subject spent being brainwashed.

Successes can be used to decrease the base time for reprogramming, or to better hide all signs of the reprogramming, as follows:

Event reprogramming takes a Base Time of 60 days divided by the level of the PAB unit. The PAB operator's Biotech Skill can further reduce this time, dividing it by two or more of his successes.

The PAB operator can also allocate successes to hide the effects of the reprogramming from later examination. Any successes allocated this way add to the target number of anyone trying to detect the mental fiddling.

A successful event reprogramming job lasts until it is detected and reversed. The victim responds to all forms of interrogation, even torture or chemical debriefing, as if the false memories were real, and standard lie detection methods, nor even spells, can spot the deception.

Even if the Reprogramming Test fails, the subject will be reprogrammed for a number of days equal to the PAB's level, before the botched job breaks down and the false memories fade, restoring the real ones. Sometimes, this can be long enough to suit the people who ordered the job done.

REPROGRAMMING MODIFIERS TABLE

Event unimportant to subject	−1
Event of vital importance to subject	+2
Subject directly involved in event	+1
Previous reprogramming tests failed	+2 per failed test
Reprogramming involves linked series of events or information	+ 1 to 4
Reprogramming involves basic attitudes, ethics, or psychology of subject	+ Subject's Willpower

For example, Sara is spirited away to a quiet clinic usually reserved for execs suffering from burnout, where she is wired up to one of Mitsuhama's own MenTokko-V engram manipulators (a Level 5 PAB). A company doctor starts working on her memories of the massacre and the reason behind it.

This involves reprogramming both a series of events and info: the briefing for and execution of the massacre, the memo that ordered it, escaping from the corp enclave, and so on—about a week's worth of memory. Sara's Willpower is 4, and she gets a +2 because of the complexity of the job. She was also directly involved in the massacre and its consequences, rather than just a bystander, so that's another +1. This makes the Target Number 7.

The doc's Biotech (Psychotherapy Concentration) Skill is 7. Rolling 7 dice, he gets 6, 5, 5, 4, 2, 2, 1. The doc got one success. The Base Time for the job is 60 days divided by 5 (the PAB unit's level), or 12 days. With only one success, the doc cannot reduce this any further. So he uses it to hide his work. Anyone trying to tell if Sara was reprogrammed will need two successes to do it.

So, Sara has been given a set of false memories that cover the events surrounding that massacre. As far as she knows now, she left Mitsuhama because of a problem with her immediate supervisor.

Detecting that someone has undergone event reprogramming requires a test using Biotech, Psychology, or a related skill. It can also be detected astrally, using a Perception Test. However, all these tests work the same way, even the astral.

The gamemaster should make this test secretly. It is unresisted, using the subject's Willpower plus the level of the PAB unit as a target number.

If the reprogrammer used successes to hide his work, then the number of successes the programmer allocated for that purpose are also added to the Target Number.

Astrally testing the aura takes only a few seconds, but if a test fails, that's it. It means the brainwashing left no traces in the aura visible to a magician of the tester's rank and skill. An initiate with a higher grade than the one who muffed the test can try again. A second test is also possible if a specialist in the Special Skill of Aura Reading is called in (see p. 65, The Grimoire). Basically, each failed test means upping the ante to try again. If an uninitiated magician fails, try again with a specialist or initiate. If an initiate fails, try again with a higher-grade initiate or an initiate of the same grade with Aura Reading Skill, and so on.

For example, more than two weeks after Sara dropped out of sight, she shows up at home, going about her business as a freelance bodyguard. The frantic snoop comms her, and is upset, but maybe not surprised, when she tells him to frag off, that she doesn't know what he is talking about. In his line of work, he's seen it before.

Fortunately the snoop has a good news team, and can call on a magician to help him out. Scoping out Sara's aura, the wiz tries to see if she's been brainwashed or not. The gamemaster makes a secret test using the magician's Intelligence, which is 4. The Target Number is 4 (Sara's Willpower) plus 5 (the level of the PAB unit Mitsuhama used on her), for a total of 9. The dice come up with zilch—nothing above a 5. The gamemaster informs the magician that no tampering is evident.

The news team doesn't buy it, given what they know, and manage to pry loose the fee for a psychometrist adept to come in and use aura reading. The guy has a Skill Rating of 8, but it's no help. He makes one success, which is not enough to crack the protection the corp doc put on Sara.

Magic has hit the problem and bounced, since no one on the news team knows an initiate. The snoop sends the magician off to try to hunt up a group that can help them, and meanwhile, he somehow convinces Sara to undergo therapy.

Mundane techniques take longer, but are often more successful. The number of days to finish a series of tests equals a number of D6 rolls equal to the subject's Willpower. This is not reduced by successes, so it stays the same no matter how brainwashed the poor jerk is, or how skillful the therapist. If the first round of tests is negative, try again, but add 1D6 to the roll for time required.

For example, Sara is being tested by a shrink with a Skill Rating 9 in Psychology, Specialization of Counter-reprogramming. It takes 4D6 days to complete the therapy and evaluate the results. The Target Number is still 9, and the shrink scores three successes. That handily beats the one success protection that Mitsuhama used, and he is able to confirm that Sara's memories have been well and truly fragged.

Reversing event reprogramming uses exactly the same techniques that were used to put it in place. Same target numbers, the whole bit. However, the counterprogramming has to use a PAB whose level is the same as or higher than the one the original programmers used. All successes go toward reducing the base time for the task, since there is no need to "hide" the restoration of original memories.

CHIP TRUTH

Most records nowadays live in the Matrix. Matrix data is the foundation of society, the basis of daily life in a zillion ways. It is also fragile as a soap bubble. Any runner knows the kind of tricks deckers can get up to in a database. It's the easiest thing in the whole, digitized world to cook up false data.

So while newsies get a lot of leads from the Matrix, the files are not much use as proof all by themselves. On top of that, a snoop has to be reeeeeal careful about using datasteals in a beat. Say he flashes private corp records as part of his proof. Next thing he knows, half a dozen police organizations are asking where he got it. If his boss has a policy against reporters committing felonies to cover a story, he may suddenly find himself both unemployed and fighting a criminal case and half a dozen lawsuits.

Fortunately, the kind of Matrix proof most useful on a beat is also the hottest. A datafile that refers to flagrantly illegal activity *and* that can be backed up by non-Matrix evidence is pure platinum in the ratings.

For example, say a snoop boosts a red-node datafile from a system over at Ares Macrotechnology. It authorizes Mr. Johnson to deal with the marketing problem they're having with Havergill Electronics, and also authorizes a drawing account for credstick certification.

The snoop traces Mr. Johnson to the turf of the Night Hunters, one of Seattle's nastier thrill-gangs. Doubtless it's only coincidence when the Hunters knock over a store out in the burbs a week later, and one of the bystanders who gets geeked is the sales VP over at Havergill.

Now all the snoop needs is a raid on the Hunters to nail any certified sticks lying around, a decker to link them up to the account in the Ares memo, and then a little blitzkrieg interview with Mr. Johnson. Voilà! A shocking tale of murder and corruption in corporate circles. Might even get some middle manager turned over to the metroplex legal system for this flagrant violation of corporate ethics.

Warning: For those who want to see how fast a story can get spiked, try doing this one at NBS (see **The Majors**, page 25). NewsNet or Seattle Spy would love it, though.

It is important to remember that no matter how ghastly the deed, if it did not happen outside corporate territory, a snoop cannot get very far trying to bring in the law. He can louse up corporate PR, maybe even interfere with its business, if the company's doing something unthinkable like breeding VITAS bugs. But whatever happens inside corp turf is under corp law.

But if the snoop can prove illegal activity on the outside, well...ever see an anthill get kicked over? Most corps would rather face a recession than a multijurisdictional felony case in Contract Court, with all their competitors and the government just drooling for a verdict that would let them send in the troops.

Fake and Bake

Spotting faked Matrix records is not that easy because there are too fragging many files in the world (and more every second). Of course, no reputable reporter would dream of faking Matrix data for a story. This subject comes up for discussion only to help characters spot any tricky files that may come their way. Just as long as everyone's clear on that.

Everybody knows a decker can modify pretty much any Matrix storage he can get his hot little cyberspace hands on. He can usually spot any fakery as well.

Files carry data forks with timestamps, access records, system tags, and hyperstorage crossindexing pointers, all of which help to validate the accuracy of the contents. Of course, the contents have to make sense when checked against reality, too. A file claiming that invisible space aliens are controlling the CEO of a corp and making him buy ammonia-based window cleaner by the tonload would be dismissed out of hand. It's tab-net stuff, the kind of thing house-spouses download while they're paying for the weekly grocery order.

A genuine file extract that has been downloaded and successfully decrypted if necessary will stand up on its own, assuming someone else has not already faked and planted it, like in an ouroboros. In an ouroboros, a "tailchaser," someone plants a faked datafile very secretly, and then goes through lots of sweat stealing it back "in public." The idea is to prove that it is genuine, because no one would go through all that trouble to dig up a faked file, right?

Faking an entry is done with a system operation (see **Shadowrun**, p. 102). Usually it's an edit, but a faked file could be prepared offline and then uploaded. The Computer Skill of the guy who faked the file is the target number for spotting the fakery.

To test for fakery, a character first has to have access to a copy of the file or to the original. It is possible to load the copy into almost any computer: a mainframe, a PC, or a deck. Make a standard Computer Test, with the Target Number based on the skill of the decker who did the fake job, as discussed above. Of course, this is another secret test by the gamemaster, who should roll the dice for a "test" whether the file being examined has been faked or not.

Successes	Result
Failure	The fake job stands up to scrutiny. The decker cannot retest. The thing is too good for him to crack.
1–2	Something about the file is altered, but it could be legitimate editing, minor file damage, and so on. The data's integrity is open to question, but there's no way to tell if it is faked or not. The gamemaster can also give a decker this answer when he tests a perfectly good file, of course. Figure that if the decker does not make at least a Target Number of 4, he might be confused by normal "wear and tear" on a legit file.
3–4	The data is obviously faked, but the decker cannot tell which parts are faked.
Five or more	Pins down the details: bad check sums, timestamps that don't match, access by passcodes that aren't in the file access table, whatever. If only part of a file has been faked, the decker can tell which parts are good and which are corrupt.

If the initial test gets a few successes (four or less), then additional tests can be carried out to try and get more info. However, the test must either be carried out by someone with a higher Computer Skill or done on a more powerful computer.

Tests carried out on a mainframe reduce the Target Number by 2.

For example, Slip N. Slide snags the datachip out of mid-air, and glances questioningly at the producer who had lobbed it to him. "What's the scam?"

"If this thing's good data, it blows the bottom out of our beat on bribery in the District Council, Slip. Check it out, willya?"

"Subzero," the decker murmurs.

Slip pops the chip into a slot on his Fuchi and jacks in. His fingers wander over the keyboard for a few seconds. The tiny tridscreen on the deck pulses with letters of light. If it's a fake, they got Da Vinci to paint it, chummer.

The editor struck a nic-stick and dragged deeply as the decker's reverie stretched on. One minute. Two.

"Ahhhhh." Slip sighs with satisfaction as he jacks out and pops the chip. "There's something in there, but it's gonna take more steam than my deck has to tell us what it is. You got any time scheduled on the big baby in the basement?"

"Give me five minutes to scream at MIS, and it's yours." The editor grabs a phone and starts dialling.

Slip has Computer Skill 6. The file is indeed altered, but the guy who did it has Computer 8! Slip gets two successes in his first test. He sees something odd, but it might just be normal system wear and tear. He wants to try it on the network's mainframe.

The tech from Information Services scowls sourly at the idea of letting the scruffy street jacker anywhere near his terminal. "This is a secure access terminal, you realize?"

"Yeah, chummer, I catch ya. Nice of ya to let me play with it."

"Hmmph. It's hardly a toy. Let me enter the passcode, then I'll turn it over to you."

"Don't strain yourself on my account," Slip says with a grin. He reaches a hand to the keyboard and taps in a sequence without taking his mischievous gaze from the tech's face. The cyberterminal screen flickers to life. Access Granted. Hoi, Slipper, whuzzappenin?

Slip is running on a more powerful machine, so he gets a second shot at the file. In addition, he's got mainframe power now, so the Target Number drops by 2, to a 6. Slip makes his Computer Test and scores, again, only two successes. If the network is going to nail down this file as a fake, they're gonna have to scare up a hotter decker.

PIX DON'T LIE

The heck they don't. Software exists that lets almost anyone whip up computer-generated trid, and a hot techie can pump out imaging that anyone would swear is the real thing.

Faking pix requires a computerized tridisynth and a test using Computer Skill or Portacam Skill. It works the same as a Pix Test, but with different modifiers. Add the tridisynth level to the Impact, but subtract the modifiers from the Impact. Modifiers work for faked pix just as they do for regular Pix Tests: subtract the modifier from the Impact.

Recording real trid takes as long as it takes. A two-minute sequence takes two minutes to shoot. Making fake trid takes a Base Time of 60 times the length of the footage: 60 minutes to fake 1 minute of footage. A skilled operator can cut this time down. When making the test, use a Target Number 4 to generate successes. Divide the base time by these successes. Whether the guy operating the image generator makes no successes or a zillion, it does not affect the Impact of the faked shot, but it does tell how long the job takes.

FAKE PIX MODIFIERS TABLE

Operation	Modifier
Altering existing pix	
Minor change	–1
Major change	–4
Generating new pix	
With stock shots	–6
No stock footage	–8
Karma	
1 point	+1D6
3 points	+2D6

Ace is one frustrated snooper. He knows that a local Mitsuhama exec is pushing contaminated endocrine analogs to local hospitals. These are useless and even dangerous drugs that could kill dozens of people, but he can't prove it. Maybe it's burnout, maybe it's hunger for the ratings. Whatever the reason, the rules go out the window and he decides to cook the evidence.

Ace slips into an editing room and parks himself at the imaging synth. He glances at the manufacturer's logo and allows himself a sour chuckle. A Mitsuhama TridMix-D. Poetic justice, anyone? He slots a collection of stock footage from Mitsuhama's PR department, and jacks in.

Ace has Level 7 portacam. He makes the test, scoring 6, 5, 5, 4, 3, 1, 1. Rerolling the 6, he gets another 6. Rerolling that, he gets a 3. His initial Impact is 15. The TridMix-D has a Rating of 4, which raises the Impact to 19. But Ace is building completely faked pix from stock footage, which drops the Impact by 6, down to 13.

Ace is faking a shot of a meeting between the exec and a low-level city official in medical procurement. He boils it down to a three-minute tridshot. The base time to generate a three-minute shot is 180 minutes. Ace scored four successes against a Target Number of 4, so it takes him 180/4, or 45 minutes.

Detecting faked trid requires a standard Portacam Skill Test by someone using some sort of equipment for playing back the tridshot. If using a tridsynth for playback, however, the test can also be made using Computer Skill. The Target Number is the Impact of the shot. A simple success is all that is needed to spot the fake job.

ON THE BEAT

Okay, so a tridsnoop is out on a beat. How does he get what he knows into the homes of millions?

FILING THE STORY

A snoop can't just go around gathering pix and proof. Sooner or later he has to *file* a story. On a hot beat that takes days to tie together, the newsie may have to file reports several times before presenting the final wrap-up. Each time he files, he has to take all the pix and proof he's gathered since the last filing, and deliver the story with enough punch to keep public interest alive. Otherwise, the story may get spiked. He'll be assigned to a new beat and as far as his producers are concerned, the story is dead.

You need another half-hour to file? What do you think this is, Gardening Tips?
—Gib Staley, Editor

No problem, right? Just hold on to all the info until the whole story is ready, right? Guess again, megabrain. A snoop pulling down a salary from a net has to deliver news when the net wants it, not when he feels like it.

Okay, so frag the nets, he'll go be a freelance investigative reporter. But it's called *news*, you catch? If it isn't new, it isn't news. So pix and proof lose their Impact over time. Wait a week to file a story and it can become a ho-hummer, chummer. Even pirate nets aren't interested in ancient history. It's a fast-forward century, folks.

Of course, *maybe* the beat will stay fresh. The snoop won't know until he files. So let's stop slotting around and talk about how to do that.

Pix

First, let's see if any shots have lost their value. The snoop makes a test for each pix he is filing. The target number is the Impact of the shot. The number of dice he rolls is the number of days that have passed since he shot the trid. If the test succeeds, the images have lost their value, and that pix is dropped from the beat.

The gamemaster may waive the test for really important pix. Pix of major public figures engaged in larceny, pix of truly unique events, secret magics, unsuspected creatures, and so on do not lose their savor over time.

A snoop can cancel the results of a test that succeeds by spending a point of Karma.

Now he adds up the Impact scores for all the surviving pix. That's his *Pix Total* for the story he is filing.

Proof

The snoop must also test to see if proof gathered via interviews may have gone stale. Stale proof is no good to the beat. Cross it off the sheet. Real proof (Impact = R) does not go stale and need not be tested.

Each piece of proof that the snoop files counts as an automatic success on the Punch Test.

Punch

Up until now, we've been looking at how to get material for a beat. When the snoop files, it's time to see how he rates at telling the story to the public. This takes a standard Leadership Test or a test using the Concentration of Reporting, or the Specialization in Trideo Reporting.

The Target Number is based on the controversiality of the story. For a given beat, the snoop player goes through the Punch Table and selects any factors that fit the story. See **Rating the Beat**, below.

Total up the numbers for those factors to get the Target Number. Keep in mind that the target can change from one filing to another. What started out Monday as a piece of minor sleaze about a local gang of goons can turn out to be a national beat involving major corporate influence by Wednesday. Then the stakes go up.

Make the test. Karma may be used to buy rerolls or successes, as usual. The successes determine how well the beat goes over on the net.

Successes	Result
Failure	Story is spiked.
1	Story shaky. If Pix Total is under 24, story is spiked.
2	Story good enough for a one-off, but lacks enough power for more coverage. If Pix Total is under 18, story is spiked.
3	Strong story. If Pix Total is under 12, story is spiked, unless at least one piece of proof was part of the filed report.
4–5	Story is hot. If Pix Total is under 6, it will still be spiked, unless at least one piece of Proof was part of the filed story.
6+	Story is nova-hot, and will not be spiked even if no major pix and no new proof is available this time.

WHEN TO FILE

A newsie usually has to file an initial story after the first day on a new beat. If the story is not spiked after that, he gets 1D6 −1 days before he must file again. If he is not ready to file a story by then, he has to negotiate with his management for an extra day. He makes a Negotiation Test with a Target Number of 5, +1 for every extra day involved. So to get an extension on the day the story is due, the Target Number is 5. By the following day, it's a 6. The day after that, it's a 7, and so on.

Each piece of real proof the reporter has uncovered on the story, whether he has filed it or not, reduces the Target Number for negotiating an extension by 1. This does not include proof from interviews, only solid documentation with an Impact of "R."

If the reporter does not file a story when it is due and fails his Negotiation Test for an extension, the story is spiked.

A snoop can file another report before the deadline, of course. If the story is still alive after the Punch Test, roll 1D6 − 1 to see when the next filing is due.

Ace files a story on covert government agencies carrying on operations in the sprawl. The initial report goes over fine, and the story isn't spiked. The gamemaster rolls 1D6 − 1 and gets a 0. He informs Ace that he has to file more on the story tomorrow. A fruitless day of pounding the pavement leaves Ace without anything worth filing. If he blows his Punch Test, the story could get spiked.

So out comes the Negotiation skill. The story is due today, so the Target Number is 5. Ace has a Matrix file retrieved from the Public Health Service computers, which shows a suppressed lab analysis of the substandard drugs. This is real proof, and reduces the Target Number to 4. Ace makes that, so he is off the hook. But the beat stays dead the next day as well. Ace has to beg for more time. This time, the Negotiation Target Number is 6, −1 for the proof, for a 5. Ace blows the test and the story is spiked.

BREAK THE NET

Print journalism had lines like "Stop the presses!" and "Extra!" Broadcast audiences see the same thing whenever the words, "We interrupt this program…" appear on the screen. This happens when a beat breaks open something so hot it can't wait for a slot on the next scheduled newscast. In the business, this is called "breaking the network."

On a major commercial net, this can only happen with approval from upper management. On a more agile independent or pirate net, it is still an important decision but one that can be made by a producer, or even the reporter himself on the more anarchistic pirates.

Basically, five or more successes when a snoop files a story with a Target Number of 10 or more means it's hot enough to break the net. The final ratings for the story will be increased by 10 points (see **The Rating Game**, below). On a commercial net, a Negotiation Test is also required, with a Target Number of 20 − the Punch Test Target Number. Reporters who file stories this hot are usually in line for raises, promotions, or fat cash bonuses.

RATING THE BEAT

The Target Number for the Punch Test depends on just what the story is about. The hotter the story, the tougher the test. Hey, you wanna take on the big boys, you better be the best.

There are four areas on the Punch Target Number Table to consider in rating the beat. Taking all these into account will generate a target number. If the target number derived from the table is less than 2, use a Target Number of 2.

If the story does not fit these profiles, the gamemaster can assign it a profile using these as guidelines, or else simply assign the story a target number based on how controversial it is, in his judgment.

PUNCH TEST

The first step in determining the target number is to consider what group or special interest, if any, the story involves. Many stories can involve multiple groups, and in this case all the different groups contribute to the target number. If different groups of the same type are involved, use the highest target number that is relevant. For example, a beat involving a local corporation and a megacorp would not get a +2 for the local and a +6 for the biggie, totaling +8, but just the +6.

Next, consider the area affected by the events the story covers. A criminal plot that involves a single neighborhood would be worth a –2 bonus to the target number. A beat that involves international ramifications gets a +4.

Next figure in the relative position of the highest-ranking individual involved in the beat. Beats that deal with ordinary people are easier to sell. This can be abused. If a snoop files a story blackening the rep of some poor jerk with no connections, it can be pushed harder than one involving a major figure, since us jerks have fewer resources to fight back. Note that this modifier is based on the highest-ranking individual even when multiple organizations are involved. If a senior corporate executive is exposed for dealings with a low-level mafioso, use the corp's rank for the modifier (a +2 in this case).

Lastly, there's the question of what the subjects of the beat are actually doing, and what they have at stake. This usually means that they are involved in criminal activity or there is a lot of money at stake, or both.

PUNCH TARGET NUMBER TABLE

Special Interest		Who's Involved	
Awakened Beings or Metahumans	+1	Low-level individuals (gang members, employees, low-ranking members, Joe Blow on the street)	–2
Charitable Organization	+2	Managers (individual gang leaders, local corporate managers, local government officials or agents, precinct police officials)	–1
Corporation		Executives (company presidents, city and state officials, local Mafia capo, minor Yakuza oyabun, senior police officials)	+1
Minor or Local	+2		
Major Subsidiary	+4		
Megacorporation	+6		
Crime		Major Executives (major corporate exec, senator or congressman, Mafia Don, major Yakuza oyabun)	+2
Individual or Street Gang	+2		
Minor Organized: Seoulpa, Triads (in North America)	+3	Supreme Executive Power (the president of a national government, the CEO of a megacorporation, a member of the Mafia *Commissione*)	+3
Major Organized: Mafia or Yakuza, Triads (in Asia)	+4		
Terrorist group	+2	Major media figures, sports stars, other newsies, people with fame/notoriety but no authority to speak of	+2
Government			
Ward/District	+3		
City/Metroplex	+4	**What's Involved**	
State/Regional	+5	Action is ethical and legal	–2
National	+6	Action is unethical but legal	+0
Covert Operations	+1	Action is illegal:	
Magician or Magical Group	+1	Misdemeanor	+1
Policlub or Political Party	+2	Felony	+2
Pro Sports	+2	Violent crime	+3
Religion	+2	Mass violence	+4
Shadowrunners	+1	Crime involves misuse of office	+1
Area Affected			
Neighborhood	–1	**The Money**	
City or Metroplex	+1	Under a million	+0
Region or State	+2	Under 100 million	+1
National	+3	Under a billion	+2
International	+4	Over a billion	+3

LAUBENSTEIN.92.

Let's look at Ace Simms' story on the street shooting of several people in that ork neighborhood in Renton. After the first day on that beat, the following factors affect the story:

- A crime by a street gang (according to interviews with bystanders) (+2)
- Metahumans (+1)
- A neighborhood is the area affected (−1)
- Private citizens and street gangers are the only folks involved (−2)
- A violent crime was committed (+3)

The Target Number is 2 + 1 − 1 − 2 + 3, or a 3. Ace can file a solid report on the beat with that kind of target number, and so keeps the story alive to pursue his lead on Humanis involvement.

Two days later, having uncovered a link between Red, the ganger who pulled the trigger, and the local chapter of the Humanis Policlub, Ace files another report. This time the target number has changed.

- Policlub involvement (+2)
- Street gang involvement (+2)
- Metahumans involved (+1)
- Neighborhood affected (−1)
- Local policlub leadership involved (−1)
- Violent crime involved (+3)

The target number is 2 + 2 + 1 − 1 − 1 + 3, for a 6. Ace might have to stretch to make enough successes on his Reporting Skill alone, but fortunately, he has several pieces of proof by now, and those give him enough automatic successes to keep the story alive.

As it happens, that story won't get any more complicated, his Target Number will stay a 6 as he moves in on nailing the Humanis creeps to the wall, and he files the story in the next few days. If, for example, the beat led him to involvement by Alamos 20,000, the mysterious antimetahuman terrorist group rumored to be behind the scenes at Humanis, the target number would go up by another +2, though the gamemaster might rule that Alamos 20,000 is replacing Humanis in the equation, which would make it a wash.

Example #2: A news team covers a normal burglary. So far the story is a typical crime beat, a once-off. The only reason it's newsworthy is that the crooks were busted while in the process of rifling the offices of a political party. The story involves:

- Individual criminals (+2)
- A political party (+2)
- Low-level individuals (−2)
- A felony (+2)

The Target Number on this unremarkable story is a 4.

Over time, one thing leads to another. The Department of Justice takes control of the case, sequestering all police reports. The burglars are linked to the intelligence community. The reporters start getting leads from an anonymous source. They find signs of a coverup, possibly involving the highest offices of the government. Eventually, the numbers look something like this:

- Federal government involved (+6)
- Entire nation affected (+3)
- President involved (+3)
- Felony and abuse of office involved (+3)

The Target Number is a 15! The snoops better have lots of proof to keep this story from getting spiked. When you figure what a Watergate would involve in the Sixth World, Woodward and Bernstein would probably have to be as deadly with firearms as they were with words to survive and see the story through.

NOTHING BUT THE TRUTH

When a story includes faked material, either pix or proof, there is a chance that the deception will be spotted. Once the story is filed, the gamemaster secretly tests this. Figure that the skills brought to bear on tests are an equal part of the target number for the beat.

Add up the numbers for Special Interest, Who's Involved, and The Money to get the skill that will be used to test faked items. So if a snoop is tackling a story involving the CEO of a megacorp, with billions riding on the outcome, it would be just as well to stick to the straight and narrow.

The target numbers for several methods of faking data were discussed in the **What Is Truth** section. These secret tests only get one crack at the data, and if they don't uncover the deception on that test, the snoop has gotten away with it. This time.

...OR CONSEQUENCES

What happens to a snoop who gets caught using faked material?

Well, first of all, the story is spiked. Dead. Kaput. But it doesn't stop there. The snoop's credibility has taken a major slam. He gets a +2 modifier to his Punch Tests. Forever. If he gets caught doing it again, that's a +4. Forever. And so on. Lastly, if the snoop is an employee of the net, as opposed to a freelancer, he faces disciplinary action.

The gamemaster can give a snoop a chance to restore his reputation. The best way is to break a major beat, playing it straight as an arrow the whole way. Frankly, this presupposes that the gamer running the snoop is really intent on getting his rep clean and keeping it that way. If the gamer just wants to clear out the penalty so he can get away with a fake-job whenever it suits him, then we figure that attitude will be reflected in the character, and his breast-beating act won't fool either the nets or the public.

THE SPIKE

Way back when news was something printed on paper, an editor killing a story stuck the printout, or typescript, or parchment (whatever they used back then) on a spike on his desk. Paper is passé, but the newsnet jargon for a killed beat is still the "spike."

Once a beat is spiked, the snoop gets no more official support from his network connections if he wants to pursue it. If he is an employee, his boss will put him on a new assignment.

If a snoop wants to pursue a spiked story, he has to do it without calling on any resources from the net. He may have to do it in his spare time, between other assignments. If he digs up more material, he can try to convince the net to re-open the beat. File the story and make the Punch Test. If the result is good enough to keep the story alive, the snoop wins the argument, and is back on the beat. If the story gets spiked again, the snoop faces disciplinary action.

OUTSIDE PRESSURE

The increased target numbers when a snoop is going after big fish reflects the pressure they can bring to bear in getting your beat spiked. This can, in fact, be roleplayed instead, which is infinitely more satisfactory. The gamemaster can hit the snoop with tax audits, credit rating errors, even goon squads or hit men. Naturally, any major corp could wipe out one of these gadflies in a minute if they weren't concerned about exposure and if they really thought the snoop could hurt them. Fortunately, it is way too raw for a squad of company police to wipe out an impertinent reporter, and the corps don't really assign that much importance to these irritants. So even assassination attempts should be in the range that the snoop and his news team can survive. Often, the opposition's goal is not to kill, which can arouse unhealthy curiosity about the unfinished beat, but to frighten or discredit the reporter instead. A snoop on a hot beat may find he is spending a good deal of time fending off attacks on his reputation or bank account, or thugs with orders to beat him to paste.

There's a payback for the snoop here. If he survives an attack, it is a piece of proof if he can document it at all, whether with tridshots, a confession by an assailant, or other materials. This does not apply to threats that come along in the normal course of the adventure. A snoop on a shadowrun into a yak safe-house cannot use attacks by its guards as proof that the gangsters are trying to shut him up.

Given that risk, many opponents prefer to avoid direct attacks on reporters. The job is dangerous enough that they may go down in the normal course of events. Let nature take its course.

30, END OF STORY

Say the beat stays alive until the snoop nails it down. What now? "30"—end of story. Another prehistoric term that's survived in the Information Age. Some stories end because they can't go any further, not because they're over. The street gang took its orders from Mr. Johnson, who worked for the Division Manager, who was following the directive from the Marketing Vice-President. And there the chain stops, as far as anyone can tell. How much higher does the corruption really extend? Company president? Corporate VP? The CEO and Board of Directors? They all expressed pious horror at the excesses of their underlings. Then they took water and washed their hands before the multitude.

One step at a time. Even Jove nods, and even the biggest big boy can take his finger off the number. A memo. A datafile. 18.5 minutes of erased tape. They'll slip. And you'll be ready.

THE RATINGS GAME

Ratings are a constant concern on the commercial newsnets, and even pirates worry about how many people are watching. When a reporter writes "30," it is time to check the final ratings for the story.

Total up all the successes in the Punch section of the Beat Sheet. Divide by the highest File Number. In other words, average the Punch successes for the whole beat.

Multiply this by the highest Punch Test Target Number that had to succeed during the beat. This usually is the last one, but not necessarily so. The resulting number tells the snoop his ratings:

0–10: A real dog. The snoop will face disciplinary action if he's an employee of the net.

11–25: Average job. No praise, no blame.

26–50: Above-average job. Snoop gets a reward if he is employed by the net.

51–60: The beat has captured national attention, follow-ups by other networks, and appropriate reactions in the real world. Snoop gets a reward from the net, and in addition, a –2 bonus on all Punch Tests for his next major beat. He can save this bonus. He doesn't have to use it on the first story that comes along. He can even save up more than one bonus at a time, but he can only use one of them on any given beat. He can decide to apply a saved bonus on any Punch Test, and once he does, it will apply to all the remaining Punch Tests on that beat.

Any characters who are exposed as criminals by the beat will be indicted if the snoop filed any proof that can be used as legal evidence. This is rather vague, we admit. It is primarily a color call by the gamemaster.

61+: As above, and appropriate legal or corporate action is taken against anyone exposed by the story. This may be formal arrest and indictment, or dismissal by a corporation with extradition to local jurisdiction. Perhaps the individual involved simply disappears or is found floating in the Sound or suffers an unexpected cerebro-vascular incident.

A reporter who doesn't care for this notion is in the wrong line of work. The puppet-masters he works to expose are ruthless about cutting their losses, and if he thinks he can play at this level without people getting hurt, he's living in a fool's paradise.

SPORTS

Why not give everyone a gun and a camera and call it a game?
—Monkeytribe: Survival Manual For Erect Bipeds, by Mullins Chadwick, Putnam-Izumo Publishers, New York, 2041

Folks sit around, folks got time on their hands, and so the corps and gummint have to find something to keep folks from getting…restless.

When it was mob-time in old Rome, folks got "bread and circuses." Nowadays, whole lotta money goes into the sportsnets and the teams they cover.

During the crashes, changes, and chaos that ripped up North America, anything that helped folks keep their drek together was valuable. Sports became *very* valuable and have stayed that way. 'Course, the bosses get a lot of their nuyen back through pay-per-view trid access, aftermarket trid and sim records, ads with big ratings, even tickets to actually see a game live. It all adds up.

BASEBALL

America's pastime made it halfway through the 21st century with only a few, teeny changes: chipped players, the collapse of the old league structure, and a three-team playoff in the World Series. And making things even more interesting, the traditionalists in North American baseball are under increasing pressure from the *zaibatsu* to open the World Series to competition with Japanese teams. But it's still basically the same old ball game.

NORTH AMERICAN LEAGUE

Even after things fell apart and the old U.S. broke up, the governments and big corps agreed to keep baseball going. That was the beginning of the North American League (NAL). The North American League championship is still called the World Series, but the order of play has changed to fit a three-conference structure. The team at the top of each conference at the end of the regular season wins the divisional pennant and goes on to play in the World Series. Two of the three regional champion teams are chosen at random to play the first game of the series. The winner of that game plays against the third championship team. The loser of the second game plays the loser of the first game, and the loser of that game is out. The two remaining teams play each other for two out of three wins.

Most baseball teams are based in the UCAS, CAS, or CFS. But just because Mexico turned into Aztlan and joined the NAN, its people didn't stop loving baseball, and the San Diego Jaguars prove it. Besides, a hot baseball team run from San Diego, a former U.S. city, lets the Azteks sneer at the anglos. Beating them at their own game, the Azzies' favorite pastime.

The Miami Sharks tap into a lot of the Cuban and South American talent that used to end up on the U.S. teams in the old days. Now a talented Caribbean League player can stay in his own country and still play pro ball.

The team no one expected to see is the Portland Lords. When a new set of franchises opened up in 2046 to expand the NAL divisions to eight teams each, a winning bid from the Hemlad Cartel in Tir Tairngire surprised the drek out of everyone. A lot of jokes made the rounds about elven players in satin uniforms, but the laughs only lasted until the Lords' first game, when they shut out the L.A. Dodgers 5–0. Yeah, the team was almost all elf, but the players were some of the toughest athletes in the Tir and they carried primo cyber. They took the Coastal Division pennant in 2048 and are a definite prospect for this year's World Series.

BASEBALL AND CYBERWARE

Unlike football, which started modding up players almost as soon as the tech was available, baseball stayed cyber-free until 2032. At that point, the rules were relaxed to let pro teams and AAA farm teams load a player with up to 3 Essence Points' worth of cyberware. The regulations also allow custom cyber, at reduced Essence costs, but only the hottest stars get that kind of investment from a team.

As an interesting aside, Japanese baseball turned to cyber a few years earlier than North American teams, for at least two reasons. First, the tech was in better shape in Japan. Second, muscle implants and other mods helped close the last gap between heftier *gaijin* players and the more lightly built Japanese athletes. Exhibition play leaves no doubt that the Japanese teams can take on American players toe-to-toe, and many bettors predict some kind of official international championship within a few years.

The usual program for a hot rookie is a year or two playing in the bush leagues unchipped. Then, if he still looks good, he gets bumped up to AAA ball and picks up some basic mods, usually wired reflexes or muscle implants. If a player gets picked up by "the Show" (the big leagues), his contract spells out the upgrades and additions he will receive to his mods. Most players and their agents spend more time on mods than on salary.

Cybered players have sent the old records to the showers. For example, "Lock-on" Lorenzo Hayes, left fielder for the Yankees, topped the records of Babe Ruth, Hank Aaron, and Saduharu Oh in 2049, and is now up to 847 career homers. Hayes has 4,195 hits so far, and so is zeroing in on Pete Rose's lifetime record of 4,256 hits. In 2042, Harry "Ironjaw" Bartlett goblinized into an ork after five years on the mound for the L.A. Dodgers. He stayed on, kept pitching, and retired in 2048 with a lifetime record of 5,301 thrown strikeouts, beating Nolan Ryan's final total of 5,299. Oddly enough, anti-metahuman jerks spent more time griping about Bartlett's race than his heavily reconstructed pitching arm. When Bartlett pitched a scorching game against the Yomiuri Giants, Japan's most revered baseball team, in the 2043 World All-Star exhibition, the newsnets of the Yomiuri corporation nearly foamed at the mouth at the Americans' incivility in expecting the Giants to face a *kawaruhito* ("changed person") on the mound.

NAL TEAMS

Eastern Division
Atlanta Braves (CAS)
Baltimore Orioles (UCAS)
Boston Red Sox (UCAS)
FDC Senators (UCAS)
Manhattan Yankees (UCAS)
Montreal Expos (Québec)
Philadelphia Phillies (UCAS)
Richmond Generals (CAS)

Central Division
Chicago White Sox (UCAS)
Cincinnati Whites (UCAS)
Detroit Tigers (UCAS)
Kansas City Royals (UCAS)
Miami Sharks (CL)
St. Louis Cardinals (CAS)
Houston Astros (CAS)
Texas Lone Stars (CAS)

Coastal Division
California Angels (CFS)
Los Angeles Dodgers (CFS)
Portland Lords (TT)
Sacramento Padres (CFS)
San Francisco Giants (CFS)
San Francisco Whales (CFS)
Seattle Mariners (UCAS)
San Diego Jaguars (AZT)

NELSON

BASKETBALL

Since the middle of the 20th century, Afro-Americans have dominated basketball, using the NBA as a voice to reach into the tension-tight inner cities even while the U.S. was being torn apart by economics and the corps. When the league was reorganized to fit the new political setup, the game remained an American show.

The North American Basketball Association is a single league divided into four regional conferences. Two conferences have only UCAS teams, split into East and West. The other two are the Pacific Conference, with teams from UCAS and CFS cities, and the Confederate Conference, made up of member teams from the CAS.

The NABA Championship starts with a series of playoffs matching the top two teams from each conference. The four winning teams from the first round play a semifinal round, and the winners of those games face off in the championship.

BASKETBALL AND CYBERWARE

Basketball is very antsy about cyber. The pattern of the game falls apart if the players are jacked up too high. Reflex increases are limited to Level 1 Wired Reflexes or Level 2 Boosted Reflexes. Unlimited muscle implants and sensory boosts are allowed, including "smartball" technology, a chipped-in combination of a ballistic computer and cyberoptic scanner that boosts accuracy in passing and shooting. The league accepted that tech in 2047, after lengthy, bitter arguments.

Weapon implants are out, and so are any complete limb replacements. Any mods that alter the height or reach of a player are illegal.

NABA TEAMS

UCAS East Conference
Boston Celtics
DC Bullets
New Jersey Nets
New York Knicks
Philadelphia 76ers

UCAS West Conference
Chicago Bulls
Cleveland Cavaliers
Detroit Pistons
Indiana Pacers
Milwaukee Bucks

Pacific Conference
Denver Nuggets
Golden State Warriors
Los Angeles Lakers
Sacramento Kings
Seattle SuperSonics

Confederate Conference
Atlanta Hawks
Charlotte Hornets
Dallas Mavericks
Houston Rockets
San Antonio Spurs

FOOTBALL

Where baseball resisted cyber, football embraced it with open arms. The first modified players suited up in 2025, their vatwork used to fix bad injuries. But after New York Jets' linebacker "Gorgo" MacGuiness shredded season rushing records after getting his legs rebuilt, and Tim Washington won the 2025 Super Bowl with a 99-yard pass from his rebuilt right arm, team owners were clamoring for new rules. Not to keep the refitted players off the field, but to let teams put cybermods on players whether they were injured or not.

The floodgates opened in 2027 and a wave of cyberjocks hit the astroturf. The 2028 season was delayed for two months while necessary emergency stadium alterations were finished. A regulation football field in the NFL is now 160 yards long by 65 yards wide. The end zones are still 10 yards long, but the distance from end zone to end zone is 140 yards. Completing a first down on the ground means moving the ball 20 yards instead of 10. The ball itself is made of denser material and weighs about two kilos, and player padding has turned into light armor (Impact Rating 3). Almost every season record for the NFL got creamed in 2027, and so did a lot of players: there were 227 serious injuries and 4 deaths. Getting used to cyber takes a little time.

Football had it kind of rocky in the years after the Crash of '29 and the merging of the U.S. and Canada. No Super Bowls or organized league action was seen from 2030 to 2037. Teams arranged their own games. Some franchises folded. Others kept going without any organized funding or coverage, nets picked up games and showed them or not, pretty much at random.

Things eventually returned to normal. No one could call the 2038 season spectacular, but something like a full schedule of games was played by teams based in the UCAS and CAS, and the Washington Chieftains won the Super Bowl.

Two pro football leagues now clash regularly. The UCAS League is the bigger one, with two conferences (Eastern and Western) totaling sixteen teams. The nine CAS and CFS franchises are organized into the Freedom League, a name chosen when secession fever was still pretty high in the countries that split from the UCAS. The winner of the UCAS League playoffs faces the Freedom League champions in the Super Bowl.

FOOTBALL AND CYBERWARE

Completely cybered limbs are out, but anything that can be implanted, grown, or grafted onto the original muscle and bone is in. Even full limb replacements that grew in a vat instead of being built on a workbench are legal. Edged, powered, or missile implants are out, but implants that increase the striking power of the natural limb are wiz as far as the leagues are concerned. Football does not limit the quantity of cyberware a player can load in. He can mod up until he's got less Essence than a Fuchi cyber-servo robot, and it's still null perspiration.

Typical mods run to boosted or wired reflexes, subdermal armor, muscle implants, boosters for natural bone and tendon, especially in tricky spots like knees, the lower back, and the neck, and so on. Mastoid implant radio links for on-the-fly directions from the quarterback or coach were legalized in 2047, as was "smartball" technology.

UCAS LEAGUE TEAMS

Eastern Conference
Brooklyn Giants
Buffalo Bills
New England Patriots
New York Jets
Cincinnati Bengals
Cleveland Browns
Philadelphia Eagles
Washington Chieftains

Western Conference
Chicago Bears
Denver Broncos
Detroit Lions
Green Bay Packers
Indianapolis Colts
Minnesota Vikings
Pittsburgh Steelers
Seattle Seahawks

FREEDOM LEAGUE TEAMS
Atlanta Falcons (CAS)
Dallas Cowboys (CAS)
Houston Oilers (CAS)
Sacramento Chargers (CFS)
Tampa Bay Buccaneers (CAS)
Orlando Thunder (CAS)
Los Angeles Rams (CFS)
New Orleans Saints (CAS)
Richmond Raiders (CAS)
San Francisco 49ers (CFS)

OTHER PRO SPORTS

The Big Three and combat sports rule the nets in the UCAS, CAS, and CFS. Other sports are bigger overseas, and even in other parts of the Americas.

Soccer remains the most popular sport worldwide, though Urban Brawl is coming up fast as number two. The quadrennial World Cup of soccer is still the most widely watched sporting event on the planet. The 2056 World Cup is scheduled for Aztec Stadium in Tenochtitlán, and Aztechnology is rumored to be spending heavy cred to build a world-beating team for the event. The big news in world soccer is the entry of Amazonia into international competition with a team that is almost completely metahuman. And against every anti-metahuman's hopes and expectations, the Amazonian team is making impressive progress in the world standings.

Some of the NAN countries have adopted lacrosse, touting it as a traditionally Native American game. And in keeping with the NAN's mixed feelings about cyber, it is no surprise that their lacrosse players are all natural. The more conservative tribal factions have enough clout to keep even physical adepts from playing, claiming it "profanes their gift" to use it that way.

One former NAN state has resurrected a more sinister athletic tradition.

COURT BALL

The Aztlan Court Ball Union claims theirs is the original form of the sacred game played by the pre-Columbian civilizations. No archaeological info exists to say whether it is or not, but the Azzies love it, and it gets a lot of play on the sportsnets in other countries too.

Rumor says some of the nastier aspects of the Aztec game have been revived, too. Back before the conquistadores brought civilization, slavery, and smallpox to Mexico, the captain of a winning team was sacrificed to the gods, sent to glory in his moment of victory. Now it may be coincidence, but in the last four years, the captains of the teams that won the Aztlan Championship have snuffed it. Lopez (Ensenada Eagles) died in a plane crash. De Brize, the Haitian who led the Zempoala Cats to victory in 2050, was apparently killed accidentally during a war between two Veracruz go-gangs. Chamac (Tenochtitlán Jaguars), washed up on a Cancun beach, apparently drowned. And of course, Xochitalco, Chamac's successor at the head of the Jaguars, brought things out in the open last year during the award ceremony. He shouted that he dedicated his win, and his death, to Tezcatlipoca and jammed a snap-blade into his own chest. Some newsies figure he must've been jazzed on something, since he cut his heart most of the way out before he fell over.

Court ball players can carry unlimited cyber, and physical adepts can compete without any restrictions. Players can use any hand-to-hand cyberweapons, and usually carry an assortment of knives, clubs, and electroprods. Because the uniform for court ball is a loincloth, leather bands on the wrists and joints, and feathers, injuries and death are common.

Court ball is played in a sunken, four-sided court, with three-man teams. No time-outs. No penalties. Only three replacements per game. Play is to seven points or the elimination of one team.

Goals are scored by shooting the ball through a ring attached to the east wall of the court. The ball may be passed. Passes and goals both require that the ball bounce at least once. Illegal passes and goal attempts (no bounce) give possession to the other team. A dead ball belongs to whichever team can take possession of it.

MAGIC AND METAHUMANS IN PRO SPORTS

Open use of magic in pro sports is illegal across the board. Spells, aid from spirits, and any other magical assistance are all banned. The biggest question from the beginning was the physical adept. When physical adepts were officially identified as a legit magical manifestation by the American Association for the Advancement of Thaumaturgy, back in the early thirties, a lot of drek started flying. Seems a couple of team owners with a bug in their headware about spook stuff brought in a "witch smeller," an adept who specializes in spotting magical energy on the astral, and ran their players past her. The adept ID'd a half-dozen top players who were physads. Most of them didn't know they were adepts, though Warren Lee, star center for the Charlotte Hornets, was from an old Ozark hill family and always made a big deal out of wearing his gitchee bags and lucky pieces off the court. Some writers figure he may have been an initiate.

This started a rash of court suits, hearings, and protests. Things dragged on until 2042, when the pro sports commissioners chartered a joint committee, which handed down a decision in 2045 that everyone embraced to their bosoms, because they were totally sick of the whole mess.

Anyone claiming to be a physical adept cannot be fired or cut for that reason, but he also cannot have *any* cyber. If a physad gets modified at all, he loses his special standing. This ruling left things pretty much up to the front office for each team. They could always find some reason to drop a player besides his magical ability, and late bloomers who got a teeny mod put in before they knew they were adept are at the mercy of the management. Where the fans accept magic, an adept or two usually appears on the local rosters. Most places, it's cyberware all the way.

We already mentioned Harry Bartlett, L.A.'s hotshot ork pitcher. He was a rarity, already a popular player when he grew tusks. Baseball is pretty conservative about metas in general, and some teams make a big noise about the sport being for "real" humans. There's maybe half a dozen metahumans in the North American League, not counting the Portland Lords, of course.

The heavier bones and musculature of orks and trolls is wizbang for football. And a remarkable number of elves are active in pro basketball. Approximately twenty-four players in the NABA are elven, and seventy-eight pro football players are ork or troll. The shadowtalk claims there is a "gentlemen's agreement" among the team owners to keep a lid on metahuman recruitment, and maybe it's true, 'cause there should be lots more of them out there.

WOMEN IN PRO SPORTS

Cyberware renders sex-based differences in strength and speed irrelevant. Skill is what matters, skill and guts. Given cyber, a top-notch female pitcher can strike out a batter as easily as an equally skilled male. Even in football, a woman with the right implants has no trouble slamming it out with male opponents.

But tradition dies hard, and a lot of recruiting depends on uncybered performance in collegiate and amateur leagues, which means women going after careers in pro sports still face major physical disadvantages. The first woman to capture a pro baseball contract was Judy Hofsted, in 2038, with the Detroit Tigers. She was cybered already, as a test subject for Anderson

Bionics. Her performance was impressive enough to prompt the more adventurous teams to scout other top female athletes.

Only about two dozen women are on pro teams today in the Big Three. Newer sports, especially the combat sports, boast a larger percentage.

AMATEUR SPORTS

Track and field is still popular in the Sixth World, but mostly on the college level. Chipped competition never got a foot in the door. Frag, they were still testing for steroids until 2014, when the new generation of training drugs came along and made testing too difficult to be practical.

Any and all pharmaceutical boosts have been legit since then, but the bosses in amateur athletics made cyber the kiss of death. This ban includes collegiate baseball, football, and basketball, but it really makes sense in track and field. Watching a bunch of people "compete" to see whose implants can toss his bod the farthest is mega-boring. But the issue got carried too far. The "purity of essence" thing is almost a religion, and the amateur sports authorities are the high priests. Even a datajack is enough to get someone disqualified, and that is fragging stupid.

Magic is O-U-T. Big meets lay on a couple of wage mages to scope competitors. Any athlete who wants to register with an organized athletics association or try out for an Olympic team gets scanned astrally to make sure he's not a physad.

UCAS athletics were opened to metahumans in 2041. Outside the Japanese-controlled areas in San Francisco, the CFS opened up at about the same time. The CAS still has a bad attitude about metas, but most of its teams, like most of its colleges, are nominally open to metahumans by now. Athletics in corporate enclaves follow company policy, natch, but there's usually a token meta or two in even the most racist organizations, especially in sports where the metas have a big advantage. Weightlifting is about 30 percent troll, for instance, as is wrestling, and Windheels Lincoln, an elf, took the gold in the 100-meter dash in the last UCAS games. His 9.1-second time is the world record, and people figure him for a big winner in the Tokyo Olympics in 2056. If the International Olympic Committee can get Japan to back off from its no-go position about metas in the competition, that is.

THE OLYMPICS

The Olympics sort of fell apart from 2032 to 2040, what with little distractions like the Crash of '29, the collapse of the U.S., and the EuroWar. The Games were revived officially in 2044, even though several different sets of Olympics were held during the disorganized period. Heck, in 2034 there were three Games, in Beijing, Buenos Aires, and Johannesburg. None of these competitions had more than twenty countries participating, and all results from these "outlaw" games were dropped from official records when the new International Olympic Committee (IOC) started the Games up again.

The Olympics are the ultimate defenders of "purity" in "amateur" athletics. Paid professionals, cybered athletes, and physical adepts are their big concern. Other probs get the big blind eye.

The Olympics were opened to multinational corporate teams in 2044, and now winning a medal is worth big corp prestige. About a fifth of all medals end up going to corporate

"amateur" athletes. Nice to know that someone who puts in an hour a week sitting at a desk, pulls down a comfy salary for doing it, and spends the rest of the time getting the best training money can buy, is an amateur.

The Olympics still run Summer and Winter Games, and only a few of the events have changed in the last fifty years. The Winter Games haven't changed at all, in fact.

Rhythm gymnastics, synchronized swimming, and yachting were cut from the Summer Games and replaced by kendo (added for the 2056 Tokyo Games, so this is still up in the air), karate/tae kwon do, jai alai, and lacrosse.

The Tokyo Hassle

Japan, *after* it won the bid for the '56 Games, announced that in keeping with the *Yamato* ideal, metas would not be permitted to compete with normals in Tokyo, but would be scheduled in special "exhibition" contests. The two elven nations, Tir Tairngire and the Shidhe Dominion in Ireland, are in a meltdown, and have damn near buried the U.N. in resolutions. Pro-meta policlubs and organizations are pressuring their governments to boycott the Games if Japan doesn't back down. The IOC has sternly waved its hands at Japan, and even threatened to form a subcommittee to study the matter intensely. The Japanese are obviously shaking in their *tabi*. Japanese corps are slotting Ghost-only-knows how many nuyen into IOC funding and the Olympic bigwigs are scared drekless of losing the money pipeline. It's anyone's guess how things are gonna turn out.

MANO A MANO

Combat sports have moved up to match major league team sports in popularity. Used to be that boxing was the only combat sport with much of a following in North America, that and the flash-'n'-trash circus that was pro wrestling. Not anymore. Maybe it's just cuz it's a tougher world out there. Maybe the way people get used up, twisted around, and spit out by this crazy way they live has made them meaner.

INDIVIDUAL COMBAT

One casualty of the times was pro wrestling. As genuine combat sports, with flashier special effects, caught on and increased their network coverage, the grunt-and-groan circuit withered away. The last spurt of activity in pro wrestling was during the tail end of the guerrilla wars surrounding the Ghost Dance, when "good guys" with names like General America and The Cowboy slammed it out with "bad guys" named Big Chief Coyote and The Dark Wizard. These days, Combat Biker has pretty much the same kind of following and the same flavor in promotion as wrestling used to.

Many individual arts feature organized activity, ranging from collegiate and Graeco-Roman wrestling, through classic oriental combat styles (judo, karate, kendo, and so on), to flat-out street fighting. The two most popular individual sports are boxing and freestyle. Bouts are broadcast on at least one of the sportsnets any day of the week.

Boxing

Boxing uses the same weight classifications it always has, but has added two ranges. A superheavyweight class (95 kilos and up) was added in 2039 to accommodate superboosted human and metahuman fighters, and boxing now offers cyber and non-cyber classes as well. Cyberboxing fiddled with rules and limits for a few years after it was introduced in 2027, then decided to heck with it. In the modified class, a boxer can load in anything he can carry. The modified class carries only two restrictions; boxers cannot modify their hands to improve the striking surface, and cannot use cyberweapons in a match. A boxer *can* get his bones and soft tissues toughened, however, so that his hand can stand up to the kind of punch that muscle implants driven by wired reflexes deliver.

The gloves in the cyber classes are heavier, and made from a more impact-absorbent material, but the added protection they provide doesn't make much difference. Cyberboxing results in ten to fifteen deaths each year and a hefty number of serious injuries.

Like always, the heavy and superheavyweight title bouts get the most coverage. Watching two guys in the 80-kilo and up range going at it seems to be what the home viewing audience wants to see.

Two competing boxing organizations vie for the audience's attention; the World Boxing Association and the International Boxing Commission. The WBA is based in Atlanta, and is basically a front for NewsNet's sports division. It is the big noise in boxing in North America. The IBC is based in Bonn, Germany, and is less commercial. It handles both pro and amateur boxing in Europe, as well as Olympic boxing worldwide.

Freestyle

Freestyle evolved gradually, as different combat styles became more and more popular on the nets. The first "official" freestyle match was broadcast in 2015 by a cablenet called SportsBlast. SportsBlast was bought up by MegaMedia in 2022, but by then other promoters and nets had introduced freestyle matches to their programming, and MegaMedia's shot at getting exclusive control of the sport and its trademarks got tossed out of court on the grounds that freestyle had entered the public domain through common usage.

Freestyle is what the name suggests: any attack a player can make with his unarmed bod is legal. Any spot on an opponent is a legal target: eyes, joints, groin, throat, you name it. Combat goes to a knockout, a disable, or a surrender. No decisions. No "ref stops contest." No rounds, time-outs, or fouls.

All I knows is, the ref was raising my right hand in victory, I looked down, and there was an eyeball in my left, lookin' at me. I don't know for sure how it got there.
— Ming Malone, 2051 middle-heavyweight freestyle champ

Freestyle uses boxing's weight classes, and also splits into cyber and non-cyber classes with the same restrictions as boxing. Also as in boxing, no (external) body armor is used.

A freestyle ring is a circle ten meters in diameter. If a fighter's entire body leaves the ring, voluntarily or not, the fighter automatically surrenders and loses. The ring's surface can be concrete, wood, canvas, or dirt.

LETHAL SPORTS

At this time, events involving deliberate combat to the death are illegal in all North American countries except Aztlan. Urban Brawl comes closest to crossing the line, but wounded brawlers are treated immediately and removed from play when badly wounded, and the object of the game is to score goals, not kill opponents. It says so right in the rules.

A number of countries and corporate enclaves promote flat-out gladiator fights; single or team combat, fought with real weapons and minimal armor, to the death. Aztlan introduced death matches between condemned criminals as a form of execution in 2039. Professional gladiators, fighting under contract, came along in 2043. Urban myths about Southeast Asian death matches have circulated for a long time. Whether they were real or not then, several Asian warlord states definitely have them now.

Mixed-style matches are what the crowds seem to like, so that's what the promoters give them. Non-cyber, heavily armed fighters against lightly armored cyberkillers. Western street fighters against oriental stylists. Norm vs. meta. "Fair fights" that match half a dozen shanghaied zeros with no combat experience against a single experienced samurai. Blood and circuses.

COMBAT BIKER

Combat Biker came along in 2013. It was thought up by a chummer named Vernon Prudhomme in Baton Rouge, Louisiana. Prudhomme needed a publicity gimmick to pump up his ailing speedway. He hired a down-and-out bunch of motorcycle "daredevils" and staged a game involving motorcycles, stunt riding, padded clubs, and "paintball" guns. He wrapped it in a lot of tinsel, and hyped it over the TV and radio. The thing caught on, and Prudhomme started joking about starting a "Combat Cyclists League."

A major sportsnet show did a five-minute filler on Combat Biker, and it caught a lot of attention. Maybe too much. The next Saturday, a go-gang called the Maulers showed up, said they were a Combat Biker team, and beat the snot out of Prudhomme's stunt riders. Their bossman, Charles "Mangler" Patterson, let Prudhomme know that for a modest payment the Maulers would stay away, so he could get on with business as usual.

Prudhomme ignored their offer, hiring his own go-gang to take the place of his battered daredevils. He dressed them in uniforms, named them the Red Devils, unpadded the weapons, and replaced the paint guns with riot weapons firing plastic ammo. When the Maulers showed up, the Red Devils smeared them into a thin paste. The funny thing is, the event actually stayed within the rules (more or less) for almost an hour before things got a little out of control.

The story made bigtime ratings on the national feeds. While most of the anchors and talkers got off on the way Prudhomme put one over on the Maulers, one newsie ran a deadpan sportsnet segment on the game before it turned into a rumble.

Prudhomme got a call from a consortium of money men, and within a year six teams were competing nationally. Combat Biker games started showing up regularly on the tube. By 2026, the game was a going concern, with a league organization, established rules, and major media coverage.

THE WCCL

The World Combat Cyclists League is the pro Combat Biker organization. Despite the name, it's a North American operation.

A Combat Biker franchise is an expensive proposition. While bike manufacturers sell machines to teams at cost in return for the publicity they get, one game can eat up a lot of iron. Add in cyber for players, the arena, medical costs, and incidentals like weapons, armor, and so on, and costs add up fast. Combat Biker is incredibly popular on the nets, and commands impressive prices for commercials, pay-per-view on ultra-close-up coverage, resale rights for sims and trid, and replays over cable and the Matrix.

The WCCL is divided into two conferences. The top four teams in each conference meet in a series of playoffs, and conference champions slam it out for the world championship in the Biker Bowl.

WCCL Franchises

Eastern Conference
Atlanta Rebels
Baton Rouge Red Devils
Chicago Lightning
Cleveland Commandos
DeeCee Shurikens
New York Marauders

Western Conference
Los Angeles Sabers
New Orleans Buzzsaws
Houston Mustangs
Oakland Hogs
Seattle Timber Wolves
Texas Rattlers

THE ARENA

Combat Biker is an arena game. Played on a football-sized field, about 150 meters long by 50 meters wide, the arena is designed as a maze divided into lanes. Some lanes are wide enough to let three or four bikes ride side by side. Others are barely wide enough for one cycle to squeak through. A track called a "skyway" runs over the middle of the field. It is about a story high, no safety railing. Some folks call it the "launch pad."

At each end of the field is a two-meter goal circle.

Within limits, each Combat Biker franchise can design its own arena layout and can change it during the off-season. The WCCL has final approval on all designs.

THE BIKERS

A Combat Biker team fields the following nine positions, with eight team members on bikes, one on foot.

Linebikers

The hand-to-hand boys. Mounted on fast, unarmored cycles, armed with maces and riot guns. Each linebiker gets his choice of an additional weapon: flail, net, whip, or bola. A team has four linebikers.

Lancebikers

Lancebikers are mounted on heavy machines, big on power, low on maneuverability. Each carries a two-meter lance, a mace, and a riot gun. Each team fields four lancers.

Thunderbiker

Armed with a fixed-mount grenade launcher on a light cycle and an assortment of boom-boom. He also carries a mace. One thunderbiker rides for each side.

Goalie

Armored like a tank and moving on foot, the goalie carries an autoshot riot carbine, a mace, and a little thing called a tetsubo. That's a heavy Japanese quarterstaff, shaped like a sawed-off lamppost and covered with big studs. When a goalie lays a tetsubo shot across the middle of a biker moving at full speed, the audience usually get to see how much guts the biker really has. A team fields one goalie, and his playing position is in the goal zone, natch.

THE WEAPONS

While weapon weights and configurations for Combat Biker have gotten nastier over the years, they are all still technically non-lethal. Fatalities average eight per season from direct weapon strikes, as opposed to the much higher figure for deaths from cycle wipeouts. All deaths are hyped as "regrettable accidents" by League flacks, natch.

Flail

A 50-centimeter haft with a 30-centimeter cable at one end. A flail has a 500-gram densiplast mace head mounted on the end of the cable.

Lance

Two meters long and 5 centimeters thick with a blunt "point," this magic wand can be used as a staff or like an old-time knight's lance (at up to 100 kph right down a playing lane).

Mace

A seventy-centimeter high-impact plastic shaft with a 750-gram densiplast headball. Every biker on the team carries one of these suckers.

Net

A two-meter-square net made of 2-centimeter-thick polycarb cable, weighted at the rim and equipped with a one-meter cable. It can snag a biker and wrap him up like the catch of the day. No real damage, but try controlling a chopper at 100 kph in a two-meter-wide lane with one of these suckers wrapped around your head.

Tetsubo

The goalie's weapon. Two meters long, tapering from about 8 centimeters thick at the head to 3 centimeters at the butt. Set with metal or densiplast bosses and a 750-gram striking head.

Whip

A two-meter bullwhip of reinforced polycarb filament, breaking strain about 1,500 kg. Besides using it as a long-distance entangling weapon, a lot of linebikers are fond of a move called the Siamese Swoop, or the Gemini: Two bikers each grab an end of the whip and barrel down a lane, clotheslining anyone in their way.

In addition to weapons attacks, any kind of unarmed attack is legal, including a "flying block"—a body block thrown at a mounted player, whether the attacker starts out on a bike or on foot.

Besides hand-to-hand weapons, bikers carry one of several firearms, all firing stun rounds.

Autoshot Riot Carbine

An autofire-capable riot gun, this is the goalie's answer when the fans start yelling for "dee-FENSE"! The goalie has a twenty-round clip of stun ammo at the start of each play. Smartgun links are standard for big-league goalies.

Grenade Launchers

The thunderbiker mounts this on his cycle, and gets three concussion grenades each play.

Riot Guns

Carried by lancers and linebikers. Short-barreled pieces, Roomsweepers, or a similar configuration. Players get a fresh three-round clip of stun ammo at the start of each play. Each player can choose to carry his weapon free or mount it on his cycle. Smart weapons are allowed, and in the major leagues, pretty much everyone has them.

THE ARMOR

Goalies wear tough armor (Ballistic 6, Impact 5). Everyone else wears lighter stuff (Ballistic 3, Impact 2). Everyone also wears helmets (Ballistic +1, Impact +1). Armor is manufactured in "home" and "away" colors, and helmets have a distinctive team-logo look. For example, the Baton Rouge Red Devils have their helmets done up like classic "devil" heads: horns, fangs, the whole bit.

THE BIKES

Linebikers ride Yamaha Rapiers or an equivalent. Lancebikers ride Harley Scorpions or an equivalent. Neither mounts weapons. The thunderbiker rides a Rapier-class bike, modified to handle the grenade-launcher mount.

Cycles may be modified to accept a vehicle control rig, and rigged players and cycles are the rule rather than the exception in the major leagues.

OTHER EQUIPMENT

All players are equipped with two-way radios, either headsets built into their helmets or cyberware. Each uniform is equipped with an emergency biotech patch under a rip-away shield. Pulling off the shield automatically activates a Trauma Patch (3).

THE GAME

Combat Biker uses a flag. An actual flag on a lightweight pole 180 centimeters long. The flagpole has a weighted, hemispherical base, and if dropped, will always roll into an upright position.

The object of the game is to do a *flagsnag*, and then get the flag into the opposing side's goal zone.

Flagsnag is like the kickoff in football. The flag starts in the center of the middle lane on the field, mounted on a high-speed bogey, a little drone on wheels that whizzes around like crazy. The linebiker's job is to snag the flag. Until one team gets possession and goes on offense, the lancers and thunderbiker have to stay out of play and in their starting positions. Once the flag is snagged, almost anything goes.

A play in Combat Biker ends when a goal is scored, or when the clock runs out. On each play, a random timer is set and runs for thirty to sixty seconds. Every play runs for thirty seconds minimum, leaving anywhere up to thirty more seconds on the clock. The random time part of the play is called *jittertime,* because the clock can run out anytime and thus affect the score. There are ten minutes of playing time to a quarter. The clock stops between plays for reloading, sending in replacements, replacing cycles, and so on.

The officiating stank! I mean, what do I have to do to get a call to go my way?
— Teddy "Terminator" Tartikoff, after riding over an opponent a record 12 times

Scoring

Actually scoring a goal—planting the flag in the opposition's goal—counts for three points. Only a mounted player can score a goal. A dismounted player can carry the flag, but if the dismounted player plants it in the goal zone, it does not count as a goal.

If, when the clock runs out on a play, the offensive team (the team in possession of the flag) is in the defense's territory, they score one point. If the offensive team is in its own territory, the *defense* scores one point. This counts whether the flag carrier is mounted or not.

If the bogey carries the flag into one team's territory during flagsnag, and for some reason the flag is still not snagged when time runs out, the opposing team scores a point.

If the flag is not in either team's possession when the clock runs out, the point is given to the last team to take possession. So if a Seattle player carrying the flag gets blown away deep in Timber Wolves territory, the Wolves are going to scramble to get that flag into the opposing team's half of the track. The opposition may try to get the flag and press for a goal, or may simply fight to keep Seattle from getting it, since they'll score if the flag is still in the Timber Wolves territory when the clock runs out.

Fouls

There aren't many. Players tagged for a foul are called out of play and must pull into one of a number of shelters built into the barriers that form the playing lanes. Cutout circuits mounted in the cycle engines let the officials kill any bike on the field, which is the standard response when a player doesn't obey an order to get off the lanes.

Three fouls by one side in a single play ends the play, and gives the opposing side one point.

A player can be kicked out of the game for a really outrageous foul. When a player is kicked out, the play ends and the opposing team scores a point. A replacement is sent in on the next play.

Combat Biker fouls include the following.

Deliberate Release of Flag: Dropping the flag on purpose is a foul. The player who does it is kicked out of the game and the opposing team scores one point.

Ramming Dismounted Player: That is, deliberate ramming of a dismounted player. Awful lot of accidental sideswiping goes on out there ("Well, I tried to miss him!"). This does not extend to the goalie, by the way, who is fair game for ramming.

Riding over Unconscious/Disabled Player: The way this gets enforced, maybe the rules should add "…more than once." Or maybe "Backing up and doing it again."

Use of Unauthorized Weapon. A player cannot use any weapons but the ones authorized for his position. Picking up authorized weapons dropped or discarded by another player is allowed, including riot guns after a player has fired his three rounds for the play.

URBAN BRAWL

In 2022, the rumble à la mode for French street gangs who wanted to settle something was a fight on a piece of neutral terra by two armed teams. The side that scored the most goals in a simple ball game won the beef. Sort of a cross between "get the guy with the ball" and the gunfight at the OK Corral.

About this time, the French corp Javert et Cie. was trying to reclaim an economically dead neighborhood in return for extra-territorial rights like those granted the multinationals. Javert was getting nothing but drek from the local gangs until some bright exec came up with the notion of sponsoring these killer ball games that the punkers seemed to like. Cash purses, assignments in corporate security, and other goodies went to the winners.

The games really gripped the gangs' attention. They lost interest in doing dirt to Javert and concentrated on working to win the contests. Things really started cooking when a mid-level exec noticed that her fellow suits were betting like crazy on the outcome of the fights. Black market vids of the fracases were hot—the suits got a real kick out of watching the street trash waste each other. A quick check with the legal department was followed by some wheeling and dealing, and next thing you know, Javert et Cie. was feeding cable coverage of "Jeu de Guerre de Ville" to pay-per-view networks all over the country. Within a few months, satcasts were carrying the games all over the world.

The gangs were organized into official teams. Non-gang players were introduced in Germany in 2024, the same year that Govinda Enterprises in Chicago adopted the game to co-opt the gangers plaguing its operations in the city's depressed zones. "City Combat Game" didn't cut it as a name for the sport in the U.S., though, so a brightboy somewhere dreamed up the name Urban Brawl.

Urban Brawlers come from almost every social class these days and even include university teams. But most brawlers still come from the streets, betting survival against escape from poverty. In some corp enclaves, felons who are tough enough may be offered indenture on an Urban Brawl team instead of imprisonment or the big sleep.

The first North American championship, "The Super Brawl," was held in 2037. European Urban Brawl was dormant at the time, since the EuroWar was giving everyone too much of the real thing. When the war ground to a stop in 2042, the corps rebuilding the infrastructure of the continent channeled a lot of returning combat vets into Urban Brawl teams. A lot of these new brawlers were hooked on the battleboost drugs and chips that were used by all sides in the EuroWar, and this pushed the game's death rate to new heights. The first international Urban Brawl World Cup was in 2046, and has been held every two years since.

URBAN BRAWL LEAGUES

Urban Brawl teams flourish in almost every nation on earth. In North America, only the Pueblo and Trans-Polar Aleut councils of NAN and the Awakened nation of Yucatan ban the sport.

North American Urban Brawl is governed by the North American Commissioner of the Internationaler Stadtskrieg Sport Verein (International Urban Combat Sport Union), based in Berlin. League franchises are limited to twenty-four teams, but every two years, following the World Cup playoffs, the top non-franchised teams can challenge pro teams for their slots.

The ISSV has a complicated formula for tracking league standings to determine the players in the biennial World Cup playoffs. National and continental championships are played under rules worked out by the franchises and the local ISSV commissioners. The annual North American Super Brawl is a face-off between the two leading teams in North America, with the contenders chosen according to their ISSV ranking.

NORTH AMERICAN URBAN BRAWL FRANCHISES
(As of 2052)

Ares Predators (Ares Macrotechnology)
Atlanta Butchers (CAS)
Boston Massacre (UCAS)
Chicago Sensations (Truman Technologies)
Chicago Shatters (UCAS)
Cincinnati Lasers (UCAS)
Denver Thunderheads (UCAS)
Detroit Nightmares (UCAS)
Havana Guerrillas (CL)
Lakota Arrows (Sioux Council)
Los Angeles Bolts (CFS)
Miami Spears (CL)
Montreal Assassins (Québec)
Mountain Dragons (Dunklezahn Enterprises)
New Orleans Tombstones (CAS)
New York Slashers (UCAS)
Norfolk Battlers (CAS)
Oakland Terminators (CFS)
Renraku Invincibles (Renraku)
Seattle Screamers (UCAS)
St. Louis Slaughter (UCAS)
Tacoma Wings (Federated Boeing)
Tenochtitlán Volcanoes (Aztlan)
Tsimshian Warriors (Tsimshian)

ARENA BRAWL

While the ISSV franchises pull in enough cred to manage the expense of street games, only the most lavishly funded non-franchised teams can afford them. Instead, they stage games in arenas or mock-ups of street zones, using non-lethal ammo (stun and gel rounds), reduced armor values (Ballistic 1, Impact 1), and dummy melee weapons doing Stun Damage rather than the real thing. Injuries are still plentiful but fatalities are rare.

Arena Brawl is fought in scaled-down game zones, in the same playing area as Combat Biker (150 by 50 meters). "Build-ings" are all one-story high, with doors and windows spotted along the walls at random.

Arena Brawl is second best. Fans can't follow the action from their seats half as well as they can when watching on trid, and the compressed playing area can mess up tactics badly. And trid rights for arena games don't sell for nearly as much as broadcast rights for street brawls. Not enough action. The brawlers don't like it either, because they run out of dodging room way too fast. Urban Brawl is a child of the streets, and the game doesn't transplant well.

THE BRAWL ZONE

Franchise games are played in the streets, in Brawl Zones selected by the ISSV before the season begins. The list of potential sites is very hush-hush indeed, and includes about twice as many zones as the league will actually need. Brawl Zones always cover a depressed area, usually an officially uninhabited area such as the local Barrens. The ISSV surveyors look for zones where the squatters are all SINless, to avoid the hassles of moving people out if the Commissioner activates the zone. A Brawl Zone measures roughly four city blocks long by three city blocks wide: official dimensions are 550 meters long by 420 meters wide, minimum, and 680 meters long by 510 meters wide, maximum. The game area must be bounded by open streets on all sides.

Teams know what cities their games will be in at the beginning of each season, but they don't know the locations of the zones. Zones are activated only twenty-four hours before a match. Residents are moved out, cameras and other gear moved in. UCAS law says any citizen in the zone can appeal an ISSV vacate notice, but not many do. Fat payments, luxury accommodations during the game, guaranteed reimbursement for property damage…heck, the poor fraggers love it. Besides, stubborn folks tend to come to grief, or so say the pirate newsnets.

Once a zone is activated, league and network techs go to work, setting up remote cameras and relay transmitters for the flocks of camera drones used to vid the game.

The teams study city maps, blueprints, and other records to try and recon their side of the zone. Brawlers can go anywhere they can reach in the zone during the game. Inside, outside, upstairs, downstairs—don't matter. The more detailed knowledge a brawler has about the area, the more edge he's got. Shadowrunners have been known to pick up hefty nuyen doing covert scouting runs into the other team's turf. Shadowrunners have also been known to get dead mixing it up with ISSV security.

Twenty-four hours after the zone is activated, the game begins.

The Brawlers

Urban Brawl players, under ISSV rules, can use any cyberware they can cram into themselves: limb modifications, body weapons, smartgun links, skillwires, just name it. When a hot brawler on a small-time team shows up sporting the latest in cybertech, it's a safe bet he's being groomed to move into the majors, and that his new team is slotting the credstick for his new cybertoys. And this happens fairly often. An Urban Brawl team can go through a lot of personnel in a season.

Thirteen brawlers go into the zone at the beginning of a quarter. Replacements are made between plays. If all the offensive brawlers on one side get taken down during a single play, by wounds or surrender, that team is the victim of a *wipeout*. The other team wins no matter what the score.

Offensive Positions

Any of these brawlers can carry the ball.

Scouts: Light armor (Ballistic 3, Impact 2, plus helmet) and personal sidearm. Four on a team.

Bangers: Medium armor (Ballistic 4, Impact 3, plus helmet) and personal sidearm. Four on a team.

Heavies: Medium armor (Ballistic 4, Impact 3, plus helmet), personal sidearm, and brawler's choice of assault rifle, SMG, or shotgun. Two on a team.

Blaster: Light armor (Ballistic 3, Impact 2, plus helmet), but carries an LMG in a gyro-harness mounting (Rating 2). One on a team.

Non-Offensive Positions

These two brawlers cannot carry the ball.

Outrider: Medium armor (Ballistic 4, Impact 3, plus helmet), a motorcycle, and a cycle-mounted assault rifle, SMG, or shotgun. Personal sidearm. The outrider can fight and can also carry any other brawler on his cycle. The ball carrier may not get a lift from the outrider!

Medico: Heavy Armor (Ballistic 6, Impact 4, plus helmet) coated with a bright, glossy, white-colored medium. No weapons at all. The medico carries a well-stocked medical kit. This is a non-combatant position. The medico cannot engage in combat, and players who deliberately attack him are slapped with a penalty. Unless he's on the outrider's cycle—that bike is always fair game.

THE WEAPONS

Personal sidearms are defined as any single-action, double-action, or semi-automatic weapon up to the Heavy Pistol class, including short-barreled combat shotguns like the Remington Roomsweeper. Brawlers can carry any amount of ammunition.

Besides the weapons and armor specified, brawlers can carry almost any other melee weapons, external or cyberware. Monofilament and electrically charged weapons are illegal. The outrider may ride any class of motorcycle and the rules allow the use of a vehicle control rig.

A brawler can pick up any discarded melee weapon and use it during play. Any improvised weapons from the Brawl Zone itself are also legal, except for firearms, monofilament, or charged weapons that happen to be found lying about.

THE ARMOR

Franchise teams register a color and pattern to which their armor must conform. Yellow or gold, which would obscure the surrender lights woven into the armor, is not allowed. ISSV rules require "at least one dark and one bright" color to minimize camouflage benefits from any particular pattern.

Regulation armor must be equipped with ISSV-approved penalty and surrender circuits. Brawlers are equipped with two-way radios, powered down to limit their effective range to the size of the Brawl Zone. Brawlers are checked carefully for implanted comm gear that might allow them to get information

from observers outside the Brawl Zone. Anyone carrying that type of gear must allow it to be neutralized during the game or be banned from playing.

THE BALL

The regulation Brawl ball is spherical, 65–70 centimeters in diameter (about the size of a soccer ball) and weighs 500–600 grams. It is made of dense plastifoam, and coated with bright gold or yellow glo-paint, "clearly visible at a minimum distance of 50 meters," according to the ISSV rules. It may be carried in the hands or tucked under one arm.

THE GAME

An Urban Brawl game is divided into four quarters, thirty playing minutes each. Each play lasts a maximum of five minutes or until one of the following conditions is met.

- A goal is scored.
- The clock runs out on the quarter.
- A ball is declared dead.
- A wipeout takes place.

If a goal is scored or the clock runs out on the play, both sides begin the next play back in their home goals. If a ball goes dead, the opposing side (the side whose ball did not go dead) has an option. They can start over at their goal, or resume play with all their brawlers in their present locations and their opponents back at their own goal. If the play ends on a wipeout, it doesn't much matter what the losing side wants to do.

The clock stops between plays, because it can take a while for a bunch of guys to walk a couple of blocks, clear casualties to aid stations, start or maintain medical treatment, reload weapons, and so on. The rules call for a team to be ready to go five minutes after the play ends. Average playing time for a game of Urban Brawl is about four to six hours from start to finish, including a ten-minute rest period between quarters and the fifteen-minute half time break.

OFFENSE VS. DEFENSE

Traditional offense versus defense doesn't work in Urban Brawl; both teams are on offense and defense at the same time. Each team carries a ball and tries to score while preventing the other side from scoring.

Once play starts, the team has thirty seconds to get the ball out of its goal block. If they fail to move the ball beyond their own goal, a freeze penalty is called on everyone on the team except the ball carrier (see **Penalties**, below). The team has another thirty seconds to get the ball out of the three blocks adjacent to their goal street, During the remainder of the play, if the ball stays in the same block for more than sixty seconds, or is carried back into its own team's goal block for any reason, the team is again hit with a penalty until the ball carrier moves into a legal block.

A team has to decide how to divide its forces to protect the ball during its travels through the Brawl Zone without leaving their goal wide open. Split the team evenly, and risk defeat by a heavy offensive push? Leave the ball lightly defended or the goal?

Any ball carrier can pass or hand the ball to any other offensive brawler at any time. If the ball hits the ground, the team has ten seconds to recover it. If they don't recover it within that time, the ball is declared dead. It also goes dead if it is picked up by an offensive brawler on the opposing team.

BRAWLER DOWN

A brawler keeps playing until he is disabled by his wounds or until he surrenders. Brawlers who surrender too easily will end up seeking other career opportunities. If they entered Urban Brawl because of a court conviction, they may get shipped back to the slam for execution of their sentence.

A brawler can trigger his surrender switch any time. The switch activates a pattern of bright yellow Neolux tubing woven through his uniform. Natch, there's a particularly broad pattern of yellow 'lux running up the spine. The surrender switch also triggers the brawler's penalty circuit, and he is under a kill penalty for the rest of the play (see **Penalties**, below). He can re-enter the game on the next play.

Keep in mind that a surrender is the same as being taken down. If all the offensive brawlers on a team go down or surrender in the same play, that's a wipeout! Game over.

Disabled brawlers can be attended by the medico where they fall. They cannot be transported until combat in that block of the Brawl Zone ceases, either by moving elsewhere or stopping at the end of the play. When the area is safe, pickup teams move in at once to evacuate any wounded brawlers.

Wounded brawlers can get first aid at aid stations located just off the field at the ends of the goal streets. Any brawler who is evaced to a hospital can be replaced in the next play. Only the on-duty physician, who reports to the ISSV, can order an evac.

A player who is not evaced but can't, or won't, re-enter the Brawl Zone at the thirty-second warning before the next play, *cannot* be replaced in that play. His team *can* replace him in the following play, but if they do, the wounded player is out for the rest of the game, even if his wounds are healed later on.

Typical field measures for wounded brawlers consist of dressings to control bleeding and fractures and heavy doses of painkillers and stimulants to get the players back into action by the next play.

Magical healing is not generally available. If a team has contracted a magical healer, once he or she applies curative magic to a player, that player cannot re-enter the game and must be replaced. Magicians are usually only retained when a team plays in a local jurisdiction that threatens legal action if severely wounded players do not receive immediate magical aid.

SCORING

A circle four meters in diameter is marked by colored Neolux and glo-paint somewhere on the street at each end of the Brawl Zone. This circle serves as the goal. The block it is in is the goal block. A team may move its goal to a different block on the boundary street at the beginning of each quarter, so the opposition is never sure where they want to hit the street when a new quarter starts.

A team scores if a ball carrier gets the ball into the opposing team's goal. The ISSV rulebook used to restrict goals to "live" ball carriers, but after the 2044 season, when there were six disputed decisions over whether the carrier was still alive when he entered the goal circle, the ISSV changed the rule. As long as the ball is in the brawler's hands or somehow attached to his body when he gets into the goal, it doesn't matter if he's alive or dead. It also doesn't matter if he got there under his own power or was blown ten meters across the pavement by the opposition's Blaster and hit the goal area in two pieces, which happened in the Boston–Seattle game last year. One of the pieces was in contact with the ball, so the goal counted.

PENALTIES

Penalties are rated as wounds, kills, or freezes. Wound or kill penalties are called on individual brawlers. A freeze penalty affects an entire subteam or team.

A wound penalty immobilizes a player for the rest of the play.

A severe rules infraction earns a brawler a kill penalty. He is kicked out of the game, and infractions that cause death or injury may be prosecuted as criminal acts in some jurisdictions. A player given a kill penalty cannot be replaced until the beginning of the next *quarter*, not the next play! If all functional players on a side receive kill penalties during one quarter, their team forfeits the match.

Uniforms are wired with a regulation penalty circuit that gives any brawler who moves while he is under a penalty a disabling shot of electricity. Any brawler who tries to disable his penalty circuit earns a kill penalty. All brawlers hear a ten-second countdown over their radios before a penalty is applied to any brawler. After the countdown, the offender's penalty circuit kicks in and his surrender lights blink on and off for the duration of the penalty.

A wounded player's penalty circuit stays on for the rest of the play. The penalty circuit of a player awarded a kill penalty stays on until an armed ISSV security escort arrives to escort the player out of the Brawl Zone. A freeze penalty lasts until the officials decide to end it.

Medico uniforms do not carry penalty circuits, and medicos are not subject to wound, kill or freeze penalties. A medico who violates the rules is kicked out of play, but is replaced immediately instead of at the next quarter.

If a freeze penalty is called on a team, any wound or kill penalties in force against the opposing team are cancelled.

If all the active brawlers on a team earn penalties simultaneously, it is *not* considered a wipeout. The ball is called dead at that point, and the other team chooses from the usual options to begin the next play.

Reasons for Penalties

Arson: Deliberately setting a fire in the Brawl Zone earns a kill penalty, and means an automatic loss for the team if the game has to be cancelled. This rule originated after an unfortunate incident in Buenos Aires.

Deliberate Attack on Disabled/Surrendered Brawler: A kill penalty.

Deliberate Attack on Brawler Under A Penalty: A wound penalty if the attack misses, a kill penalty if it hits.

Illegal Intelligence: Any team receiving information from outside the Brawl Zone during a game forfeits the game. The ISSV has a pretty good lock on jamming technological means of cheating, but magic is the big problem here. An astral magician, or even a spirit, could relay information to brawlers. While the ISSV employs astral security firms to prevent this, one of the paranoid fantasies of the ISSV is that overly skillful or lucky teams are actually getting reports via astral space that help them find (or avoid) opposing brawlers. (There hasn't been a verified case of magical cheating since the EBMM scandal in Bonn in 2043.)

Insufficient Offense: If the ball carrier is still in his own goal block sixty seconds after the play begins, a freeze penalty is called on every member of the team except the ball carrier. The penalty stays in effect until the ball carrier leaves the goal block. He and his fellow brawlers have to catch up with each other as best they can after that.

The penalty also applies if the ball carrier is in any of the three blocks adjacent to his goal street two minutes after the play begins.

Likewise, if the ball carrier spends sixty seconds in the same block, a freeze penalty is called on his side until he moves into a different block.

An official can also call insufficient offense if, in his opinion, the ball carrier is not making an effort to get the ball to the opposition's goal. This rule is enforced pretty loosely, but basically prevents ball carriers from going to ground in basements, or skipping back and forth between the same two blocks trying to avoid contact with the opposing team.

The clock stops on insufficient offense if the ball carrier is engaged in combat. That is, if a ball carrier spends thirty seconds in a block, then gets caught in a fight, the clock stops until the ball carrier is out of combat, whereupon he has thirty seconds remaining to vacate the block.

Leaving the Brawl Zone: A wound penalty.

Roughing the Medico: Deliberately attacking a medico earns a kill penalty. If the medico is wounded or disabled, a replacement medico is sent in immediately.

Roughing the Officials: A kill penalty is called on any player who attacks an official.

Unauthorized Ball Carrier: If the medico, the outrider, or a player mounted on the outrider's bike takes possession of the ball, or the ball carrier mounts the outrider's cycle, the ball is called dead at once. The opposing side may choose from the usual options to begin the next play.

Unnecessary Destruction of Property: This penalty rule is designed to cut down on damage that the ISSV will have to pay for later. Shooting at a car because someone is using it for cover is fine. Doing it just for the frag of it draws a wound penalty.

Unsportsmanlike Conduct: A wound or kill penalty, at the discretion of the referees. This rule includes arguing with a decision, interference with a media device, and so on.

Use of Unauthorized Firearm: Picking up someone else's gun earns a wound penalty.

OFFICIALS

Two to four officials cover each city block of the Brawl Zone. Officials wear Partial Heavy Armor coated with white glo-paint and marked to show their status as referees, technicians, or biotechs.

Officials' armor is wired with a wizbang set of pickups that let them scan the Zone through any of the fixed-mount cameras. They can also check the action through the signals from any of the hundreds of surveillance drones that buzz through the Zone catching the action for the folks at home.

Officials carry tasers to defend themselves from the occasional crazed brawler.

SIMSENSE

Realer than reality. Realer than life. RealSense™
—Fuchi Electronics advertising slogan, 2049

Artificial Sensory Induction System Technology (ASIST) first hit the scene in 2018, as demonstrated by Dr. Hosato Hikita of ESP Systems in Chicago. ASIST today is a central element of simsense, cyberdecks, rigging, skillsofts, med-wares, and a bucket of other tech. A simsense is not the same thing as a skillsoft just because they both use ASIST, anymore than a trideo is a computer, even though they both use video.

Simsense lets a person experience something that happened to someone else. As far as the user can tell, he or she is really there, going through the same changes as the actor/artist who recorded it. Simsense does not enable expert system responses, the way skillsoft does, or adjust moves and responses to physical input/output the way skillwires, rigs, and decks do. To put it in a nutshell, simsense lets a person *imagine* that he or she is doing something, but doesn't actually let that person do it.

Commercial simsense gear appeared in the mid-20s, originally available only as a status toy for the rich folks. By the late 2030s, the tech got hotter and cheaper, and sims began to build a popular audience. Finally, in 2046, MegaMedia brought out Honey Brighton's novahit, *Free Fall.* The sim combined state-of-the-art ASIST, production values to the max, and a star who was marketable with a capital M.

Sim has not conquered the whole media scene, not by any means. The technical specs for simsense transmission via trid limit it to a few of the high-ticket Matrix nets. The bandwidth and playback gear for real-time sim transmission is not cheap, and studios charge a bundle for licensing on their sims. So though simsense has taken over the entire theatrical release market that movies used to own, trid still keeps the movie cams running, grinding out new flat and holo product.

Simsense takes a lot of post-processing. A wet record, the raw sim output from a performer, needs to be tweaked up and toned down before it delivers what audiences pay to feel. That's true even for output from tried-and-true simstars like Honey Brighton or Rita Revak. The tech for this is not cheap. Even a basic ASIST signal processor like the Truman Reality 500, an old warhorse that has been in production without any major design changes since 2037, will still set you back about 50,000¥.

BASICS OF SIMSENSE

Simsense operates in two major spectra of response, or *tracks*, which are sensory and emotive. When a user plays back the sensory track, it triggers brain responses that match the "physical" responses of the artist who originally performed on the tape. The emotive track does the same thing with the neurological changes that trigger emotional responses.

The sensory track is measured on the *proprioceptive/extroceptive* (or PC/EC) scale.

Proprioceptive: PC for short. Sensory stimuli caused by muscle tensions, posture, blood pressure, balance, and so on. Basically, these signals are caused by stimuli from within the body.

Extroceptive: EC for short. Sensory stimuli originating outside the body.

There's no hard-and-fast line dividing proprioceptive and extroceptive stimuli. In fact, most things we experience involve a mix of both types of perception.

PC/EC is measured on a scale of 0 to 10, where 0 is virtual sense-deprivation, and at 10, the primary stimulus on the sensory track wipes out all other signals.

Sensory input is not just one PC/EC signal, however. There are sensory tracks for sight, sound, smell, kinetics, kinesthetics, and so on.

---

aaaaaaaaaaaaaaaaaaaaaaaaaaaaaa aaaaaaaaaaaaaaaaaaaaahhhhhhhh —Another satisfied customer

---

The emotive tracks are measured in terms of the neurobiological systems that activate or suppress a particular emotional response. The major emotive tracks are sympathetic, parasympathetic, adrenal, thalamic and hypo-thalamic, limbic, and so on. A good emotive track mixes all these to produce a single response. For instance, the adrenals will activate whether a person is about to fight or have sex, but there is more to both than just the adrenal activity.

A really accurate simulation involves both sensory and emotive tracks. For example, sim techs talk about "urge" (sexual thrill) as if it were a single sensation, even though urge, like any sensory event, is a complex interplay of a whole mess of sensory and emotive tracks. Saying that a star like Rita Revak "gives good urge" means she can produce a rich mix of responses when called on for this kind of reaction. And likewise, when someone says Irena Naylor, the top-rated simthmixer at Abbey Productions, does the best urge in Hollywood, it means she is adept at augmenting the wet record across all tracks to produce a finished product that can induce user meltdown.

First-generation simsense could only handle the sensory track. It was not until Fuchi brought out its RealSense™ system in 2037 that emotive signal-processing showed up in commercial sim.

Simsense recordings are classified as Baseline or Full-X. Baseline offers only the sensory tracks. Users receive the sensations of the original performer, but their emotional responses are their own. "Full experience" (full-X) handles both sensory and emotive tracks.

SIMSENSE PRODUCTION

Technofetishists (aren't we all?) may get misty-eyed over the EC/PC modulator circuits of a Yamaha 95000-V simsynth ("simth") or the signal parameters of a Truman Dir-X playback unit, but there is more to simsense than the tech. Hot sim needs a hot star. A lot of simstars are lightweights, built to specification by the studio hype factories and some talented tech with a top-line simth. But the real talent has that charismatic and highly marketable something known as "star quality."

THE PERFORMERS

A simsense *performer* is the one in the production wired with the cyber to make an ASIST recording. Anyone else in a simsense is just part of the scenery. Slang in the sim biz describes other actors as *flats* (actors who stand around providing background in a scene), *props* (actors who interact verbally or physically with a performer), and *targets* (actors in either a fight scene or a love scene with a performer).

Most performers are only cybered to produce baseline. Many sims skip the emotive track entirely and just come out in a baseline version. Sometimes the studio mixes down an emotive track in post-production. Only the top simstars are wired for full-X, 'cause they're the ones who can turn in emotional performances with mass appeal.

Most sims center around one or two wired performers. Only rarely are more than a half-dozen involved in a single production.

Only the main characters in a sim are wired, and so the audience experiences the story from their point of view, or POV. No one wants to experience the last days of Pompeii as a spear carrier. The leading man and leading lady are always wired, and the typical sim is directed to produce the maximum amount of action from a star's POV. Antagonists and even supporting characters may also be wired, because there is a decent market for simsense as the sidekick, and even more for the villain. The usual drill is to release a simsense using the top stars' POVs, and if the sim is a hit, the studio will release "expanded" recordings that include the POVs of other characters.

PERFORMANCE METHODS

Performers have to stay in tiptop condition. People are not going to pay to feel flab, lower back pain, or short wind. The studios keep a close eye on their simstars' health, often locking them into restrictive contracts that *severely* regulate personal behavior.

For baseline performers, the action is all there is to it. For full-X performers, the action is barely the beginning. A full-X simstar has to *become* the character, has to actually feel the emotional responses. Oh, the final polish gets put on by a technician running a simsynth, but a star who cannot lay down the basic emotive tracks will not stay a star for long.

Creating the emotive track requires mental gymnastics that make old-style "method acting" look like improv. Simstars use all sorts of tricks to induce the desired emotive responses, most commonly meditation, biofeedback, hypnotherapy, and medication. More drastic techniques include magic and high-gain simsense conditioning. A couple of stars are rumored to use BTLs to keep their edge. But any of this stuff that messes with basic emotional drives can chew a person up and spit out the seeds. The glitterworld of simsense is littered with casualties, performers who could not keep up the pace.

STAND-INS AND SPECIAL EFFECTS

Because the whole reason for simsense is to sell a star's own experiences to the public, stand-ins just will not cut it most of the time. In simsense, it's not as easy as putting make-up and a wig on a stunt-double and using a long camera shot for the action sequence. A simsense "double" is someone whose perceptive set is a close match for the star's own sensorium. A tech can fudge a response on the EC side of the tracks, but the proprioceptive parameters have to be a real close match or there's no point in even trying. It is not enough for a double to look like Honey Brighton. Anyone can do that by spending a few thousand nuyen in any body shop in the western world. The double has to "feel" like Honey Brighton; has to feel like she does to herself.

The usual gimmick to get this is called *stacking*. To stack a sim, studios first run the stand-in through the action, taking a baseline recording of that experience. Then they play back the experience for the star, and do a full-X record of the star's experience. This has two spinoffs: it filters the stand-in's sensory track through the star's sensorium, which will smooth out minor differences in the PC/EC sets, and, of course, as a full-X, it adds the simstar's emotive tracks to the recording. The output from stacking becomes the wet record for the final product.

Stacked experiences start to wear thin about three levels deep. That is, a record of a record of a record is as far as one can go—any more stacking and the first experience starts getting blurry, like a daydream. People can do their own daydreams for free. Simsense makes money by providing the poor clowns on the other end of the cable with dreams they cannot have for themselves.

Studios keep big libraries of sense-patches: stock experience records from stars or stand-ins, similar to stock footage in video. These can be used in stacking, or injected directly into a simsynth during editing. The big studios scout for *patchers*, people with useful sensory parameters, pay them to have a baseline simrig installed, and then pay by the piece for usable sense patches. They especially like patchers engaged in high-

risk, sensation-rich activities. A studio lucky enough to find a cooperative shadowrunner who is a close PC/EC match for a star can send their expensive performers through the life-and-death experiences of a typical run without risking their investment.

When a sense patch is not available from a live source, a studio can create computer-generated patches. This process is known by the redundant name of *pseudosim*. "Not a simulation, but an incredible imitation," as a waggish tech once remarked. Pseudosim costs a bucket. It takes up mainframe time like crazy and the programming is complex. A major sim recorded live, with sets, extras, stars, and all usually costs less than a pseudosim of the same script. Pseudosim is sometimes used for short sense-patches, when nothing in the database is quiiiite right. But the primary role of pseudosim is in special effects. For example, suppose Honey Brighton is to have a scene with a dragon. The studio tries to sign Dunklezahn, but the Great Media Dragon holds out for a BIG percentage. The alternative is to generate pseudosim of the experience and stack it through Honey's sensorium.

MAGIC AND SIMSENSE

Big-budget simsense productions use a lot of magic for special effects, rather than pseudosim. The record of the star's reactions to the illusory experience is as real as if the experience actually happened, because the sensorium cannot tell the difference between a high-quality illusion spell and reality.

There are drawbacks, natch. First thing is finding a magician who is willing to play ball, and who knows just the spells the studio is looking for. Next problem is budget, because magicians who specialize in simsense work like to set their prices just cheaper than the cost of a pseudosim program. On top of that, repeated takes can quickly wear out both the magician and the star. Even worse, multiple hits of really powerful spells like stimulation can be psychologically addicting and put the star at risk. But the bottom line is that magically induced experiences repeatedly test out with audiences as "realer" and more satisfying than pseudosim, so the studios shell out the nuyen.

Magical illusions work just fine for the actors in simsense, but magic itself does not record worth a hoot. Astral elements simply don't show up in an ASIST recording. A sim of a magician casting a spell may have some pretty neat sensations to it, but will not teach anyone how to go about casting the spell. It's the same problem that keeps popping up every time someone tries to make a skillsoft for magic. As far as ASIST is concerned, there ain't nothing going on.

Sims involving magical plot lines always use special effects for astral sequences, because astral perceptions just don't show on the recording.

THE DIRECTOR

The director in films is the number-one boss most of the time. A sim director has to take what his performers give him. "Differences in artistic vision" usually come out in favor of the actor. After all, it's his or her vision (and hearing, and smell, and so on).

The director has to judge whether the raw recordings made on the set have what it takes for big sales when the editing is done. Most sim directors make this judgment the way film and vid directors have for years, by checking out "rushes" at the end of a day's recording. Some directors try to speed up the process by using an ASIST interface that hooks them directly into the performers. They can sample the performers' responses as they are being recorded and make decisions about retakes on the spot. The big disadvantage to this approach is that the director's mind can turn to mush from being exposed to hours of wet records every day.

A sim director has to be able to get inside the mental processes of his performers to understand how they will perceive a given scene. Often the most difficult part of his or her job is directing the action of the script to make the scene provoke the effect he wants from the performer's point of view. Overall, cameras give you less trouble, any day. Cameras do not collapse with the screaming meemies after the fourth or fifth take.

Once the wet records for the sim are in the can, the director of a simsense is almost always in charge of the editing process that turns the sim into a commercial-quality product.

THE WET RECORD

The output from a performer's simsense rig is called a "wet record" in the business. Wire up Honey Brighton, Nicky Saitoh, or whoever has the best draw for the script being shot, and put them through their paces, recording every highly paid pulse, twist, and twitch. After a few weeks, or months, the result is a wet record.

The same principle applies to shooting baseline sim in the backyard "starring" Newbie Nobody, of course. It just costs a few million nuyen less.

A wet record can gobble up gigapulses of storage. Baseline simsense takes one megapulse per *second* of experience; a full-X recording three times that. The memory alone costs a bucket. The wet record also includes stray breaks in the performer's concentration, hangovers from the party the night before, and various forms of mental "background noise." The wet record has a long way to go before it's ready for the sense-decks and sim-theatres of the world.

WHAT GOES INTO SIM?

Keep in mind that a sim tells a story from the POV of a single character. The user sees with the character's eyes, hears with the character's ears, feels with the character's skin. Big difference from a movie—no voice-overs, music tracks, camera angles, and so on; instead the user gets flashbacks and even dream sequences. Some sim makers are big on internal dialogue, too, where performers spell out their thoughts by talking to themselves. Internal dialogue is added in post-production by dubbing the performer reading the script into the experience record.

ENTERTAINMENT SIMS

Sim stories are usually heavy on action: lots of exertion, lots of unique experiences, stuff that drives the senses. "What makes simsense work," said studio suit Vincent Prosser, "is fighting, feeding, and fornicating. Anything that gets in be-tween those parts of a script is a waste of memory."

Expensive costume epics are big in the market right now, full of knights and ladies in the best tradition of Hollywood history (nobody has fleas and everybody bathes). Sims pitting brave corporate agents against scummy shadowrunners are hot items in the corporate enclaves.

Romantic sims also corner a big market, ranging from soft-edged plots heavy on flirtation to stuff that is just a notch shy of the raw porn market.

Comedy is a weird area in sim. Very few people like to experience comedy as the fall guy in a joke, and so comedy sims usually feature performers watching other people get caught in comic situations, or maybe even putting them there.

Highbrow sims are usually the kiss of death at the box office, but occasional exceptions have been known. Martin Zabriskie's remake of *Romeo and Juliet* was a big success, though critics complained that the two lovers in the original never got quite as close, quite as often, as they do in Zabriskie's version. Anton MacArthur's monoPOV sim of *Macbeth* was good for a lot of nuyen, too, especially when the actor took that final dive in his private jet for real. Seems like the curse of the "Scottish play" survived into the simsense era pretty much intact.

Commercial sims, like films before them, treat time as a flexible commodity by using fades, cutaways, and flashbacks. It is also possible to edit a sim to increase or decrease the perceived rate of action, within limits. A minute of repetitive action in the sim can be stretched until the users feel they've been slogging through the jungle for hours, without actually spending hours of sim time reproducing that experience. Users definitely notice the technique, but accept it as a convention, much the same way moviegoers accept montage shots.

Sim pacing usually starts fast and stays fast, concentrating on the action. PolyPOV sims find pacing and balancing the action a real challenge, because the studios generally want time to run simultaneously from all POVs. If the sim is tracking a heroine, a love interest, and a villain all in the same story, the action in scenes where the performers are not interacting with one another have to be timed pretty closely. For example, while one user experiences the heroine's drive at high speed through the city, a second user may be experiencing her boyfriend's risky helicopter-landing at the villain's hideout. A third user experiences the villain as he arms up to fight it out with the boyfriend. Then, during the fight between the villain and the love interest, the heroine's POV deals with her fight against the kung fu masters guarding the road to the villain's hideout, and all three POVs must mesh for the final showdown.

Not all sims use this format on a polyPOV, natch, but it is the way the big-name producers have decreed things will work, and so that's usually the way it is.

DOCUSIMS

While sim takes too long between recording and release to make it the standard in realtime news reporting, documentary sims do exist. The biggest market is in sports: fans are eager to buy the sim of the winning quarterback in the Super Bowl, or the world champion freestyler's title bout. Star athletes can pull down big nuyen for exclusive rights to their recordings of winning events, and most of them have baseline simrigs implanted to cash in on that market. The corp wars are another prolific source of docusims. After most major battles, a sim of combat experiences from the highest-rated clashes is available.

Other branches of the entertainment industry have jumped on the simsense bandwagon. A number of rock stars pump up their incomes by selling simsense rights to their live perfor-mances. Rock fans have always been ready to pay to be near their idols. They are willing to pay even more to *become* them! Several of the hottest rockers, notably Concrete Dreams, ME-109, and Maria Mercurial, have turned down offers in the millions of nuyen for simsense recording rights. The Dreams and 109 have cited their contempt for the way simsense substitutes fantasy for reality. Ms. Mercurial, always an enigmatic lady, was quoted as saying that certain aspects of her performance would not be very pleasant for fans to feel.

Some studios keep baseline performers on retainer and send them off to places where interesting (and often dangerous) events are taking place. Then, a few weeks or so later, a tape like *The Month In Review* will come out, featuring sims of major goings-on from the last thirty days. Stories on these sims usually focus on happenings with high sensory values: natural disasters, jetliner crashes, macroflash social events, and so on.

EDUCATIONAL SIMSENSE

Though a sim is not a skillsoft, training sims are pretty common. Baseline recordings of all sorts of tasks can be used as part of educational programs. Basically, these function like skillsofts without the algorithmic enablers and expert systems that let skillsofts actually take over responses and actions for their users. Using a sim of a lecture by a noted professor is just like going to that lecture. A user will remember it as clearly as if he or she had been sitting there. The recordings are usually taken from top students, cleaned up and augmented in a quick post-production process, and sold.

Lab sessions get simmed pretty regularly, too, though some argue that a sim of a hands-on experience does not cut it as a teaching tool.

The big goal for producers of training sims is to come up with something that will teach people magic, but because, as we mentioned before, the astral side of magical perceptions does not come through on simsense, this goal remains unattainable so far.

SIMSENSE POST-PRODUCTION

THE SIMSYNTH

The heart and brain of the simsense editing process is the ASIST signal processor, or *simsynth* (or just "simth"). A tech feeds a wet record into a simth, smooths the rough spots, modulates the high points, and eventually produces a commercially salable *experience record*, the finished form of the simsense. "Realer than reality," as the Fuchi flacks like to say in their ad copy.

Fuchi and Chicago-based Truman Technologies have been duking it out for years to see who is leader of the pack in simths. Fuchi held a slight lead for awhile, especially after they brought out the RealSense™ format. But ain't that the way it always goes? Some brightboy gets a hot idea, makes it big, then gets lazy and whammo! He's not Ichi-ban Number One no more.

Three other simth manufacturers currently threaten Fuchi's lead; Truman is near to overtaking them, and Yamaha and Zeemandt, GmbH hover close behind.

Truman broke the POV barrier just two years ago. Up until then, all simsynths were monoPOV. That is, a simth could only process one point of view. If a studio wanted to release three versions of a recording, making the experience available from three different character perspectives, three post-production units would be tied up to make all three come out simultaneously.

On a polyPOV simth, multiple recordings can be processed simultaneously, which means big savings on production costs. On top of that, polyPOV makes it possible to edit experience records interactively with each other. In other words, a tech can make sure that the passion of the two lovers in the big scene is matched to the last thundering heartbeat if the studio desires.

Simths come in all sorts of configurations, from the little baseline portables found in most home recording units that use built-in CPUs and cheesy sensory-mix modulators, up to mainframe-driven monsters like the Fuchi Kosmos or the Truman Inner-I series. Professional systems are always modular, allowing interfaces to a master mainframe and a host of peripherals: EC/PC modulation controllers, sense-patch playback and sampler units, emotive enablers, and so on. The typical setup in a studio like MegaMedia will set a person back a few million nuyen, easy.

CPU CONTROLLERS

Only bottom-of-the-line household simths have built-in CPUs. The rest allow for control inputs from a PC or mainframe. The better the CPU, the better the mix. Studios tend to keep the mainframes that drive their simths isolated from the Matrix, or else defended with very nasty IC, indeed, because the thriving black market in pirate sims, especially for wet records from big stars, is rich bait for the entrepreneurially minded decker.

The CPU also functions as a sense-patch sampler, recording and storing sense-patches from the experience record if the simth has patch-extraction capability.

PATCH INJECTION DRIVERS

A patch injection driver makes it possible to feed sense patches into the record on the simth. These can replace part of the wet record or be combined with it. It takes a good editor to smooth out differences between canned patches and wet records, but it can be done.

Say the star was just not having a good day, and his imitation of burning desire would not heat a cup of soykaf. Null perspiration. Cue up the patch injection driver and mix in a sense patch for "Urge (male)—level 9" with an EC boost to intensify the tactile track as the hero's ladylove flows up against him. Now just twiddle the signals, and the audience almost surely won't realize that this is the same embrace they experienced in *Artic Express*, when Rita Revak melted down Karl Kalashnikov's circuit breakers.

Pseudosim patches are just more of the same, even if the signals involved started out in a computer instead of a person. Early pseudosim was pretty horrible—either unconvincing or overmodulated enough to cause nasty neurotic side effects. Nowadays, audiences still tend to dislike sims that make too much use of pseudosim, especially when it's injected straight into the record without the filtering effect of stacking. But pseudosim patches used only to augment or even to replace small portions of real sim that are not up to standard usually get by, especially when a retake is not possible.

In some cases, it is possible to "dub" sequences that only show up as problems in post-production. This involves stacking the flawed segment through the simstar, to try and intensify or clarify the response. This technique rarely works as well as a complete retake, but it is much cheaper.

EXPERIENCE OUTPUT SAMPLER

The output from the simth is routed to an experience output sampler. This peripheral cuts the final sim onto its storage medium.

The usual medium for simsense output is an optical memory chip. However, CD is much cheaper, and preferred for low-end releases if the output will fit into the available 500 Mp of storage available on a compact disk.

OUTPUT FORMATS

A finished experience record can be sampled, that is, recorded, in one of two formats: Direct Experience (Dir-X) and ASIST Control Transport (ACT).

Direct Experience Format (DIR-X)

Dir-X is the same basic format as the wet record, but instead of raw sensory/emotive tracks, it is the final form of the sim. Dir-X is certainly the closest thing to being there, as far as the user is concerned. Within the limits of the technology, the user *becomes* the performer he or she is experiencing.

Dir-X is incredibly expensive. A full-X Direct Experience recording eats up 3 Mp per *second*. That means that a feature-length, sixty-minute recording occupies about 18,000 Mp. That's thirty-six CDs worth of storage! The chip alone costs a fortune!

Studios use Dir-X for master recordings, for theatrical release, and for pay-per-use Matrix transmissions of simsense. Rich sim freaks (oh, sorry, connoisseurs) make up a small, direct-sales market for Dir-X recordings.

ASIST Control Transport (ACT)

For the rest of us, ACT is the way to go. ASIST Control Transport is the basis of almost every portable and trid-installed simsense player on the market. ACT is essentially a stripped-down version of the experience record. Instead of storing the whole experience record, ACT only samples specific bands of the tracks. It also uses some very fast data-compression techniques that reduce the storage requirement. ACT needs only about 1 percent of the storage required by the Dir-X format. The major problem is that all this massaging dulls down signal clarity pretty severely.

For the translation to the user, ACT simsense decks use enablers and modulators that directly manipulate the sensory and emotive systems of the user. These restore the experience intensity that the data reduction took out. So in addition to the compressed experience record, ACT loads a command set that addresses the playback deck's interface peripherals, and tells the deck how to tweak the user's systems directly to approximate the original signals of the experience record.

A good ACT player like the Sony Beautiful Dreamer can deliver approximately 85 percent of the signal content of a Dir-X recording, if the unit is equipped with a personalized interface driver tuned to a specific user. A cheapo deck, like Truman's widely available Dreambox, delivers about 50 percent of the Dir-X standard. Only the rawest sensations come through with any impact. Of course, the user can always jack up the power controls on a deck to get a more potent version of the experience, but this is like turning up the volume on a cheap audio player. Playback is "loud" but badly distorted, and overdriving the deck can cause disorientation and mood swings, not to mention damage to the playback unit. And some of the knock-offs imported from various havens of pirate tech are downright dangerous at any signal strength.

Due to the impressive data compression achieved with ACT, CDs and chips are used about equally to package the product in this format.

POV PLAYBACK MODES

Whether in Dir-X or ACT format, simsense output can be either monoPOV or polyPOV. MonoPOV sim is still the traditional output mode, but polyPOV is quickly overtaking it. Depending on the features of a sense deck, a polyPOV sim can be played back in any of several ways.

Polyphase POV-Select allows a simsense user to switch from one POV to another during play. This is the typical mode used in simsense theaters, for example, and audience members can experience the story from the point of view of any of the performers, switching POV at will.

High-end personal decks, both Dir-X and ACT, now come with POV-Select as a standard feature.

The ACT market was a natural for polyPOV sims. PolyPOV goes beyond single-user POV-Select, allowing two or more people to experience the same recording on a single deck, with each user getting into the POV of a specific character.

A single user with multiple datajacks can try simulPOV: experiencing multiple POVs simultaneously. Episodes of disorientation following extensive "simulPOV" use are common, though some users (or abusers) insist it leaves them with greater insight and actually strengthens their personality. Tests by several consumer organizations have produced conflicting results.

SENSE DECKS

Simsense players, or sense decks, come in many configurations, from cheapo monoPOV ACT units soldered together in some back alley to rack-mounted full-X critters with as much silicon as a cyberdeck. Whatever the format and whatever the price, commercial sense decks have some things in common.

ASIST INTERFACE

A sense deck must have an ASIST interface to handle output. This component makes the user feel the sensations recorded on the sim. The best interfaces include ranks of sensory and emotive enabler circuits, each driving a specific subsection of the principle tracks. Cheaper units try to cram multiple functions into fewer circuits, with predictable loss of output clarity. But then, you get what you pay for.

---

*See the pyramids along the Nile/
See the Louvre and Mona Lisa's
smile/Just remember darling, all
the while/It's not really happening
—Early simsense ad jingle*

Whether a deck uses Dir-X or ACT, the ASIST interface can be "tuned" to a specific user's neurobiology. This increases the apparent reality of the experience for that user, though it may make the signal seem distorted to others.

RAS OVERRIDES

Sense decks are equipped with a Reticular Activation System Override, also called a "locomotor cutout." It does double duty.

The override cuts back input from a user's own sensorium, numbs it so that it does not interfere with the experience of the sim. Pain/danger stimuli remain pretty much at full strength, so that users will not sit in a burning building ignoring the heat and smoke. But sight, hearing, taste, and certain levels of touch are filtered out almost completely.

Similarly, the Reticular Activation System is the interface between the brain and the voluntary muscles. A sense deck suppresses most muscle activation commands, to prevent users from lurching around and crashing into things while reliving a simsense. Minor muscular actions are filtered through, to let people shift to avoid muscle cramps and notice other minor needs.

Disabling or modifying the RAS overrides on a commercial deck is a misdemeanor. Going around in public hooked up to a deck without the RAS is also a misdemeanor, comparable to "drunk and disorderly." Driving while using a sim is about on a par with DUI. Because simsense is not much fun if a user's own senses keep clashing with the recording, these laws are not considered much of a problem.

LEGAL CONSTRAINTS

Similar laws govern simsense production standards in most North American jurisdictions. Signal intensities, simultaneous stimulation, and perhaps inevitably, some areas of subject matter, are all regulated.

PEAK CONTROLLERS

In order to be sold legally in most jurisdictions, a simsense experience must be filtered through a licensed ASIST Peak Controller before being recorded for sale. This device smooths any deviance in the signal to comply with legal requirements. Because even the best ASIST peak controllers can cause abrupt drops in signal strength and clarity, most conscientious sim directors and editors prefer to keep their output within legal limits by design and retain the integrity of their product.

California Hots and Bootleg Sims

Intensive lobbying by various production companies continues in the legislatures of the UCAS, CAS, and California to try and raise or eliminate the limits on simsense modulation. California did relax some of its restrictions this year, but at the same time required recordings made under the more liberal standards to be clearly marked with a government advisory. Some adroit advertising turned the warning label into a selling point: "The story too bold, too powerful, for the weak of mind. Or heart! The Surgeon General has advised that this recording may be too much for those who can't take REAL living." These "California hots" are still illegal in the UCAS and CAS, and are therefore popular black market items in those countries, carrying a Class A Cyberware offense rating.

A market exists for unfiltered sims, of course. Fans will pay handsomely for bootlegged wet records from their favorite stars. Finished sims also show up on the street in unfiltered form, rather like the "European versions" of movies back in the more uptight days of the 20th century.

SUBLIMS

Ever since the mid-20th century, people have been fiddling with the idea of subliminal messaging: images, text, pictures, and sounds delivered below the threshold of normal perception. Crusaders trying to protect the public from insidious, "invisible" advertising as well as smart suits in ad companies have kept the subject hot.

A lot of data storage went toward proving that sublims were non-existent, all-pervasive, ineffectual, diabolically effective, and many additional adjectives. Whatever may have been true about sublim in video, film, and holos, simsense makes sublims very, very effective.

The big problem with sublims in their original form was that if the message was really *sub limen*, below the threshold (of perception), then the mind did not necessarily retain the message for long or give it any importance. But simsense can play games with the threshold, move it up, down, streeeetch it out. And a sublim that is nothing much by itself can be a very big deal indeed when coupled with a tickling little surge of urge.

Subliminal messaging is tightly controlled in most jurisdictions, though rumor has it that special cuts of sims are made to order for showing within extraterritorial corporate enclaves. The users get all manner of glowing corporate slogans with their entertainment, juiced up to the max.

SIMSENSE ABUSE

Legal, commercial sims, not to mention high-intensity sims like California hots or bootleg wet records, are subject to a good deal of abuse. For many users, the only relief available from a dull, often poverty-stricken life is to jack into a simdeck playing back the latest romantic epic of their favorite simstar. Psychological dependence on sim is an exceedingly hot topic of debate, with the preponderance of evidence proving beyond any doubt that such a thing is simply not possible. Of course, the funding for a preponderance of the studies producing this evidence comes from the same corporations that produce simsense.

At present, with the exception of a few local laws governing the sale of sims to minors, no controls are placed on abuse of legal sims, and abuse of hot or bootleg sims carries no penalty beyond the one for simple possession.

BTL

The other illegal spinoff of ASIST is the BTL, the Better-Than-Life chip, dreamchips. BTL involves high-amplitude ASIST outputs with direct stimulation of response centers in the limbic area, the "pleasure center" of the brain. This involves both more extreme signal modulation than a commercial sense deck can generate and a number of modifications to the output signal as well. A tech can modify an off-the-shelf simsense deck to produce BTL signals, but must replace most of the factory circuitry to do so.

Similarly, a BTL program is a very different critter from a normal experience record, though a simsense can be the "foundation" for a BTL. Tracks are added that do not occur in nature, and the signal intensity is generally jazzed up across the board.

Only a BTL recording played on a BTL delivery system will produce the classic BTL experience. If only one component in the playback is modified for BTL, the user gets a distorted experience, maybe pleasurable, maybe not. But without the proper combination of components, users cannot get the massive neurobiological distortions that real BTLs cause.

Three overall types of BTL programs are possible, and any of them can be recorded in either of two BTL playback formats. The program classifications are as follows.

BTL/Simsense Mix

A simsense that has been modified to produce BTL responses. This is a simsense story line become BTL fantasy, called tripchips and fairy tales on the street. When the RAS overrides are cut out, they are called walkie-talkies, because users will be able to move freely, interacting with their environment based on the action going on inside their heads.

Track Loops

Track loops induce an extended episode of one sensation or event, emotive, sensory, or both. Typical track loops are euphoric, sexual/sensual, or aggressive in nature, though pretty much any experience can be burned into a loop. Street names tend to reflect the nature of the experience, and for some reason, typical street names include a color: Blue Passion, Red Meanie, Cool White, and so on. These are the commonest BTLs on the street. The RAS controls are usually cut out on track loops, so that users can move around freely under the influence of the chip.

Personafixes

These are the newest thing in BTLs, and maybe the most dangerous. A combination of simsense and skillsoft technology that modifies the basic personality responses of the user, the

simplest ones involve behavior modification along some particular psychological line: aggression, passivity, paranoia, lust, and so on. Rumors of experimental models combining sophisticated expert systems with high-level skillsofts claim that personafixes can actually create an artificial personality, even ones based on powerful figures from history. No one has been able to document this rumor, though, so it is probably just another urban myth. Street names include talking head, odd mod, and P-fix. Playback formats are direct chip input and dreamdeck playback. BTL chips use two basic playback methods.

Direct Chip Input: This is exactly what the name implies: a chip designed to be jacked directly into a datajack or chipjack. The microprocessor and data storage for the BTL are built into the unit. Typically, the whole unit is designed to burn out after a single use, and is controlled by a timer to prevent traumatic overexposure to the BTL signal. But people's tolerances differ, and what is a survivable exposure for one user is a ticket to the recycling center for another. Chips can be easily jiggered with a microtronics kit to cut out either the overload circuit or the timer or both. Chips cooked for continuous play are called dreamgates on the street, and are usually a one-way gate at that.

Dreamdeck Playback: Also what the name implies. The format requires a sense deck modified to deliver BTL output and a chip with an ACT format program modified to produce BTL signals. Again, the typical chip for this playback is rigged to self-destruct after one play, but a microtronicist can quickly disarm that. Most users set a timer on the deck to avoid overdosing, but all they have to do is switch that off to get their ticket punched. Dreamdecks cost more up front, but they are the Eurocar Westwind of BTL abuse, because they can replay a user's favorite BTLs over and over again.

"Realer than *Reality.* Realer than *Life!*"

Fuchi Electronics is proud to announce the release of the *Dreamliner* series of RealSense™ experience players. The engineering artistry of our cybernetic designers combines with the performing artistry of the hottest stars in Hollywood to offer you a universe of experience such as you have never known.

When you jack into a RealSpace™ experience record on a *Dreamliner* deck, your reality becomes something that only the most sensitive souls can appreciate. And with Fuchi's revolutionary MultiPOV interface, you can share that sensation with someone close to you.

Direct interface ASIST Attunement is available for a nominal charge from any factory-authorized Fuchi outlet -- to make the reality of RealSense™ even more compelling, even more personal.
Step out of your world and into...reality.

FUCHI

REALSPACE
BY
FUCHI

NEW TWISTS

Somewhere in a special corner of dreamchipper heaven (or hell) are bright little biotechs coming up with new and better ways to fry neurons. Two of their latest brainstorms are personalized BTLs and implanted chips.

Any BTL program can be personalized when it is created, fine-tuned to massively affect a particular person. At present, personal BTLs are almost exclusively a vice of wealth, but the technology for this sort of thing is notorious for becoming cheaper with time. A personalized BTL can addict the user within a half-dozen doses. Fortunately, it is also somewhat less destructive to the neurobiology of the user. Once hooked on a personalized BTL, street stuff becomes only marginally satisfying, and users cut off from their personal supply have to jack mass quantities of other BTL to avoid withdrawal symptoms. This, in turn, can cause accelerated trauma and side effects.

In the last few years, an increasing number of BTLs have been directly implanted as headware. While this, too, remains a vice of the well-heeled as far as voluntary usage goes, some shuddery cases have come to light where involuntary implants have been used to control the victim. The implants in one case had two programs, either of which could be triggered by an external radio signal. One was a very powerful track loop, releasing huge amounts of endorphin. Instant ecstasy. The other, as might be expected, fired pain receptors all over the sensorium simultaneously.

GETTING CLEAN

Extended BTL use can result in many unpleasant side effects, including multiple personality disorders, catatonia, mania, or a syndrome in which a user cycles randomly through both, and loss of long-term memory, culminating in classic amnesia. Flashbacks are also common, especially when the user jacks a single BTL program repeatedly. A final side effect is synesthesia, which is sensory crossover, in which the victim experiences one stimulus in terms of a different sense. Taste becomes sight, sound becomes touch, and so on.

These are all real good reasons to stay off the chips—or to get clean if a person is hooked. Extreme effects of BTL use can be mental collapse, various forms of psychosis, and breakdowns in brain neurochemistry resulting in death. Most BTL-related deaths, however, are caused by accidents suffered while under the influence, malnutrition or dehydration because of extended BTL use, or suicide.

Withdrawal is difficult because an early effect of BTL use is that endorphin production is suppressed when a user is not jacking the signal. Shortly into withdrawal, the chipper suffers heightened sensitivity to all stimuli accompanied by an extremely low threshold of pain. The time required for this effect to diminish is directly proportional to the duration of BTL use and the frequency with which the user jacked. Heavy users may also suffer damage to nerve tissue requiring repatterning therapy or even tissue implants.

Lastly, extensive psychotherapy may be necessary, especially for users suffering from P-fix addiction, or a personalized habit.

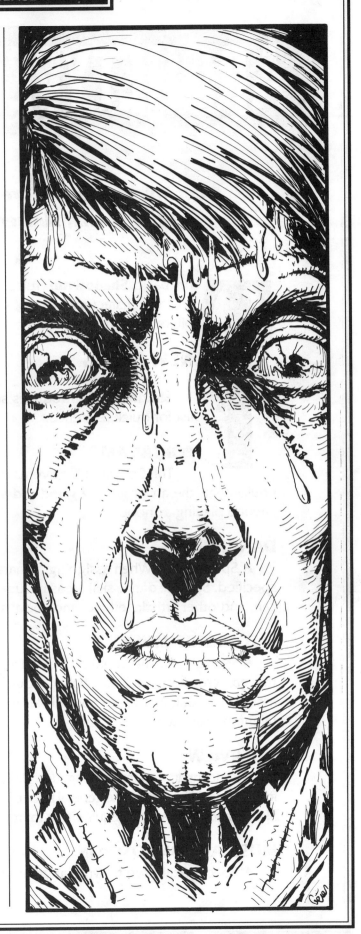

ARCHETYPE ADDITIONS

Oh my, so much more of me to go around!
—Lady Lynx, simsense star

The basic **Shadowrun** rules provide information and guidelines for creating character archetypes. **Shadowbeat** expands the basic rules, and offers some new goodies players and gamemasters may find useful.

NEW SKILLS

Shadowbeat introduces some new skills, outlined in the following list for quick reference.

PORTACAM

This Special Skill governs the use of video and trideo cameras, editing equipment, the art of getting good trid shots, and so on. This skill is essential for anyone playing a snoop.

DANCING

A Special Skill. When assigning a character Dancing, the type of dance must be specified. Specific dance skill areas include ballet, modern, ballroom, Native American, and other artistic, ethnic, and social styles.

ELECTRONIC MUSIC

A Special Skill. This could be treated as a Specialization of the Computer Skill, but the gamemaster should probably require would-be composers or performers to assign Electronic Music as a Special Skill instead, because not all programmers will be talented musicians.

INTERVIEW

A Concentration of the Interrogation Skill. One Specialization is Trideo Interview. Some form of this skill, whether the general Interrogation Skill, or one of the forms of the Interview Skill, is another essential requirement for reporters.

MUSICAL COMPOSITION

A Special Skill used to write anything from pop songs to grand opera.

MUSICAL INSTRUMENT

For this set of Special Skills, a specific form of the Musical Instrument Skill must be chosen. Players must choose among winds, guitars, keyboards, strings, and percussion, using the Concentrations of Acoustic, Electric, and Synthesizers. Specializations are for playing specific instruments such as electric guitar, acoustic violin, and so on.

A separate skill is recommended for other unique instruments. These include ethnic instruments, such as the Japanese koto, one-of-a-kind instruments, such as the throbber, and so on.

MUSICAL PRODUCTION

This is a Special Skill involving business negotiations in the music business, including arranging tours, designing productions, booking gigs, and other crass, management-type tasks.

REPORTING

A Concentration of the Leadership Skill, with specializations including Trideo Reporting and Print Reporting. This is the third skill in the "holy trinity" for the would-be reporter.

SINGING

A Special Skill covering singing. Concentrations include Chant, Rock, Classical, and Pop. Specializations govern specific genres, for example, Gregorian Chant, Native American Chant, Metal Rock, Opera, Blues Shouting, and so on.

SPORTS

Sports Skills are Concentrations of the Athletics Skill. Concentrations increase knowledge of rules, strategy, and specific moves. Urban Brawl Skill would be an Athletics Skill Concentration. Specializations govern specific moves or tactics. Football Passing or Combat Biker Flagsnagging are Athletics Skill Specializations.

NETWORK AFFILIATION

Freelance snoops may have an affiliation with a network. Freelancers are not employees, but have good connections to a network, and may possibly be employed regularly as a stringer. A character can be affiliated with many different networks. For example, a muckraking freelance vidsnoop might buy an affiliation with a major for the stories he can sell on the big network, and a pirate for the stories the major spikes.

A character with network affiliation has access to assistance from the network during an adventure in pretty much the same way a runner can call on assistance from a gang or tribal connection: 2D6 people will show up to help on request.

However, assistance comes in the form of "good citizens," network employees devoid of street skills or criminal tendencies. These typically consist of technicians, drivers (with their vehicles), research assistants, and even security. Network employees cannot provide and will not include hot deckers, riggers with panzers, streetwise fixers, or samurai. The quality of assistance and the tech to back it up will depend on the network itself. A driver borrowed from a pirate probably has a battered commuter car, while transport from a major will be appropriate for the occasion: hot car, helicopter, or Lear jet. On the other hand, pirate folks are usually less finicky about petty matters such as legality than would be the salaryman who would show up from one of the majors.

All network folks sent to help the snoop will have attributes and appropriate skills rated at 3.

In addition, someone affiliated with a network can usually sell stories to that network more easily than elsewhere, and his or her reports will receive wider coverage.

Affiliation with a pirate net costs 10,000¥.
Affiliation with an independent costs 15,000¥.
Affiliation with a major costs 25,000¥.

NETWORK EMPLOYMENT

A full-time reporter for a network is provided a salary and a lifestyle, and all the reporter has to do to keep it up is file at least one story a week (or work on one filed story if the network employee is not a reporter). This position provides all the benefits of network affiliation plus the comforts of home. Of course, hose up once too often and it's adios, amigo.

An employee of a pirate net preserves his or her anonymity and lives the free life of the SINless. An employee of an independent or a major is part of the system and has a perfectly valid SIN, whether he or she wants one or not, and must even pay taxes! Not to worry—the taxes are covered by an employee's lifestyle. Additional income is taxed at 20 percent. And any runner or citizen trying to evade the tax had better not get anyone in the government ticked off. Audits can be so nasty.

Minor jobs include an anonymous staff reporter, a technician, a security specialist, and other, similar positions. A major job places an employee in a position as a featured reporter, a field producer for a news show, or a major member of a news team. The class of job and the level of the network that employs a character determines the lifestyle that salary provides and the cost of that option for the archetype.

EMPLOYMENT TABLE

Job/Network	Lifestyle	Cost
Minor Job/Pirate Net	Low	1,000¥
Major Job/Pirate Net	Middle	10,000¥
Minor Job/Independent	Middle	10,000¥
Major Job/Independent	High	100,000¥
Minor Job/Major Net	High	100,000¥
Major Job/Major Net	Luxury	500,000¥

Disciplinary action may mean a demotion from a major job to a minor one, or simply getting fired from a minor position. A good job of reporting may result in a promotion to a major position if a character is currently just another minor schlub in the pool. Really good work in a small network can generate job offers from larger nets.

This aspect of employment is best handled by roleplaying. Simply lousing up one story will not usually get a person canned, and breaking one hot story in a year is not enough to turn a person into the net's ace reporter overnight. A consistent record of achievement (or failure) is what does it. A really spectacular failure, especially if the person gets caught faking proof, will usually put an end to an otherwise promising career.

ROCKER STATUS

If a player wants to run a rocker, he or she can buy status in the music biz (see p. 13) when creating the archetype. The available statuses and their costs follow.

NEWBIE: 0¥

Free, chummer. If all someone wants to do is pick up an instrument and start wailing, go for it. Newbie is the initial status of anyone pursuing a career in rock who does not buy a higher status when building the archetype.

OPENER: 100¥

This character has a teensy-weeny reputation in the local markets. His albums are not total drek and he does not get passing-out drunk in the middle of a set. Beyond that, no one is sure if he's got what it takes.

SELLER: 1,000¥

This rocker has had at least one recording sell in decent quantities, and he can usually get a gig when he needs one. At this level, rock even pays well enough to pay the rent on a Low lifestyle.

SOLID: 10,000¥

When people need a professional to back them up on a recording, fill in at a club, or play at a bar mitzvah, they call this character. He can live a Middle lifestyle on the income from his music.

STAR: 100,000¥

Like the word says: this rocker plays the hottest clubs, does tours, makes personal appearances. It can be a little tricky mixing this with shadowrunning, because people tend to recognize him or her. "Hey Vern, isn't that…?" "Yeah, it sure is! Wonder why he just blew the door off our R&D facility?" Rock maintains a High lifestyle for the character.

NOVASTAR: 500,000¥

This is one of the top-rated rockers in the country. Why he or she is running in the shadows is anyone's guess, when he lives a lifestyle of Luxury and his face is known to almost everyone over the age of five. But, hey, it's his money and his life.

SINS

Rock stars, pro athletes, and reporters all function to some extent within the system. Being SINless in these professions allows the system to use them up and grind them down without too much trouble.

Characters without a SIN who get money for their services take a 50 percent cut in the payoff. This cut is taken by unscrupulous managers, and is also the result of the erosion of fees paid as cash scrip, certified credsticks, and so on.

SINless characters who receive a lifestyle as part of their position must reduce that lifestyle by one level. That means a SINless rock seller would still be on the street, for example, and a SINless novastar is living only a High lifestyle. Naturally, characters can upgrade their lifestyle out of their own funds.

Anytime SINless characters are required to make tests for social interactions, such as a rocker looking for a booking or a reporter applying for an interview, add +2 to the test target numbers. This adjustment may also apply to other SINless characters, of course (sadistic grin).

SINNERS IN THE SHADOWS

What's the flip side? A character with a SIN but who is living a double life, partly in the light and partly in the shadows, faces many problems.

First off, keep in mind that purchases made with official SINful credsticks can be traced. If the character transfers money from a SINful account to a certified (SINless) account, apply the rules for fencing loot (**Shadowrun**, p. 148). Profit from SINless activities goes through the same laundering process as boosted credit. If the characters fail to take the correct precautions, he or she simply points all the tracers that live on his legal account straight at his shadowbank. Not good.

Taxes are paid on the lifestyles characters receive as part of their contracts. Characters with SINs are expected to pass on 33 percent of any additional income paid into their SINful accounts to the local taxing authority. Evading taxes is a popular pastime, but if the character is investigated by the government or other authorities for any reason at all, there is a chance his little "accounting error" will be discovered. Roll 3D6, and subtract the character's skill in Accounting or Law, or the Accounting or Law Skill of any fixer-type contact the user maintains.

What? The guy didn't keep a hot mouthpiece online? Gee, that's too bad.

The result of the dice roll and modifier for skill is the number of months of upkeep on the character's official lifestyle that must be paid as a fine. For example, a snoop with a minor job in an independent network has a Middle lifestyle. He has also collected assorted payments under the table for shadowruns he made while investigating stories. He gets busted and his SIN is investigated. He has a fixer on retainer with a Law Skill of 4. The player rolls 3D6 with a result of 12. He subtracts his skill : 12 – 4 = 8. A Middle lifestyle costs 5,000¥ a month, and so 5,000¥ x 8 = 40,000¥ in fines and penalties.

Oh, dear.

GEAR

Image you can buy. Guts, you can't.
—Anonymous cybersnoop

L ike riggers, media people have their own set of toys, ranging from video and trid equipment for the snoop's scoop, to unique musical equipment that could make a newbie a novastar. This section covers all the angles.

The broad categories of equipment follow the order of presentation in this book. Within those groups, the listing of gear moves from the simple to the complex.

SIGHT

This section provides information about trideo recording and editing equipment. This is the snoop's toy store.

PORTACAMS AND CYBERCAMS

Portacams can be very small, the main limitation on size being the lens structure and the medium the camera uses to store images. State-of-the-art in storage media is the optical storage chip, which can cram an enormous amount of data into a few cubic centimeters. Lenses are harder to miniaturize, but even they can be shrunk down for the right price.

All the portacams listed here have multi-functional lens systems that adjust automatically to low-light conditions, and can select thermal imaging when needed.

Portacams can be hand-held or mounted on a variety of bases. Using a manual portacam occupies at least one of the operator's hands. Cybercams do not have this restriction.

Cybercams are simply portacams with a tridlink interface, allowing the user control through a datajack or via camgoggles. These can also be either hand-held or mounted on a base. The base is cybered so that the user can control the camera's aim via the jack.

Fuchi VX2200 Manual

One of the nicer low-end portacams, the VX2200 meets the minimum specs for a professional tridsnoop. The manual model fits comfortably into one hand, and all the controls are easily accessible in the pistol grip. The VX2200 uses miniCDs to store images, and cannot connect directly to other storage media or to transmitters. Images must be copied offline using a CD player.

The biggest problem with the VX2200 is that it is difficult to mount on a portacam base, and shots using a base lose 2 points of Impact.

Fuchi VX2200C Cybercam

The cyber version of the VX2200, this portacam is equipped with a tridlink interface.

Sony HB500 Portacam

The professional's choice, the HB500 is a manual portacam. Controls are built into the pistol grip, but the portacam includes a remote-control unit that can be carried or worn on the wrist when the portacam is mounted on a base. The HB500 is equipped with a universal mounting bracket that mates with all standard bases.

The HB500 consists of a lens housing measuring six centimeters in diameter by eight centimeters long, with an optical memory storage transport that adds another three centimeters to the length of the unit. The pistol grip can be removed when the remote-control unit is in use.

The HB500 can be connected directly to an offboard storage transport or a transmitter for live trid.

Sony CB5000 Cybercam

This is the tridlinked version of the HB500.

AZT Micro20 Microcam Series

The Micro20 achieves its tiny size by using an electronic-imaging lens emulator. It measures about 4 centimeters by 3 centimeters by 2 centimeters, too small to fit standard portacam bases. The user needs AZT's Micro30 series of bases for hands-free use. The camera and base have a Concealability Rating of 8.

The Micro25 is the cybercam version.

Bionome Tridlink Adapter

This tridlink adapter can be fitted to a manual portacam to allow for datajack control.

PORTACAM BASES

Portacam bases come in a number of configurations, allowing any wannabe to stick a portacam or cybercam on a base, strap it on, and start tridding. Most bases are hand-held, shoulder mounts, head mounts, or chest mounts.

The best mounts include gyrostable gimbals and movement compensation processors that help offset the effects of rapid movement while shooting.

Kodak GAC-25 Shoulder Mount

This unit fits either shoulder, using a rather clumsy system of straps. It has no gyro-stabilization capability and cannot be cyber-controlled. Its manual controller can be hand-held or worn on the wrist or belt.

Cinema Products Steadicam™

Cinema Products is the most popular accessory manufacturer among professional camera operators. Their Steadicam™ technology, proven over half a century, provides a four-point countermeasure against the effects of motion, combat, and other violent movements made while shooting.

Their bases are equipped with manual or cybernetic control inputs and are specifically designed to accommodate cybercams like the CB5000.

Shoulder-mount Cinema Products bases are designed to fit either the left or right shoulder. A left-side unit will not fit comfortably on the right, and vice versa. The units are also available in a chest-mount configuration and a head mount that can be fitted to any helmet or to a Cinema Products head-mount brace.

AZT Micro30 StaticBrace

This compact base unit is designed for Aztechnology's Micro20 portacam series, available in wrist and chest mounts. The Micro30's motion compensation processors provide a two-point countermeasure against the effects of motion while shooting.

CAMGOGGLES

Camgoggles can control a cybercam and/or portacam base without using a datajack. The user has to be wearing them, natch. They come in many configurations, either monocular or binocular, and extra nuyen buys a set that looks just like ordinary glasses.

Fuchi I-C-U Autocam Controller

This binocular controller straps on easily. The autofocus shot-acquisition system allows the operator to view the scene through the camera rather than with his own vision. While using this controller, the operator suffers a +2 to all target numbers for any activities other than shooting trid, because the controller throws off his perspective.

Zeemandt Luxor Monocular

This lightweight controller covers only one eye, but is otherwise identical in function to the Fuchi I-C-U. Because it allows a portacam operator to use his own point-of-view in tandem with the camera's, the penalty to target numbers for "seeing through the camera" is only +1.

Sekrit Sistemz No-Sho Camtroller

Sekrit Sistemz has an excellent reputation for no-fault covert surveillance equipment. The No-Sho Camtroller is built into camgoggles that look like an ordinary set of glasses, either reading lenses or shades.

CYBEROPTICS

Cyberoptic portacams are simply high-quality cybereyes equipped with the options needed for professional trid. A cybersnoop usually carries an implanted portacam, a state-of-the-art hi-res electronic magnification subsystem, and the thermographic and low-light eye options. Eyecrafters offers a special package to the industry, routing image storage directly into headware memory, or through a datajack into an external store such as a chip or CD drive.

Cyberoptics can be fitted with a smartcam processor (see below). The Dr. Spott model is used by most cybersnoops.

SMARTCAM

Built into a cybercam, a smartcam is a powerful co-processor that corrects tridshots for motion, lighting conditions, focus, and, to some extent, even composition. Smartcam improves the Impact of Pix Tests by 2 points (see p. 41). A smartcam option is available for cyberoptic units as well.

A smartcam adaptor can be installed in any portacam or cybercam.

A character using a tridlinked camera requires a smartcam implant to get the 2-point Impact bonus.

If the operator is using camgoggles or is using a datajack but does not have the smartcam implant, then the bonus is only 1 point.

TRANSMITTER LINKS

These units can be built into a portacam or carried externally and connected to the portacam when desired. They allow live transmission of trid to the network, still a rare occurrence for news coverage. Only the most important stories are fed into the network "live and direct."

Unsecured transmitters use public frequencies or cellular systems to transmit data. Secured systems employ error-correction algorithms to eliminate errors in transmission and encryption schemes to avoid interception. The receiver for a secured transmitter must be programmed with the decryption scheme that matches the encryption used by the transmitter.

Short-haul transmitters have a maximum range of two kilometers and are generally used when transmitting to a mobile unit in the field. They are eminently portable and have a Concealability Rating of 6.

Long-haul transmitters have a range of approximately fifty kilometers. They are portable, but too large to be concealed effectively.

Uplink transmitters feed to a specified satellite and transponder code. They are not portable, and require a one-meter dish to operate.

Field reporters who use transmitter links often employ a combination of units. For example, a reporter might use a short-haul unit to connect to a van or temporary base where a long-haul or uplink unit is installed, which relays his signals to the network.

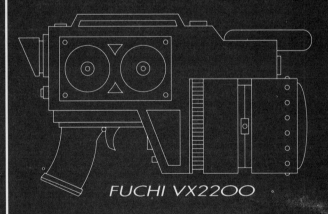

TRIDISYNTHS AND MIXERS

Various editing devices are used legitimately to prepare footage for broadcasting, and, less legitimately, to fake tridshots. The best units can increase the effective skill of the operator by up to three extra dice.

Vertex Netsynth Tridmixer

A solid, dependable editing tool. This unit does not provide any skill adds, but in the hands of a hot mixer, that's no problem.

Fuchi Holo-Edit 7200

The Holo-Edit has a superb expert system that adds 1 point to the operator's effective skill. It also uses Fuchi's patented holovization system, which can scan a flat image and generate a 3D presentation of that image.

Sony TFX-10000 Imaging Generator

The sports car of tridisynths, this unit has a built-in 500-Mp dedicated processor that adds three dice to the operator's effective skill.

PIRATE EQUIPMENT

Pirates need special toys to get their subversive trash onto the networks. All prices given are "street list," which means a brisk round of haggling is almost mandatory. Almost more uncertain than the price, supply versus demand can also vary wildly from place to place and week to week.

Electromagnetic Transmitter

These transmitters can broadcast signals on the radio, VHF, and UHF bands of the spectrum. Besides broadcasting pirate signals, a simple adjustment turns one of these into a peachy wide-spectrum jammer capable of messing up transmissions in the area the transmission covers.

The basic unit has a range of about five kilometers. Every additional five kilometers of range doubles the cost of the transmitter. Units cannot cover a range greater than five kilometers unless they are hooked up to a source of industrial current, which means that mobile transmitters must stand still to transmit to a larger area.

Transmission Sampler

Transmission samplers are actually anti-piracy devices, used to triangulate the source of illegal broadcasts. See page 28 for details.

Satellite Injection Uplink Station

This is an illegal trideo uplink transmitter, equipped with security penetration logics that allow it to infiltrate a transponder circuit on a satellite. It is non-mobile and requires a one-meter dish.

Cable Signal Formatter

A CSF allows a pirate signal to be injected into a cable network, replacing the legitimate signal, at any optical-cable booster node (see page 28). ECM in this context refers to the ability of the signal formatter to avoid computer checks of the network status, or to report false locations for its position in the net.

MEDIA EQUIPMENT TABLE

Portacams and Cybercams	
Fuchi VX2200 Portacam	1,000¥
Fuchi VX2200C Cybercam	1,300¥
Sony HB500 Portacam	2,200¥
Sony CB5000 Cybercam	2,700¥
AZT Micro20 Microportacam	2,500¥
AZT Micro25 Microcybercam	3,200¥
Bionome Tridlink Adapter	700¥
Portacam Bases	
Kodak GAC-25 Shoulder Mount	200¥
Cinema Products Steadicam™	
Shoulder	1,800¥
Chest	1,800¥
Head	1,800¥
AZT Micro30 StaticBrace	
(for the Micro20 Portacam Series)	
Wrist	2,200¥
Chest	2,200¥
Camgoggles	
Fuchi I-C-U Autocam Controller	400¥
Zeemandt Luxor Monocular	700¥
Sekrit Sistemz No-Sho Camtroller	1,000¥
Cyberoptics	
Eyecrafters Opticam Package	20,000¥ (Essence 5)
Dr. Spott Smartcam Implant	10,000¥ (Essence 2)
Smartcam	
Smartcam Link	2,500¥ (Essence 5)
Smartcam Adapter	1,500¥
Transmitter Links	
Unsecured Transmitter Links	
Short-haul	4,000¥
Long-haul	6,000¥
Uplink	1,000¥
Secured Transmitter Links	
Short-haul	6,000¥
Long-haul	9,000¥
Uplink	1,500¥
Tridisynths and Mixers	
Vertex Netsynth Tridmixer	8,000¥
Fuchi Holo-Edit 7200	10,000¥
Sony TFX-10000 Imaging Generator	13,000¥
Pirate Equipment	
Electromagnetic Transmitters (Radio/TV/3V)	
Non-mobile	5,500¥
Mobile	7,500¥
+ECM Rating (1 to 6)	+2,500¥/rating point
Transmission Sampler	1,000¥
Satellite Injection Uplink Station	1,000¥
+ECM Rating (1 to 6)	+3,000¥/rating point
Cable Signal Formatter	2,000¥
+ECM Rating (1 to 6)	+1,500¥/rating point

SOUND

Amplification systems, recording gear, and musical instruments are the focus of this section: hardware to delight the heart of any rocker on the planet.

MUSICAL INSTRUMENTS

A comprehensive table of prices for musical instruments would cover several pages. Instead, we offer the following generic rules for pricing instruments. Ideally, this system will prove flexible enough that if someone wants an electrified Greek bouzouki with a synth master-controller interface built in, the rules will allow the gamemaster to set a price.

Acoustical Instruments

Instruments come in three overall quality ratings. "Cheap" instruments limit the skill of the player to a 4. No matter how high the player's skill, on a cheap instrument he or she may only roll a maximum of four dice for the skill rolls. "Average" instruments can support a skill of up to 6. "Fine" instruments put no limit on the user's skill.

In addition, instruments are rated as Common or Rare. Common instruments are typical in the culture where they are purchased, whereas rare instruments are not available on every street corner.

Common instruments in North America include all the instruments normally found in a symphony orchestra or pop-music band. Rare instruments are those peculiar to a different culture: Japanese kotos, Indian sitars, Indonesian gamelans, Russian doumbeks, Scottish bagpipes, as well as historical instruments and any custom instruments the musician has made to his or her own specification.

Keep in mind that hopping a plane to a different country may turn a rare instrument into a common one, but if the local technology base is lower than North America's, then refinements like electronics or synth interfaces will go up in price, or even be unavailable.

Instruments also have a Complexity multiplier from 1 to 5. The size of the instrument, the number of moving parts, difficulty of construction, and range of sound all contribute to Complexity. See the Complexity Table below for examples.

COMPLEXITY TABLE

Rating	Typical Example
1	Bamboo flute, penny whistle, simple drum, triangle, cymbals, gongs
2	Tambourine, western drums, chimes
3	Typical strings, guitars, brasses, woodwinds, Celtic harp
4	Xylophones and vibraphones, pianos and other keyboards, concert harp
5	Pipe organs, calliopes

Electric Instruments

Price electric instruments using the same rules as for acoustical instruments. However, because technological components replace more expensive materials and craftsmanship, reduce the instrument's Complexity multiplier by −1 point. The minimum complexity for an instrument is 1.

Amplifiers and speakers for electric instruments are bought separately, as are digital direct-recording outputs that store the music without using an analog speaker to generate actual sound.

Synthesizers

Master controllers are priced in the same way as electric instruments, that is, using the pricing system for acoustical instruments but subtracting 1 point from the Complexity multiplier. The slave synthesizer is priced according to its quality, plus an additional modifier based on the number of channels, or "voices," it can support.

Amps, speakers, or direct digital outputs are bought separately.

A professional synth supports a minimum of eight "voices." Monovocal (one-voice) synths are just toys. Multivocal (many-voiced) synthesizers with fewer than eight voices are something for amateur night. Top rockers will have twelve, sixteen, or even more voices on their synths. The sheer flexibility and power of a high-end, multivocal synthesizer adds

Of course all of our music is programmed. It takes thought to compose and program music. Any moron can just plug in and go.
—Billy Synapse of The Newrons

power to a performance. If one or more of the rockers in a band has a really good instrument, the impact of the performance increases. Of course, cheesy equipment has the opposite effect, and so if a rocker is using a low-end synth, it will lower the impact of the performance, or the group's performance.

SYNTH IMPACT MODIFIER TABLE	
Type of Synthesizer	**Impact Modifier**
Monovocal synthesizer	–4
Less than eight voices	–2
Eight voices	0
Twelve voices	+1
Sixteen voices	+2
Twenty-four or more voices	+3

The skill limit for playing a synthesizer system is based on the lowest-quality component in the system. For example, if a rocker has a fine controller, but is still using average slave synths, then he can only use a skill rating of 6 or less. Once he upgrades his synthesizers to match the controller, he can perform with a skill higher than 6.

Synthlinks

A synthlink requires a datajack and an implanted synthlink interface system. The user "jacks into" a synthlink control deck, the master controller for the slave synthesizers. Actually, there is no physical connection to the control deck. The synthlink interface and control deck communicate through a short-haul cellular connection, allowing the user full freedom of movement, unencumbered by cables.

Slave synthesizers, amps, speakers, and so on are configured the same way for a synthlink as they are for a manual controller.

Autosynths

An autosynth, also known as a music generator, is a synthesizer master controller driven by an expert system. Like a Song-O-Mat, an autosynth can be programmed to drive slave synths in response to a set of parameters. The programming in an autosynth unit is not the cut-and-paste "composition" of the Song-O-Mat.

An autosynth is designed to "jam" with a live performer. It responds to both musical input and programming. That is, the rocker can simply set up the parameters for the autosynth and it will play background while the rocker performs, or he can compose the accompaniment in advance and program it into the unit. This is more like a "pickup-band-in-a-box" than the more sterile "rocker-in-a-box" of the Song-O-Mat.

Autosynths are priced according to the effective performance skill of the expert system, but the autosynth's skill can never exceed the highest "live" music skill of the rocker it is accompanying. That is, if a rocker with a skill of 4 is using an autosynth with a skill of 6, the autosynth expert system can only contribute a skill of 4 to the performance. The autosynth system does not let the rocker roll more dice!

Similarly, if a rocker has more skill than the autosynth, then the rules for group skills apply to the performance.

Autosynths are useful because they can drive multivocal synthesizers (see **It's Only Rock and Roll**) for musicians who are not skilled with synths.

SOUND SYSTEMS

Most basic sound systems include microphones, amplifiers for electric instruments, speakers to produce the actual sound, and mixers to tie the pieces together. More exotic equipment includes direct digital output interfaces, polycorders, sampling consoles to edit recordings, and other goodies.

Modern sound equipment uses a cable-free, cellular connector system that radio-links the equipment over signal-locked, checksum-protected digital channels that are highly resistant to noise or interference. Connections for physical cables, mainly optical cable in a protective sheathing, are still installed on equipment for situations where the cellular system is not dependable.

Acoustic Modulators

The ultimate in analog sound controllers, acoustic modulators tie into sound systems to balance amplifier power, mixer control, and speaker performance, and can create optimal acoustics or special acoustics designed according to highly flexible parameters in virtually any space. Want a warehouse to sound like Carnegie Hall? Or vice versa? This will do it.

Acoustic modulators increase the Impact of live performances by +4, but their effects are purely analog and so do *not* increase the impact of recordings, which are based on digital technology. Therefore, the Impact bonus does not affect the Performance Rating for purposes of distribution payments (see p. 14).

Acoustic modulators are rated by the size of the area they can modify, and are not available in ratings bigger than a hall system (see **Amplifiers**, below). They include auxiliary speaker systems that double the weight and volume of standard speaker arrays (see **Speakers**, below).

Amplifiers

One amplifier is needed for each electric instrument or synthesizer system being hooked up. Amps need speakers and speakers need amps, so check out the info on speakers below.

The availability of good technology has made the question of quality in amps almost irrelevant. If an amp has survived on the market, it is a good amp. Amplifier pricing is based on power. Make that **POWER!** An amp does not have to be guaranteed to melt down fusion plants a kilometer away, but it sure could be fun to try.

Anyway, amps are rated by the size of the space they can effectively fill with sound. An amp in a space smaller than its rating can put out volume fit to melt brains.

Small amps can drive the signal for a single room. They are used for practice and for studio recording, and are the economical choice when volume is irrelevant, especially when the music is being recorded directly to digital media. Small amps and speakers are essentially the same equipment found in a good home audio system.

Club amps are powerful enough to fill a typical club.

Hall amps will fill a concert hall that seats between three and four thousand.

Stadium amps can handle the demands of a full-sized sports arena seating up to fifty thousand.

Superstadium amps are like stadium amps, only louder. For those who like auditory damage in large doses, these are the way to go.

Direct Digital Output

This is an optional device that can be interfaced to an amplifier (for recording an individual instrument) or to a mixer (for recording the band's entire output). A DDO connection writes digital musical signals direct to digital recording mediums such as a CD transport, optical storage chip, a SAN for recording directly into a Matrix system, and so on.

A direct digital adaptor takes analog output and converts it to digital. For example, the feed from a digital-to-analog speaker output on a mixer would require an adaptor to be transmitted directly as a digital signal.

Microphones

Standard microphones are body mikes with rechargeable battery packs providing three hours of use on one charge. The physical mike is a cylinder about 15 centimeters long and 3 centimeters in diameter, weighing 250 grams. Top-quality mikes are "tunable," meaning they can be set to react to only one particular voice or sonic pattern, using an ultra-high-speed sampling microprocessor to filter out extraneous input. This eliminates problems with feedback and picking up other performers' singing or instruments.

Larger mikes mounted on traditional booms or stands are still used, as are handmikes. These microphones have remained much the same size, for convenient handling and visibility.

As a rule, one mike is needed for each vocal artist in a performance.

Mixers

One mixer is needed for each sound system unless each amplifier is hooked up to its own speakers. Mixers are priced according to the number of input channels they can support. One channel can connect to one amplifier or one microphone. For example, a band with two electric instruments, three synthesizer systems, and two vocalists, each with a mike, will need a mixer with seven channels.

All mixers have output channels for speakers, usually one output for each amplifier connected to it, though a band can get away with fewer speakers. Multiple outputs allow fancy effects like "moving" sounds from one speaker array to another. All professional-quality mixers have built-in direct digital output as well as digital-analog output gates. Some have built-in polycorders.

Mixers designed for live performance only can get away with having digital-analog outputs only, used to drive the speakers.

Multitrack Sampler

Samplers store numerous recordings on chips, and can play them back in various combinations, either one at a time or over multiple channels. Samplers can mix multiple signals into one output, and they are the equivalent of the old mixers used in 20th-century studios.

Standard top-of-the-line studio units accommodate up to sixty-four channels, with custom units allowing even more. Less expensive units usually run eight- or sixteen-channel configurations.

Samplers can be tied into a synthesizer system using a standard OMNI connector. They can also tap digital records stored on a personal computer or mainframe. Recordings can be stored directly in a sampler using a standard optical storage chip of any capacity, and most samplers have inputs for six chips.

The best samplers are rigged for control via datajack, and DNI-only units are very small—approximately 50 centimeters long by 20 centimeters wide by 3 centimeters high.

Units with manual controls are much longer. Figure that the unit is 10 centimeters long for every two channels supported, by 50 centimeters wide by 10 centimeters high. So a thirty-two-channel sampler would be 160 centimeters by 50 centimeters by 10 centimeters.

Polycorders

Polycorders are the most common sound-recording system on the market, the equivalent of a late 20th-century cassette recorder. They come in a variety of sizes and shapes, from pocket-sized (or smaller) to rack-mounted components for music buffs. Typical models have a built-in microphone and a jack for input from a remote microphone. Higher-priced models also have a datajack connector to allow recording from cyberaudio implants. Cheap polycorders can only accept miniCDs, but even these have mostly been replaced by units with both a read/write CD transport and a direct chip encoder, so that either disks or chips can be used.

Playback is through a built-in speaker (in portable models) or output to a component sound system. The hottest models feed a modified ASIST signal over a datajack connector so that music can be played directly on the auditory nerve, bypassing analog sound systems altogether.

Speakers

For the classicist, speakers are still one of the most important aspects of a rocker's sound system. As "Lightning" Lance Braunstein once remarked, "It don't mean a thing if it ain't audible in the next county."

Speakers are rated the same way as amplifiers. The limit on a sound system's total performance is the weakest link in the chain of amplifiers and speakers. If the rockers are playing through club amplifiers, then they only get club-level sound, even if they have a bank of superstadium speakers. Similarly, if they have hall speakers, then they cannot get the full advantage of more powerful amps. They can try, of course, but technology has yet to find a cure for "blowing the speakers," and pushing a speaker past its rating turns it into junk in short order.

The prices given below are for an array of speakers. The equipment can be one box, or several. In a system larger than club size, the array always consists of more than one speaker. While electronics technology has shrunk most other components, a speaker can only shrink by a limited amount and still produce quality sound. Acoustical processes do not miniaturize well.

	SPEAKER ARRAYS	
Size	Area (cubic meters)	Weight
Small	1	10 kg
Club	2	20 kg
Hall	6	60 kg
Stadium	12	120 kg
Superstadium	18	180 kg

A mixer can feed one speaker array for every digital-analog output. An amplifier can feed a single speaker array directly, though most bands mix everything through a central array. Most concert halls and sports arenas have built-in speaker arrays and mixer systems.

INSTRUMENT COSTS

Let's look at how the system works. Take that old standby, the guitar. This is a common instrument. Looking at the basic instrument prices on the chart below, we see that the base price for a cheap instrument is 50¥. An acoustic guitar has a Complexity multiplier of 3, so a cheap guitar, made of compressed plastic pulp, knocked off on an assembly line, costs 150¥.

If the rocker were buying a fine guitar, we'd take the basic price of a fine instrument (5,000¥) and multiply that by the Complexity, for a list price of 15,000¥. The rocker has a handmade instrument of excellent quality.

This pricing system does not even begin to address such priceless collector's items as Stradivarius violins or original Fender Stratocasters, which are worth hundreds of thousands, maybe millions, of nuyen. But those instruments are not for sale off the shelf anyway.

Okay, so rockerchum has an acoustic guitar. Only now he notices he is playing with an electric band! So he goes shopping for an electric guitar. Say he goes for an average instrument. The basic price is 500¥. Guitars have a Complexity of 3, but electric instruments reduce Complexity by 1. So an average electric guitar will run 1,000¥.

The band is playing club gigs for now, so a club speaker system will suffice for output. Amp and speakers run another 1,400¥. If the rocker buys a sound system equipped with the cable-free cellular linking system, it ups the price by 50 percent, to 2,100¥.

The band decides to switch to an all-synth sound, so our rocker is back in the stores pricing synthaxe controllers and racks of slave synths. An average controller costs the same as an electric instrument, so that's another 1,000¥ for a controller. The band is trying hard to make it into the big time, so the rocker has to spring for at least an eight-voice synthesizer, or the band's performance impact goes down. An average eight voice synth costs 500¥, plus 100¥ per voice, and 500 + 800 = 1,300¥, for a total of 2,300¥. Fortunately, speakers is speakers, so the sound system he's been using for the electric guitar will work just fine.

This same process works for any other kind of instrument. It does not take custom instruments, fancy casings, special effects, and other personal touches into account, but haggling over these goodies is a perfect opportunity for roleplaying and making Negotiation Tests.

SOUND EQUIPMENT TABLE

BASIC INSTRUMENT PRICES*

Quality	Common	Rare
Cheap	50¥	250¥
Average	500¥	2,500¥
Fine	5,000¥	25,000¥

*Actual price = Basic Price x Complexity. Electric instruments and synthesizer controllers reduce Complexity by 1.

Synthesizers
Cheap	150¥ + 25¥ per voice. Max voices = 8.
Average	500¥ + 100¥ per voice. Max voices = 16.
Fine	5,000¥ + 500¥ per voice. Max voices = 32.

Autosynths
Skill 1–3	1,000¥ per skill point
Skill 4–5	3,000¥ per skill point
Skill 6–8	5,000¥ per skill point
Skill 9–10	10,000¥ per skill point

Synthlink Equipment
Synthlink Interface	2,500¥ (Essence Cost: .5)
Synthlink Controller	
Cheap	1,000¥
Average	10,000¥
Fine	50,000¥

SOUND SYSTEM COMPONENTS

Acoustic Modulators
Small	8,000¥
Club	15,000¥
Hall	35,000¥

Amplifiers
Small	100¥
Club	400¥
Hall	1,200¥
Stadium	5,000¥
Superstadium	12,000¥

Direct Digital Output
Built-in DDO	+500¥ to base price
DDO Adapter	+700¥ to base price

Microphones
Body Mike	100¥
Hand Mike	100¥
Mike Stand	50¥
Mike Boom	75¥

Mixers
Basic unit (4 input and 1 digital-analog output channels)	1,000¥
Per additional input channel	+200¥
Per additional output channel	+500¥
Built-in Polycorder	+300¥

Multitrack Samplers
4-track Sampler	1,200¥
8-track Sampler	3,200¥
16-track Sampler	8,000¥
24-track Sampler	14,400¥
32-track Sampler	22,400¥
Manual Control Only	Base Price
Direct Neural Interface Control Only	Base Price x 2
Combined Manual/DNI Control	Base Price x 2.5

Polycorders
Microcorder (3 x 3 x 1 cm)	1,000¥
Minicorder (5 x 3 x 1 cm)	700¥
Pocket sized (10 x 5 x 3 cm)	200¥
Hand-held (20 x 8 x 4 cm)	100¥
Rack-mount Component	1,500¥
Sprawl Blaster (built-in small speakers)	200¥
Sprawl Fuser (built-in club speakers)	1,200¥
MiniCD Transport Only	Base Price/2
ASIST Direct Neural Playback	Base Price x 3

Speakers
Small	100¥
Club	1,000¥
Hall	5,000¥
Stadium	12,000¥
Superstadium	25,000¥

PROGRAMMABLE ASIST BIOFEEDBACK (PAB)

PAB units are strictly regulated. Unauthorized use is governed by the military technology law (Class J weapon offense). All PABs are restricted. List price to authorized purchasers is as shown below. Street price starts at three times the list price, but is subject to Negotiation (isn't everything?).

Programmable ASIST biofeedback units are required for event reprogramming (brainwashing), as described on p. 47. Any PAB with a Rating 3 or higher can only be used at maximum effectiveness in an intensive care facility. Otherwise, its effective Rating is 2.

PABs with a Rating of 2 or less are quite portable. They fit into a briefcase and weigh only a few kilos. Larger units are about the size of a desktop PC and weigh about ten kilos.

PAB PRICE TABLE		
Unit	Rating	Price
Galil Ruach-Aleph Reprogrammer	1	10,000¥
Mitsuhama MenTokko-II Engram Manipulator	2	15,000¥
Ares CyberMed Psychscanner	3	25,000¥
EBMM Therapeutic ASIST System	4	40,000¥
Mitsuhama MenTokko-V Engram Manipulator	5	60,000¥

SIMSENSE GEAR

SIMSENSE RIG (SIMRIG)

A simrig is a cyberware implant that makes wet simsense recordings available in baseline (records sensory tracks only) and full experience, or full-X (sensory and emotive tracks). Non-cyber versions using induction 'trodes instead of a datajack are available, but produce only baseline records. 'Trode recording quality is not high enough for commercial use.

Simrig output can go to any digital or optical storage format: CD, headware, or optical memory chip I/O module. Output can also be routed through a simlink. Baseline recording requires 1 Mp of memory per second of recording, and full-X requires 3 Mp per second.

SIMLINKS

Simlinks are relatively short-range transmitter/receiver systems designed to carry simsense. The maximum range for a simlink is about 1,000 meters if using a high-powered unit, and most are limited to 100 meters or less.

Simlink transmitters can be cyberware or external. The receivers can hook up to a sense deck, allowing a user to experience the wet record in realtime, or a simlink recorder, which can produce a wet record with the same storage requirements as a simrig.

Simlinks are usually used by the production staff during a simsense recording to monitor a performer's POV. They can also be used to monitor other individuals equipped with a transmitter, for example, to follow an agent's progress over a dangerous piece of turf.

Simlink transmissions can be encrypted, decrypted, and subjected to the same surveillance measures and countermeasures as any other form of data transfer.

SIMTHS

Simsynths, or just "simths" are simsense editing systems ranging from self-contained units with minimal flexibility and power to large, modular workstations operating in tandem with a mainframe CPU and various peripherals.

A typical baseline home-use simth, the Fuchi Reality-500, is a self-contained unit, 1 meter long by 30 centimeters wide by 15 centimeters high, weighing about 15 kilograms. It contains a 100-Mp CPU, a monoPOV input jack, a monitor jack for the operator, a control keyboard, a six-band EC/PC modulator with a maximum Signal Rating of 6, and an ACT Experience Sampler. It can be used as a sense deck as well as a simth, of course.

A typical major studio configuration might consist of: interface to a mainframe computer; a high-end studio-quality simth such as the Yamaha 95000 or Fuchi Kosmos (any simth of this quality will have multiple monoPOV inputs, inputs for peripherals, including sense patch injectors, track enablers, and so on, and monoPOV and polyPOV outputs); ACT and Dir-X monitor connectors for the operator; racked EC/PC and emotive enablers, usually between twenty-four and forty-eight in each major spectrum, with signal-handling capacity up to a Rating of 10; and samplers to record the simth output.

ASIST ENABLERS

ASIST enablers are the signal generators and modulators that alter or enhance the EC/PC and emotive tracks on the simth. Scores of different enablers work on each track: visuals, tactiles, thermals, gustatories, and so on for the sensory, and various neural system and subsystem enablers for the emotive.

Enabler output is measured on a scale of 1 to 10.

A home simth usually has no more than six enablers, all dealing with pretty gross levels of experience and rarely rating higher than 4. Studio simths may have twenty or thirty enablers, all rated a full 10, hooked up to the simth, allowing any given experience to be fine-tuned to an amazing extent.

PATCH INJECTION DRIVER

This unit injects sense-patches to the simsynth. Most injectors interface with a CPU or other source of bulk memory which stores the patches, though some cheaper models have a few hundred Mp of built-in storage.

SIGNAL-PEAK CONTROLLER

This signal processor is required by law in the production of commercial simsense. It modulates the final output to the experience sampler to ensure that the product conforms to regulations on signal intensity, fluctuation, and areas of simultaneous stimulation.

DIR-X EXPERIENCE SAMPLER

This is a recorder that produces Dir-X format simsense recordings. Output can be to any digital or optical medium, and storage requirements are the same as for simrig wet records: Baseline = 1 Mp/second. Full-X = 3 Mp/second.

ACT EXPERIENCE SAMPLER

A recorder that produces ACT-format simsense recordings. Output can be to any digital or optical medium. Storage requirements are 1 percent of Dir-X: Baseline = 1 Mp/100 seconds. Full-X = 3 Mp/100 seconds.

SENSE DECKS

Playback units for simsense are called sense decks. Personal units are usually limited to ACT format, with Dir-X used only by theatrical units. However, some high-ticket decks capable of both ACT and Dir-X are now becoming available for home use.

Commercial Dir-X decks in theaters are connected to an ASIST multiplexer feeding an optical cable net to individual receivers mounted by the patrons' seats. Some establishments are experimenting with direct broadcast of the signal.

Most older decks are equipped for monoPOV playback, but an increasing number of polyPOV decks are available in all price ranges.

Portable ACT decks are about 10 centimeters square and 3 centimeters thick, and have only limited signal outputs. Tabletop or rack-mount units have more versatile circuitry and better power supplies, and provide cleaner signals.

Most sense decks can interface with the user through standard datajacks or induction 'trodes. The signal through a 'trodeset is diffused and less intense: a real simhead will get a jack implanted if he can possibly afford it.

SIMSENSE GEAR TABLE

Simrigs

Baseline Cyberware Simrig	300,000¥ (Essence Cost 2)
Full-X Cyberware Simrig	500,000¥ (Essence Cost 2)
Baseline Induction Simrig	50,000¥ (Essence Cost 2)

Simlinks

Rating 1 to 10 (Range = 100 meters x Rating)

Internal	70,000¥ + (10,000¥ x Rating)
	[Essence cost: .6 + (Rating x .05)]
External	25,000¥ + (5,000¥ x Rating)

Simths

Truman Reality-500 (monoPOV Baseline)	25,000¥
Fuchi RealSense™ Kosmos XXV	250,000¥
Truman Inner-I	200,000¥

Simth Peripherals

ASIST Enablers: Rating 1 to 10 (Signal Strength)

EC/PC Enabler	Rating x 10,000¥
Emotive Enabler	Rating x 25,000¥
Sense Patch Injector	25,000¥
Signal Peak Controller	15,000¥

Experience Samplers

MonoPOV ACT Format	15,000¥
MonoPOV Dir-X Format	75,000¥
PolyPOV Samplers	+25% per additional POV

Sense Decks

Truman Dreambox (monoPOV ACT)	350¥
Sony Beautiful Dreamer (monoPOV ACT)	1,200¥
Sony Beautiful Dreamer II (polyPOV ACT)	1,800¥
Fuchi Dreamliner (polyPOV ACT)	2,500¥
Truman Paradiso (polyPOV ACT and DIR-X)	75,000¥
Fuchi RealSense™ MasterSim (Commercial Dir-X)	125,000¥
ASIST Dir-X Multiplexer	2,500¥ + (100¥ per channel)

Simsense Recordings

(All prices shown are for baseline recordings. Triple prices for full-X.)

ACT Recordings

Cheap or Instructional Recording	1¥/minute
Average Entertainment or Documentary	2¥/minute
High-Quality Entertainment or Documentary	2.5¥/minute
Current Hit	3¥/minute

Dir-X Recordings

Average Entertainment or Documentary	90¥/minute
High-Quality Entertainment or Documentary	100¥/minute
Current Hit	150¥/minute

STORAGE MEDIA

COMPACT DISKS

Six centimeters in diameter, a standard high-density/double-sided digital compact disk can hold 500 Mp of stored data. HD/DS CDs can be edited and rewritten on any standard drive or transport system. Retrieval is woefully slow compared to optical storage systems, and CD drives are generally used only in very cheap personal computing and entertainment systems.

HEADWARE MEMORY

Cybercams, either internal or external, can be configured to deliver imaging signals to headware memory for storage. This feature is often used by newsies on a covert beat who find it safer to use eyeshots instead of external portacams. Headware is also used extensively in simsense production, with the wet record transferred to an external datastore after each take.

OPTICAL MEMORY CHIPS

Regardless of capacity, the standard OMC measures 2 x 3 x 1 centimeter. Commercial configurations are available in increments of 10 Mp up to 100 Mp, then in increments of 100 Mp up to the gigapulse level (1,000 Gp). OMCs are used for data storage in state-of-the-art portacams, audio systems, and other media equipment, as well as on cyberdecks, personal computers, sense decks, and so on. They serve the same function as diskettes in 20th-century PCs. OMCs are small enough to be concealed almost anywhere on one's person, and can be carried plugged into a datajack for output from other cybersystems.

HD/DS MiniCD	10¥ (holds 500 Mp)
Headware Memory	100¥ per Mp
Optical Memory Chips	.5¥ per Mp

DATA STORAGE REQUIREMENTS

Regardless of the physical media used for storage, the amount of storage required for various forms of information is always the same. It does not matter if a user has a CD, an OMC, or his own lovingly implanted dome-chrome. It's a digital world, chummer, and a megapulse is a megapulse.

DATA STORAGE TABLE

Data Type	Storage Required
High-resolution video imaging	1 Mp/minute
Trideo imaging	5 Mp/minute
High-resolution trideo imaging	10 Mp/minute
Normal spectrum sound	1 Mp/minute
Extended spectrum sound	3 Mp/minute
Wet Record Simsense	
Baseline	1 Mp/second
Full-X	3 Mp/second
Dir-X Format Simsense	
Baseline	1 Mp/second
Full-X	3 Mp/second
ACT Format Simsense	
Baseline	1 Mp/100 seconds
Full-X	3 Mp/100 seconds

TRIDEO SERVICES

For those who wish to buy trid services a la carte, as it were, prices follow. The base price for SINless users who wish to purchase services via bribery is five times the list price given here. This price will appear in parentheses () in the price list. A successful Negotiation (6) Test can reduce this figure. Every success reduces the SINless price by 10 percent. The maximum reduction possible when using the Negotiation Skill is 50 percent of the SINless price, and so more than five successes does not provide any additional benefits.

TRIDEO SERVICE PRICE LIST

Trideo Service	Cost	Notes
Basic Service	50¥(250¥)/month	Free at Low Lifestyle.
FAX	100¥	Free at Middle Lifestyle.
High-Speed Matrix Access	200¥(1,000¥)/month	Free at High Lifestyle.
Large Field Holophone	1,500¥	Free at Luxury Lifestyle.
Large TV/3V Display	1,000¥	Free at High Lifestyle.
Multistation Trideo	500¥(2,500¥)/month/per station	Free at High Lifestyle (3 stations) and Luxury Lifestyle (6 stations).
Multiphonic Sound	2,500¥	Free at High Lifestyle.
Premium Cable Access	100¥(500¥)/month/channel	Free at Middle Lifestyle (3 channels), High Lifestyle (6 channels). All access free at Luxury Lifestyle.
Premium Matrix Access	200¥(1,000¥)/month/channel	Free at High Lifestyle (3 channels), Luxury Lifestyle (all channels).
Premium Matrix Interface	1,000¥(5,000¥)/month	Free at Luxury Lifestyle.
Satellite Reception	100¥ for dish 100¥(500¥)/month/channel for decryption	Free at Middle Lifestyle (3 channels), High Lifestyle (6 channels). All access free at Luxury Lifestyle.
Simsense Interface	10,000¥	Free at High Lifestyle (requires Premium Matrix Access and High-Speed Matrix Access).
Vidphone Service	50¥(250¥)/month	Free at Middle Lifestyle.

GLOSSARY

Axe n. A musical instrument. Often refers to a guitar, but not exclusively.

Eyeshot n. Video recording made using a cybereye. Images are of lower resolution than those made with an external camcorder, but it is much easier to take eyeshots covertly.

Flat n. (simsense slang) From an old theatrical term for a piece of scenery. An actor in a simsense who is not wired for sim recording, but merely forms part of the background for a scene. An extra.

Indy n. An independent (but licensed) broadcasting station or network.

Jittertime n. Any time in a Combat Biker play after the first thirty seconds, i.e., a randomly timed period of the play.

Major n. A major broadcasting network.

Mucknet n. A newsnet, usually a pirate net, specializing in investigative reporting, often undocumented and downright libelous.

Newsdecker n. A decker who operates as part of an investigative news team.

Newsie. See **Snoop**.

Pirate n. An unlicensed, illegal broadcasting station or network.

Polyphase POV-Select n. A simsense recording carrying multiple POVs (qv). The user can switch from one POV to another at will.

POV n. (simsense slang) Abbreviation of "Point of View." Refers to the experience recording of a single performer, their point of view of the story. A monoPOV recording contains only a single experience record. A polyPOV recording contains the experience tracks of more than one performer.

Prop n. (simsense slang) From the theatrical term "property," something an actor handles in a scene. An actor in a simsense who is not wired for sim recording but who interacts with a wired performer.

Simsynth n. An ASIST signal processor, used to edit raw simsense recordings for commercial release.

Simth n. A simsynth (qv).

SimulPOV v. Experiencing multiple POVs (qv) on a simsense recording simultaneously. Early studies indicate danger of personality disorder developing from this practice.

Snoop n. A reporter. **Cybersnoop:** a reporter cybered with video gear. **Vidsnoop:** a reporter who uses external video gear.

Synthlink n. A music synthesizer operated via direct neural interface.

Tabnet n. A "tabloid" net. A publication or broadcast specializing in scandal stories or sensational tales of the unknown. Of course, in the world of **Shadowrun**, many of the weirdest stories are true.

Target n. An actor in a simsense who is not wired for sim recording, who interacts with a wired performer in a fight or love scene.

Throbber n. A synthesized musical instrument that generates ultra- and subsonics designed to affect the human nervous system via sound.

Vid n. Any image-recording medium: film, digital, tape, holo, or flat.

Wax n. The music recording industry. Also, a recording, whether distributed on physical media or via the Matrix.

Waxworks n. A recording company, usually a major recording company. Big, corporate recording companies are also called "waxcorps."

Wet Record n. A raw simsense recording taken directly from a performer.

Pix

Timestamp	Impact	Fake Number	Description	File Number

Proof

Timestamp	Impact	Fake Number	Description	File Number

Punch

File	Target Number	Successes

Ratings

Average
Punch Successes _____

Highest Punch
Target Number _____

Ratings _____

Permission to photocopy for personal use.

Pix

Timestamp	Impact	Fake Number	Description	File Number

Proof

Timestamp	Impact	Fake Number	Description	File Number

Punch

File	Target Number	Successes

Ratings

Average
Punch Successes _____

Highest Punch
Target Number _____

Ratings _____

KA·GE.

THE LAST WORD IN SHADOWRUNNING.

SLOT AND RUN.

You're busy. Staying alive in the sprawl is a full-time job, so we'll make it quick.
You need to jack into the Shadowrun Network©, the only org licensed by FASA to give you what you need: the latest news, info and rumors from the streets of 2051.

WHAT'S MY CUT?

You want a pretty certificate? Go join a corp. We're not some drekky little fan club.
We're a network, with an accent on the work. For your donation of $16.00, you'll get four issues of our quarterly newsmagazine, **KA·GE**™ (Japanese for shadow). **KA·GE**™ is 32 pages of chiptruth that covers the streets from every angle, whether you want magic, matrix, or Mossberg. We give you fiction, new gear, spells, contacts and archetypes, all wrapped around a tough scenario. You'll also get the hottest paydata on FASA's new products, long before they hit the streets.

THIS AIN'T BTL.

Sign me up! For my $16.00* membership I'll receive:
- ·Four 32-page issues of **KA·GE**™ with: Info on conventions and tournaments.
- ·Access to restricted FASA information
- ·Stats on more and better tools of the trade and a chance to connect with other runners.

The three things I most want to see are:

__ Detailed scenarios __More archetypes __ Equipment __ Cyberwear
__ Short scenario ideas __Non-player characters __More spells __Corporate Info.
You tell us, Chummer _____ __Locations/Maps __Organization/Gang Info

Name _____
Archetype _____
Address _____
City _____ State _____ Zip _____

Send $16.00*, in Check or Money Order only, to
Shadowrun Network
2101 West Broadway, #305, PO Box 6018
Columbia, Missouri 65205-6018

Canadian, Puerto-Rican and Mexican Members please add $4.00
shipping & handling. All others outside the United States add $6.00.